FOX BITES

Content Warning

On a couple of occasions characters use ableist and homophobic language. There is also one instance of racist language. This is unfortunately accurate to the time and setting of the story. We provide this information in advance in good faith so readers can be prepared.

Acknowledgements

Funded with help from The Literature Wales Writers Bursary

With Special Thanks to Crystal Jeans and Chris Winters for their feedback on various drafts and redrafts of this story

Desmond Barry, Rob Middlehurst, Philip Gross, and Chris Meredith for their guidance during the early days of this book's inception

Alex Haagaard for providing a fount of interesting medical knowledge and great suggestions

Emily Rose Harrison for her wonderful illustrations and support

And Susie and Rich for their patience and encouragement

FOX BITES

Lloyd Markham

PARTHIAN

Parthian, Cardigan SA43 1ED
www.parthianbooks.com
First published in 2024
© Lloyd Markham
ISBN 978-1-914595-17-2
Editor: Susie Wildsmith
Cover design by Emily Courdelle
Contents page and Fox Bites illustrations by the eminently
commissionable Emily Rose Harrison. She is a multi-disciplinary artist
with a background in fine art, printmaking, and textiles based in
Cardiff, Wales
Typeset by Elaine Sharples
Printed and bound by 4edge Limited, UK
Published with the financial support of the Welsh Books Council
British Library Cataloguing in Publication Data
A cataloguing record for this book is available from the British Library
Printed on FSC accredited paper

*Dedicated to the people of Zimbabwe,
my family, and childhood friends*

Particularly those no longer with us

I have never stopped missing you

Black Diamond Fox Bite

or

A Giant Rests Beneath A Hateful Sun

Red Spiral Fox Bite

or

On Your Naked Back, In The Heat of Alien Saliva

Long Dogs Under The Hot-Eyed Heavens

Horned Up & Saintly Boy Blues

End Of The Dino War

Hot Snap

You: A Silver-Eyed Sorcerer

Hot Spit

Amber Altar Fox Bite

or

Heavenly Insects Dissolve Our Pain

Cupboard Boy Blues

An Omen Veiled In Moth Dust & Paper Clippings

White Column Fox Bite

or

Ears Cupped To The Drum Of Your Soul, Plucking Out The Darkest Sour Notes

What The Heart Wants . . .

A Mask Tightens, Squeezes Out The Bad Dreams

Prey: Numb

You: A Silver-Eyed General

You: A Silver-Eyed Host

Curious Souls Entwined Under Pearly-Eyed Night

Blue Opal Fox Bite

or

All Your Arrows Dipped In Sweat And Blood, Aimed Heavenwards, Ready To Piece The Moon

A Lion & A Jackal Look Into The Void

Our Flowers Unbloomed, Lodged Tight In Clenched Throats

Dissolving Dreams

Let Go?

Loss Whispered To White Petals

Prey Willing

You: A Silver-Eyed General

Bang

Agate Eyeball Fox Bite

or

Daggers Held Close, Our Malachite Roots Search The Sky

Upside Down: Your Foolish Head Planted In The Earth

The Dictator & The Stag Beetle

You: A Silver-Eyed Bumpkin

You: A Silver-Eyed Fool

You: A Silver-Eyed Mind Eater

Shadow Pact & Stitch-Lipped Boy Blues

Turquoise Prism Fox Bite

or

Bleeding Out On A Chair Of Viridian Wires

Prey: On The Run

You: A Silver-Eyed Tyrant

You: A Silver-Eyed King

Justice?

Leftovers

His Eyes On Empty Space, Your Eyes On The Moon

The Flame Out Yearning Heart Boy Blues

. . . it claims in unexpected ways

Emerald Vein Fox Bite

or

Holding Hands In A Whirlpool Of Strange Metals

Our Frail Constructs, Pull Tight Each Other's Seams

Paper Chain Into Darkness

Promises Whispered To Midnight

Ochre Heart Fox Bite

or

Our Spirits, Ribboned Into Shining Scraps, Float Away From Us

The Dinosaur Boy Blues

Our Outlines Traced By Ash-Dipped Fingers

The Girl In The Shadow

 Let Go

Out Of Orbit, Our Cracked Hearts Bleed Out

The following is a work of fiction

*It is inspired by events from the author's life,
but it is not an account of it*

*Nor are any of the characters veiled depictions
of people the author has known*

It's a bad dream, friend

*Step into it with love and know
there is light on the other side*

Our greatest mistake was believing that knowing was the same as understanding.

– Brother Antal of The Bronze Cast,
extract from *The Final History Of The Triumvirate of Metals*.

Black Diamond Fox Bite

or

A Giant Rests Beneath
A Hateful Sun

Caleb is everything Taban is not. Tall. Tanned. Muscular. Possessing wide blue eyes full of expression and light. Wide blue eyes that are weeping.

Pale, short, sickly, Taban has never wept. In his fifteen years alive his face has been an uncrackable mask. Neutral or neutral-smile. A little dash or minus sign. Sometimes with a slight curve, but usually like this → '–'

His narrow eyes are near-black brown. They don't let the light in. They don't let anything out. Even when Taban wants them to.

Caleb's mother, Gertrude, stands next to her grieving son, hands shaking, sharply inhaling, containing something violent inside. Her shark-fin quiff has gained new streaks of grey.

'Sorry we're late,' Taban's mother says. 'Traffic was a nightmare.'

'It's okay.' Gertrude squeezes Ann's hand. 'We've still got fifteen minutes. Catch your breath.'

A dusty wind blows. Ann's auburn mane flickers up like flames and for a moment the stagnant smell of oil from the nearby petrol station is displaced by the heavy stink of cattle shit.

Ann's nose curls. 'Yuck.'

'Probably a farm upwind,' Gertrude says.

They turn to face the structure behind them. The Harare Fifth Church of Saint Maurice. White and green – the paint could use a touch up. The little cross sticking out from the top of its triangle roof is the only indication it's a church and not a farmhouse.

Apart from the TOTAL petrol station opposite, The Fifth Church of Saint Maurice is the last building before the city breaks up into rural expanse. Pockmarked tarmac, brick, and concrete give way to sun-bleached grass. Lonely 2-to-4 lane highways melt into the horizon.

3

Ann smiles sadly. 'Don't know why we're doing a service at this old place really. My brother was quite godless.'

Gertrude doesn't register the statement. Her mind has been re-abducted by grief.

Ann's smile dissolves into a grimace. 'I guess Mom and Dad would be glad. Weird seeing the old place after all this time.'

Seeing a break in the conversation, Taban attempts to say something to Caleb, who is staring at his shoes, face wet with tears. He wants to say, 'I'm sorry. I love you.'

Instead his mouth hangs open for a moment, then quickly shuts. He wanders a few metres back to the car, where his father, Cormack, is having a smoke.

Cormack points across the road. 'Check out the old madala.'

On the sidewalk by the petrol station, a craftsman sat on a grass mat – soapstone sculptures splayed around him – is focused on a prowling tsetse fly. The bug affects disinterest – like a cat slinking nearer and nearer its master's plate. The man doesn't buy the act. Bony fingers twitch. Thwap. A rolled-up copy of the *Daily News* flattens the blue buzzing orb against the head of one his sculptures.

The old man spots Taban and Cormack watching. He waves – smile surfacing from his greying bristle beard.

Cormack waves back. His thick moustache crests – revealing a smile awkward and unequal to the old man's sincere toothy beam. Looking both ways, he crosses the street.

A short conversation follows sprinkled with Shona and slang: *Shamwaz. Mushe. Tatenda.*

Cormack returns with a *nyaminyami* necklace. 'Heard these little snakes are meant to bring good luck.' He places the charm around Taban's neck.

'Why didn't you get one for yourself then?' he asks.

No answer. Another awkward smile.

Taban stares at the sculpture splatted with diseased insect guts.

It's of a jackal.

Or maybe a fox.

Even here it is laughing at his pain.

Perhaps it is right to.

A voice, not his own, quiet, internal: **You asked for this.**

Ann calls to them, 'We better go in. It's starting now.'

Taban heads towards the church. Cormack stubs out his half-finished cigarette, pops it into his top pocket, and follows after.

A priest, tired, overworked, greets them by the door and hurries them to their seats at the front where the seven-foot-long casket of the gigantic Uncle Athel dominates the room. He is dressed like his mourners – formally, in a manner he would've hated were he still alive. His face, usually earthy and red, is drained – the only face that isn't sweaty in the freakish off-season heatwave.

Gertrude, Ann, Taban, and Caleb each take a seat. Taban in the middle, Ann is to his left, Caleb to his right, Gertrude at the end of the row, by the aisle – closest to her beloved Athel. Cormack hovers. There is no room for him. Someone rushes over with a chair, apologises for the mix up in the seating arrangement. He sits down – an awkward appendage to the row, obstructing the aisle.

The priest stands at the podium and attempts to transmute the life of the man who lies silent and boxed before the congregation into a story – into a sequence of soothing words. His tone is distant and professional. He is in a rush. He has many more funerals to get through.

Caleb raises his hands to his face as if trying to shield his eyes from a searing, painful light. His gentle weeping turns into a howling sob.

Taban tries again to say something, but cannot. Instead he lightly squeezes his cousin's shoulder. He thinks that this is something he should do. A way of performing his love for Caleb who he admires more than anyone. A way of performing his sorrow for the loss of Athel who was dear to him. A way of suppressing his shame – his guilt.

Taban feels guilty.

He is responsible for this tragedy. Most here believe that Athel's death was an accident – that he'd accidentally overdosed on his medication after having one too many drinks the evening before. Others whisper that it was an intentional act. That he just couldn't bear losing the old family farm – after spending so much effort and treasure to repurchase it. But Taban knows the truth. It is all his fault. Athel's death was the result of a curse that is running out of control – a curse he let into the world.

Taban can feel the presence of the swollen moon above them. Ever since that horrible evening it has hung brazenly in the daylight sky. Though no one else seems to notice. Every morning he wakes to find it larger.

The Black Diamond Fox Bite by his collarbone itches.

It smells of charcoal.

It looks like this →

The text describes three 'casts'. [1]

There are the Bronze Cast – who are gardeners. Though 'gardener' is a bit euphemistic. 'Geo-engineers' would be a more accurate analogy given the abilities described. Their symbol is the Sickle & Tree.

There are the Silver Cast. They are 'guardians' and sometimes 'metallurgists' – soldiers and scientists. Their symbol is the Snake & Dagger – which in the past has unfortunately led to a lot of spurious and culturally insensitive speculation. In the 1990s some academics from our country noted that the fragment was found in the Zambezi and predated known records of the Tonga people's Nyami Nyami legends. Based on this and this alone they leapt to theorise that their serpent guardian legends must have originally been 'inspired' by this tablet or perhaps 'passed down' from the people who made it.

To these theories we simply say: the tablet also predates all Viking myths by thousands of years and features extensive descriptions of a 'World Tree' and yet no one has attempted to claim that this must mean that all Norse Mythology must be credited to the makers of this strange broken slab. Some academics reveal more about themselves than their subjects when they use amazing discoveries like the Zambezi fragment as a pretext to explain away the accomplishments of other cultures.

Finally, there are the Gold Cast – 'overseers' and artists. 'Overseer' here seems to be a role that combines administration, diplomacy, and regulation. Bureaucrats and painters essentially, with a slight mystic air, and some allusions to supernatural abilities. Their symbol is an eye within an eye.

The fragment insists that all three casts are equal in stature, but placed separately into roles best suited to their skills.

Funnily, it is this and not the heavenly trees or miraculous powers which we find most difficult to believe.

---

1. *There is an interesting ambiguity as to whether the author of the fragment is talking about social classes or beings literally 'cast' from molten metal.*

– Extract from *Psychopomps & Heavenly Portals*
by Casper and Birgitta Andreassen.

Six years earlier
In a cupboard
Under a
Sink

Amber Altar Fox Bite

or

Heavenly Insects
Dissolve Our Pain

Cupboard Boy Blues

Taban is awakened by a burning in his throat and a stinging in his toe. In the corner where the moths dwell something glimmers. A tiny being. Six gold wings wrap around its body like a cocoon. It hangs upside down – its gnarled twig-like leg hooked into a crack in the door. It sways in front of the keyhole, the only source of illumination in the cramped cupboard where Taban is imprisoned.

'Hey,' Taban whispers. 'Did you nip me, little bug ... person?'

Silence. The boy wonders if he is seeing things.

Then a single yellow eye pops out from behind the veil of folded wings.

'No,' says a voice that comes from all around. 'A fox did that. Naughty creature. Comes and goes where it pleases. Bites who it pleases.'

'Oh,' says Taban. The drum of his left ear throbs. He'd had a bad infection when he was little. Doctors pulled a thick congealed candle of black blood-wax right out of his head. Ever since then his left ear hears – or rather *feels* – frequencies that others cannot.

'Say,' continues the being. 'You seem sad. Why don't you make a wish? I have a master – a king – in another world who can grant wishes even in this one. So long as they're made *sincerely*.'

'Would you please talk quieter, Sir? Ms Cowley might hear you.'

'Only the selected can hear my voice, boy. No need to worry.' The being flutters down from its perch – two wings flapping, four covering its face. It leans in close. A spindly cobalt-blue hand waves, beckons. 'Why not make a wish? You can whisper if you like. So no one will hear.'

13

'No. I don't want anything. Please go. You're going to get me in trouble.'

'My, my. This Cowley seems to cause you much discomfort. Why don't I make her disappear? I can do that. As a demonstration. I get the impression there are a lot of people you'd like to—' The creature clicks its silver-tipped fingers. 'Disappear.'

Taban shakes his head, covers his ears. For a moment he thinks he hears a rasping bark-like chuckle behind him.

The little winged being backs away. 'Perhaps now is not a good time. But, consider what I have offered. Should you change your mind, merely say so with all your heart. King Solomon answers all prayers. Farewell. For now.'

The creature bows and is gone – sliding through some curtain-like fold in the shadows.

Taban shivers. The pipe that digs into his back has gone cold. Someone is running the tap – probably washing the paint brushes. How long has he been in here? His mind always goes funny when it's locked in this cupboard.

The school bell rings. The door unlocks.

Taban unfolds himself from under the sink and stands up. He dusts off the grit in his blonde hair and straightens up his grey school uniform.

'I hope you have learned your lesson, Taban Grayson?' Mrs Cowley scowls. 'No more disrupting art class.'

Dressed in her usual funeral-black outfit, Ms Cowley is slim and has a mousey face that Taban has never once seen smile.

'Yes Ms Cowley,' replies Taban, his voice pitched at its usual near-monotone flatness. 'I promise not to paint the ocean purple when the instructions say blue again.' He does not bring up that the only reason he did this is because he is colour-blind and cannot see the difference between some purples and some blues. One time he had tried to explain his condition, but she got very angry and told him he was making up excuses. So the boy knows not to try reasoning with her.

Ms Cowley's eyebrow twitches. 'That defiant expression of yours is infuriating,' she says. 'Just because your mother is a teacher don't think I won't send you to be caned by the headmaster.'

Ms Cowley always finds these deep meanings in Taban's face. He does not know what to do. It's just his face. He doesn't know how to make it move in a way that will please her.

Taban skirts past the other children – who are rapidly exiting the classroom – to his desk. It is an old thing. Still has a hole for an ink pot. That and two decades of graffiti. He lifts the lid and takes out his pencil case – checks it. Someone has snapped his colouring pencils in half. As expected. Eleventh time since Cousin Caleb moved away. He closes the case and puts it in his school bag. Then a soft, 'What?' reverberates around the classroom.

Taban turns to see Hilde, the only other child still in the classroom, staring at her feet.

Ms Cowley's face is performing its most dangerous expression – betrayal.

Hilde is both a swot and good at sports. The latter should make her popular at Highveldt, but she is almost as unpopular as Taban. This is because she doesn't talk much and when she does she is often blunt in a way people think is mean. And even though she's more expressive than Taban she often chooses not to be – giving neutral looks when people expect smiles. Also she is a black girl with white parents – which the other kids insist is weird even after learning how adoption works and everything. And there was a nasty rumour going around that she was found in a coffin as baby. Which wasn't true. It was a quarry – which is where they get metal and rocks.

Her, Taban, and Caleb all used to be friends.

Since Caleb moved away she's stopped talking to him.

Such is the way.

'What do you mean you forgot your swimming costume?'

'I really thought it was in my kit bag, Ms Cowley, I don't know what has—'

Ms Cowley sweeps her hand as if pulling shut a little zipper on Hilde's mouth.

The child falls silent.

Cowley smiles. 'This afternoon was our last opportunity to practise before the Swimming Gala this weekend, Hilde.' Her voice is gentle and calm. 'Jackal House is behind this year and this event is our only chance to catch up. We're hardly going to manage that if our star swimmer can't remember her costume.' Cowley closes her eyes, rubs her temples. 'I expect this sort of carelessness from the other students,' she adds, voice cracking a little. 'But not you!' She gives Hilde a strange look. Sad, angry, but full of affection. The sort of expression a more typical adult might make before forgiving a remorseful child.

Cowley snatches Hilde's arm.

'Taban, get the ruler.'

Taban pretends not to hear. He knows what comes next. He doesn't want it to happen.

'Taban!'

He crumbles. 'Y-Yes, Ms Cowley.' He runs to the teacher's desk and fetches the wooden ruler from the top drawer. It is at least a generation old – numbers long since faded. Taban wonders if Cowley had, in her own school days, used this same ruler to draw straight lines where straight lines needed to be.

If he knew how to make a face that performed remorse Taban would do so. Instead he wears his usual neutral mask as he hands Ms Cowley the ruler. She takes it, raises it, slowly guides it through the air until it is just above Hilde's arm – like a golfer preparing a swing.

Hilde scrunches her face, squirms.

'Girl! Look at me! Look at me!'

She complies. The two lock eyes. Ms Cowley's expression is wistful, nostalgic. It seems like some small light of mercy might break through its hardness. Instead a low growl rattles up from her throat.

'You stupid!' Crack.

'Stupid!' Crack.

'Girl!' Crack.

Hilde flinches with every strike.

'Remember your swimming costume this weekend.' Ms Cowley releases her raw, red arm. 'Now get going!'

'Yes, Ms,' says Hilde, bolting out of the classroom.

A part of Taban wants to run after her, wants to say, 'I'm sorry.'

A tiny part even wants to add, 'I love you,' – a phrase he hasn't said aloud for a long while.

The boy used to say, 'I love you,' to his friends and family all the time. Because it is true and something he feels. But a little over a year ago he said it to Caleb in front of some older boys Caleb was trying to impress and Caleb became so angry that he did not talk to Taban for over a week. Taban had asked his mother why this was. She explained that it was not so much *what* he had said so much as *how* and *when* he had said it. That as he grew older he would understand when it was okay to say, 'I love you,' and how to say it in a way that wouldn't disturb or embarrass the people he loved. Based on this information, Taban concluded that he should simply not tell anyone he loved them until he was absolutely certain he could do it properly. Now the words sound strange – dying in his chest before they reach his lips.

Such is the way.

He nods and leaves as if it didn't happen.

He pretends it didn't happen.

It didn't happen.

Caleb wouldn't have let it happen.

As Taban is about to step out the door, Ms Cowley's voice pins him in place. 'Taban, before you go …' The words are spoken slowly, quietly, with the confidence of someone who knows they do not need to project their voice to make their audience listen. She bites a loose strip of skin from her nail, and then continues. 'I've passed along what you said to Headmaster Horlick and we're going to put a stop to it. Thank you for speaking up. One thing we absolutely don't tolerate here at Highveldt is bullying.' She suddenly claps her hands together. As she pulls them apart moth dust and moth limbs fall to the floor. 'Bloody pests!' she says, waving her hand to dismiss him.

As soon as Taban steps outside the room, a hand shoves his face against the red-brick wall of Room 32B and holds it there. The hand in question belongs to Hendrick Eugene Boeker. Hendrick has sea-green eyes and blonde hair. He's very athletic. His father was once a professional rugby player. His four older brothers all excel at sport. Rugby, cricket, soccer, swimming, cycling, running – the Boekers are good at all of it.

'Howzit, Tabby! What colour is my uniform?'

'Grey.'

'Sut! Wrong, it's blue!'

'It's grey, Hendrick. Colour-blindness doesn't work like that.'

'Na, Tabby, it's blue. Hey everyone! This is blue, right?'

Some other kids have stopped to watch. 'Ja,' says one of them, smirking. 'Looks blue to me, Hen.'

'You hear that, Tabby – it's blue.'

Taban knows his only escape is to play along.

'Okay. I guess it's blue then.'

'Stupid! Everyone knows it's grey, Tabby!'

Some of the other children laugh. Others roll their eyes. They've seen this routine before.

Satisfied, Hendrick unpins Taban and walks off in the direction of the Central Grounds.

Taban's face stings, bleeds. He closes his eyes, sucks in air, and flushes the event from his mind – squashing it down into some deep pit in his stomach.

It didn't happen.

Caleb wouldn't have let it happen.

He continues on his way – walking around the corner to the Southern Grounds where, ever since Caleb changed schools, he sits on the veranda outside the school library and eats his lunch alone. The veranda is made of blackish-grey stone that gets searing in the hot-dry season. It overlooks the Southern Grounds – a sparse patch of unkempt grass and paper thorns that gently slopes towards a fence shrouded in haggard bushes, beyond which are the school swimming pools.

It's a desolate view. Apart from one small bit of green sprouting from the centre – an acacia sapling – branches spread like two open palms, raised to catch as if the sun was a falling cricket ball. Its bough is painted white to shield it from sunlight and the termites. Taban wonders if that actually works or is just a superstition. He's been observing the tree for months – wondering if it will die. And, if it dies, could he tell just by looking?

He sits on the edge of the veranda and eats his potato chip sandwich – the only way he can eat chips because getting grease on his fingertips makes him anxious. He thinks of next Monday – the first day of the summer holidays when he will be going to the Mana Pools game reserve with his mom. There he will get to see his cousin for the first time since Caleb's family moved out to the farm nearly a year ago. He can't wait to talk to him. He needs to talk to him. He needs to tell him how things have changed. Maybe he will even figure out how to properly say that he loves him, that he misses him.

Taban hears footsteps. He turns to see Hilde emerging from the toilets next to the library. She looks like she's been crying. She does not acknowledge him. Instead, she too sits on the edge of the veranda – a metre or so away. She picks up a stick and scratches pictures in the dry dirt by her feet. Taban has seen these pictures before. Back when they were friends Hilde had explained to him that these pictures were old Viking letters called Runes. She had found them in a book owned by her adoptive parents – who both taught at the university near Taban's house.

As Hilde draws, sunlight bounces off the bruises blossoming on her arm – making them look shiny, rubbery.

Taban again feels the urge to say something – to indicate his regret, his sorrow. 'I'm sorry the teacher hit you,' he says. 'I'm sorry I brought the ruler.'

'Shut up,' she replies.

Taban shuts up.

The scratches in the ground by Hilde's feet are almost

entirely a mystery to him. He does recognise this one symbol though → '<'. Hilde told him once that it means 'injury' or 'pain'.

Around Hilde's feet there are rows and rows of '<'.

Taban packs away his now empty lunchbox and leaves her to her runes.

After meandering for a minute, not really sure where to sit since his preferred spot was taken, he settles on the edge of the Central Grounds – sitting on one of the benches that line its southern perimeter.

A person that used to play with him and Caleb way back in Grade 1 is sat on another bench several metres away talking with Hendrick. Daisy. Blonde. Pretty. Outwardly normal – though back then she secretly liked to eat ants. She would spit on her finger and spear them – trapping them in her sticky saliva. Taban and Caleb used to help by riling up the nests with chongololo carcasses and drawing the insects to her. But then one day the teacher caught them and they all went home with red arms. After that she didn't speak to them any more.

Once Taban had asked Daisy why she liked to eat ants. She said it was because they were alive and she liked living things. Eating dead things was gross – like filling yourself with death. She also confessed that one day she would like to eat a really big ant – the size of a baby if possible. To punch a hole through its eye, pull out its black-green guts, and devour it.

Taban's toe begins to itch again.

<<<

An Omen Veiled In Moth Dust & Paper Clippings

That night Taban dreams that Ms Cowley disappears. That one day during school she vanishes in a cloud of moths, leaving only dust and scuffed glasses.

In the dream, the shy insects that inhabit the cupboard under the sink – the ones the other kids call gross, whose wings they rip off in fits of idle cruelty – swarm out of the cupboard and cover her head to toe. She is not bothered by this. She does not seem to even register their presence as she continues marking homework.

Then, one by one, the moths fly up and out of the window, taking pieces of her with them. The pieces of Ms Cowley look like torn bits of paper – flat, weightless, two-dimensional. Each one a puzzle-piece fragment. The gap between her eyebrows. The knuckle of her left index finger. Her right nostril. As the last scraps of her are removed, Taban thinks he sees relief on Ms Cowley's face – which is now nothing more than an eyeball and some lips. She looks like she is achieving some blessed release. Taban also feels relief. Relief that he is not going to be put in the cupboard any more. Relief that he, Hilde, and all the other children will no longer get whacked with rulers.

When he awakes from this dream it is still dark out and he experiences three immediate sensations. The first: disappointment that the dream is not real. The second: a strange sense of shame about that disappointment. The third: the itch in his toe. He pulls the covers off his bed and in the moonlight spots a mark. An orange wound. Its edges are crisp and clear and glow like they have been drawn into his flesh with glittering ink. The wound is shaped like something he saw in a church once – when their neighbour and family friend, Eve, got married.

Like this →

Putting aside the hotly debated issue of whether the fragment predates the invention of cuneiform, what can be translated from the ancient fragment is deeply mysterious. The text has all the content of a great myth. In fact some of it even feels like quite precise, calculated echoes of Viking and Christian mythology. Shadows of Yggrassil, Fenrir, Loki. The apple tree of Genesis. Seraphim.

All the more perplexing that it would be found deep in the riverbed of the Zambezi – a continent away from the cultures most associated with these mythologies.

But the content of the fragment is not as inscrutable as its stylistic form.

It doesn't read like a poem or religious verse, but like an instruction manual or engineer's schematic. Dare I say that some parts even read a bit like a sales pitch? It implores the reader to build the gateway it describes and promises all sorts of heavenly boons. Eternal life. Universal knowledge. Etc.

At least most of it reads like this.

Parts of the fragment are overwritten. It's as if someone hurriedly scratched something new on the tablet – like you might jot a note on an old receipt.

These parts are mostly unintelligible. But there is a fearful urgency.

These sections read like a warning.

– Extract from *Psychopomps & Heavenly Portals*
by Casper and Birgitta Andreassen.

Red Spiral Fox Bite

or

On Your Naked Back,
In The Heat of Alien Saliva

Long Dogs Under The Hot-Eyed Heavens

The sun's gaze sweeps over the ragged midday wilderness of the Mana Pools National Park. The air hangs hot and heavy over everything like a see-through plastic film. The Grayson family car weaves past a large pile of disintegrating animal shit. Taban's not sure what creature it came from. Something big. Buffalo maybe? Or perhaps elephant? He hopes not. One year, at night, a bull elephant ransacked their camp and had to be driven away by rangers with rock-salt shells. 'Old Gandanga' was a known menace in these parts. Grown mad and violent with age, he'd been ostracised from his herd, and had taken to raiding camps for sweet-smelling fruit. Apparently, that's just something that happen to old bulls sometimes. Taban recalls Gandanga's eyes, lit up by campfire – sad, dark pearls in a roiling ocean.

The car makes a metallic gurgle. Something within rattles. Fourth time since they left Harare. This pea-green 1950s Beetle was not built for deep potholes and dirt-track roads. 'It's going to break down any minute now,' Taban's mother mutters. 'Any minute now.'

Taban ignores this. He is staring out the window at the passing trees and imagining a different world: caverns of clear crystal deep beneath the earth spiral down in criss-cross patterns before coalescing in a vast hall, in the centre of which the molten core of the world is suspended – held in place by a network of lights that emit mysterious energies. Around this hovers a halo of floating platforms. Buildings shaped like globular stalagmites cover the surface of each. One by one people drip from the strange houses and gather in the streets. Men, women, some who are neither, all of dark complexion

27

dressed in white robes. Together, in accordance with the morning ritual, they sing.

Is there a point to this ritual? Taban hasn't seen that far ahead yet. It is just an idea – a lingering image that rises to the surface of his mind when things are quiet. He has a lot of ideas like this. He doesn't know what to do with them. They leave his brain feeling clogged and slow. This one is reminiscent of a show he watched that morning. What is it called? *Spartakus and the Sun Beneath The Sea*. That was it. That old French cartoon had captured his imagination. Now his imagination has captured it back, cannibalised the bits it liked, without him even asking it to. His mind is greedy. It wants to swallow everything.

Taban's forehead aches. His skull buzzes – as if a fly is trapped inside. He winces his eyes closed. When he opens them he sees a figure out in the bush. An animal. It looks a bit like a fox, but unlike any fox Taban has ever seen. Tall as a man. Unnaturally long and thin – as if its grey flesh and patchy white fur have been stretched over a skeleton that is not its own. Its mouth is wide – twisted into what looks like a smile. The animal stares unblinking at Taban. A command forces itself into his mind.

Become Conduit.

Taban tries to turn away from the window but his head is heavy, his neck stiff. It's like he's pulling against some magnetic energy.

Must look away.

He wrenches himself from the animal's gaze. All around there is the sound of sporadic gushing wind. Then he realises – it's not the wind but his breath.

His mother has stopped the car.

'Taban, are you okay?' she asks.

'There's something out in the bush.'

'Where? I don't see anything, my boy.'

Taban points out the window to the spot where he'd seen the creature. There is nothing there now.

A sickly iron taste lingers on his tongue. He puts a finger in his mouth.

Red.

His gums are bleeding.

<<<

Horned Up & Saintly Boy Blues

As they pull into the campsite, Taban is surprised that Caleb does not come to greet him and his mom. Only Aunt Gertrude and Uncle Athel are there smiling and waving as Ann parks the car. Gertrude wears the unspoken dress-code of Dehannas matriarchs – polo shirt, flip-flops, and cargo shorts. She has a glass of wine in one hand which she narrowly avoids spilling as she pulls Ann in for a hug.

'How was the trip up?'

'Okay. Was a bit worried that the car was going to crap out but it all worked out in the end.'

'And Cormack?'

'Oh. Yes. He couldn't come. Work stuff.'

'Typical. Your husband is a workaholic, Ann.'

The two women share a knowing look. Taban recognises that they are engaged in a performance where they pretend to not know the truth – that his father always finds an excuse to avoid these annual camping trips regardless of how busy things are at the recording studio. Ann once told Taban that this was because Cormack didn't like the bush. During the war for independence there was an incident where he got separated from the other soldiers and ended up lost in the wilderness for several days. The experience 'spooked' him.

Uncle Athel, smiling, laughing, scoops Taban up onto his shoulder.

'How is my boy?' he asks.

Uncle Athel is a giant with long muscular arms, big hands, a bulbous nose, and thick eyebrows. His skin is tanned and veiny. He is dressed as ever in khaki shorts, a sleeveless vest, and a broad-brimmed hat. Indiana Jones as performed by the BFG – as Cormack once described him after a few beers.

'I'm good,' says Taban, 'Where's Caleb?'

Athel's smile strains – like a ship that's been rocked by a sudden wave.

'He's sulking!' Gertrude points to a red two-person tent at the far end of the campsite. 'Why don't you go and say hi? Maybe you can snap him out of his sour mood.'

'Okie doke.'

Athel puts him down and Taban darts in the direction of the tent on the very edge of the clearing. It is a long way from the big green tent that serves as the kitchen and the long blue one where Gertrude and Athel are staying. Even its entrance is faced away in an obvious statement of protest. One thing Taban appreciates about Caleb is his lack of subtlety – he isn't difficult to read.

He unzips the tent and peers inside.

Caleb is lying on his back looking at a magazine with a half-naked woman on the cover. He looks different from when Taban last saw him several months ago. His limbs, while still gangly, are more muscular and his skin is almost tanned as brown as his thick bush of hair. The biggest change though is his expression. He is frowning. It is a sad, heavy frown that appears to have resided on his face for a long time.

'Hey.'

'Jasis!' Caleb jumps up and quickly stuffs the magazine under his roll-up mattress. 'Taban? It's just you, is it?'

'Yup.'

'Yurrrrr. Don't sneak up on me like that. If Ma had seen this I would've been in big trouble.'

'Why? It's just a magazine.'

'Ja, but it's real naughty. One of the Grade Seven Prefects gave it to me.'

'What's so naughty about it?'

'The girls in it are naked.'

'So? Girls are naked all the time.'

'Ah. When you're older you'll get it, Tab.'

'You're only nine months older than me.'

Caleb rolls his eyes. 'Don't worry about it. Anyway how have you been? How's Highveldt?'

'Rubbish.'

'Oh.'

Caleb is silent.

Taban wonders if he is expecting him to elaborate, but doesn't know where to even begin.

Caleb sighs. 'Well it isn't Saint Vitus so it can't be that bad.' He stands up, brushes past, and walks in the direction of the green kitchen tent. 'Come, let's get cokes.'

Taban nods. Before following after he looks in the direction of where Caleb has hidden the magazine. He feels a strange urge to rip it up.

<<<

End Of The Dino War

Bedtime. Back in the tent. Taban unpacks a box of plastic toys from his satchel and spreads them out in front of Caleb. The little electric light Athel engineered for them makes the toy soldiers and dinosaur figurines cast twisted, amalgamated shadows – plastic bodies merging into dark forms.

'Do you want to play Dino War?'

Dino War is a game Taban and Caleb have been playing since they were six. Although it is less a 'game' and more a long-running collaborative story they act out with toys. Taban has aspirations of turning it into a strategic computer game one day with a campaign mode that would take the player through the key battles of the war.

'Na.' Caleb doesn't look up from the comic he is reading. 'Tab, that stuff is for dorks. Also the game is over. The green guys won.'

'I was thinking we could begin again many years later with a twist – the Arcosaurs have now become corrupted by power and the surviving Terrorsaurs must redeem themselves by overthrowing them.'

'Slow down. What does "redeem" mean? What does "corrupted" mean?'

'They're words from the bible. "Redeem" means "become good", "corrupt" means "become bad".'

'You use too many big words. And didn't we already make the Arcosaurs bad at one point?'

'No, that was just when a spy had taken over their army from within.'

'I can never follow your stories, Tab.'

'Please, Cal.'

'No.'

'Come on!'

'No! Don't whine. It's weird when you whine in that robot voice of yours. You sound like a retard.'

Externally, Taban wears his neutral mask. Internally he is in pain. 'Retard' is the sort of thing Hendrick would call him. He packs away the box, takes a book out of his satchel, and curls up in his sleeping bag. But he can't focus on the words. All he can think about is how weird Caleb is acting.

'You talk differently now,' he says.

'How?'

'You sound older.'

'Ja, well at Saint Vitus you've got to talk like the big guys or you have a rough time.'

'You sound like Hendrick and all the other bullies at school.'

'Little Hen? Really? That guy? He didn't seem so bad. Always nice to me. Anyway, God, you're a wuss – just hit him and he'll leave you alone. I know his type – all show. You don't know what real bullies are like, Tab. Highveldt is soft.'

Taban feels an urge to reach over and put his hands around Caleb's neck and squeeze. Then, as suddenly as the urge came it is gone, leaving only a lingering sense of shame.

'Is it okay if I turn off the light?' Caleb asks. 'I'd like to go to sleep now.'

Taban wants to explain to Caleb how he is wrong. He wants to explain how much nastier Highveldt has got since he left. How isolated he has become. How much he misses him. How he wishes everything could just be restored to the way it was. How much he loves him. But he doesn't know how to make a face that expresses that or a voice that rises to the occasion. Instead he just says, 'Sure,' in his typical, neutral way. Then Caleb flips the switch by the entrance and the light goes out.

< < <

Hot Snap

A few hours later Taban is awakened by hot breath. At first he thinks it is the wind, cutting through the thin tent, but then realises that whatever is blowing against his cheek is too moist, too warm.

He sits up. Outside, two white lights shine in the dark, their edges wavering, unfocused. They approach. The breath approaches with them – grows hotter.

The eyes and the breath are one thing.

It is in the tent.

The fox. It coils, slithers. Its bones crack and shift. As if it is reforming itself with every motion. It is on top of Taban. Liquid pours from its open jaws – which unhinge like a serpent's.

A thought punches into Taban's mind.

Become Conduit.

Teeth fall towards him.

He closes his eyes.

<<<

You: A Silver-Eyed Sorcerer

Taban is Solomon. He has always been Solomon. This broad chest, these silver eyes, are his. As is the rifle in his hands. President Andrew's troops are in the valley below. He has lured them to exactly where he needs them. He just has to signal. Then his soldiers will fire from the surrounding bush. He peers around – confirms that no unvetted eyes are watching. Then he removes his glove and places on the earth a white hand at odds with the rest of his complexion. The bite on his palm glows, itches. The power within him surges. He has grown much more adept at using it since that night in the tomb of the Bronze Man. The night when he knelt before the tree. Ate fox flesh. He imagines the officer in charge of the battalion below. He starts with his hairy toes and works his way upward. Once he has a good mental image of the man's entire anatomy he focuses on the specific part he is interested in – the heart. He explores its chambers, feels out the thickness of its blood, tastes its contents. Iron. Glucose. Copper. Salt. Oxygen. Tiny traces of cyanide – a smoker. Solomon could kill this man painfully – block one of his arteries and cause a fatal heart attack. He'd be within his rights. Scanning the man's synapses he can see that he has tortured dozens of captured revolutionaries. Instead he simply wills the officer's heart to stop. Energy pulses into the ground.

'All done?' whispers Ibn.

'Yes,' says Solomon.

Down below a commotion breaks out among the counter-revolutionaries as their commander collapses dead in the grass. As planned snipers fire from the south and west. Solomon's left ear bleeds. The doctor is sucking black rot from his throbbing head – rooting around in his skull and scraping, scraping, scraping. Taban wonders if his head will ever be clear of all this poison.

Wait.

Taban?

<<<

Hot Spit

Dirt. Taban feels dirt on his cheek. His skin is wet with an unknown fluid. At first it is heavy, sticky. Then it turns viscous, dribbles off his body, and sinks into the earth.

'This is why I told you to be patient,' says a voice that comes from all around, a voice which makes his left ear throb. 'You moved too quickly and his mind rejected it. He needs to be willing.'

Shut up, Pollinator. The last time we tried things your way we took too long and the host spoiled. The seeds of the tree died in them before they could germinate.

'It couldn't be helped. There was no way to account for how they would respond to such a traumatic event. Sometimes the weather just isn't right.'

A low growl.

Whatever. The soil of this world is trash. I don't think a conduit could ever grow here.

Taban creaks open his eyes. He sees vague lights and shapes hovering in the moonlight. Teeth? Wings? Golden irises? Silvery fur waving in the midnight breeze?

'He is waking. Let's get going.'

The shapes drift away.

Taban is alone somewhere out in the bush. He rolls onto his back. Above, the night sky's constellations are clear. For a moment they look like the orderly circuit diagrams his father brings home when he has to repair something ahead of a show. Then they don't. They are random splatter. Yellow on a blue-black canvas. Then they do again – if he focuses, strains his eyes. The stars waver like a Magic Eye picture book, between signal and noise. Taban sits up, looks around. He is ten metres from the campsite. There is something glowing by his toe. No. Not *by* his toe. *On* his toe. It is the orange mark – the one the winged person in the cupboard said was a Fox Bite.

There is also a new glowing mark on his thigh.

It is red and thin and coils around and around.

Like this →

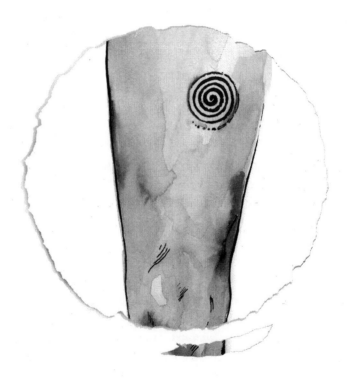

A light approaches. A small torch. Caleb. Taban can just about make out a concerned look.

'Tab? Jasis what are you doing out here?'

'I'm not sure. I think I was dreaming.'

'You're not sure? Were you sleepwalking again? It's dangerous out here at night. You have no idea how much I panicked when I got up to go to the loo and saw you weren't in the tent. This may be a game reserve but it's still the bush. You'll get chowed. Come on, let me help you.'

Caleb grabs his hand and pulls him up. Taban nearly topples right back onto the ground.

'Woah! Steady, steady.' Caleb says, catching him. 'You really are out of it. Come on let's go.' Caleb wraps his arm around Taban and half leads, half carries him back to camp.

Taban stares at the glowing marks – the Fox Bites. 'Caleb, can you see those?' he asks.

'See what?' Caleb replies, looking around.

Caleb is topless, thick scars snaking along his ribs.

'What are these?' asks Taban, pointing.

Sadness flashes across Caleb's face. Then immediately it is gone – subsiding beneath that new hard frown. 'It's nothing. Got into a fight at school. Mention anything to anyone I swear I will klup you.' He gestures to the tent. 'Come on – get in.'

Taban flops on top of his sleeping bag.

'Do you need water or something? I could get it from the kitchen tent.'

'No. It's fine, Cal. Thank you.'

'Alright. I'm going off to the loo then. Absolutely busting now.'

Taban watches Caleb walk away. Soft footsteps and soft torchlight fade into blackest night – leaving him alone in the dark with his glowing bites and the dampness of mysterious fluids.

Nordic Runes. Hebrew Pictographs. Phoenician Characters. And that's just naming the three most well documented.[1]

The Zambezi River Fragment features a unique writing system that feels like a scattershot of a hundred cultures separated by thousands of miles and multiple millennia.

It's like someone took a 5000-year snapshot of our planet and averaged all of our languages into a single script form.

The Zambezi River Fragment seems almost *designed* to be translated.

Which begs the question – what message could be so important?

---

1. *We must take a brief moment to acknowledge the excellent work being done to analyse the fragment in the context of Asian languages by our colleague Lǐ Xīnyí at the University of Hong Kong.*

– Extract from *Psychopomps & Heavenly Portals* by Casper and Birgitta Andreassen.

White Column Fox Bite

or

Ears Cupped To The Drum Of Your Soul, Plucking Out The Darkest Sour Notes

What The Heart Wants …

A fist keeps hitting Taban's face. Over and over. Thwack. Thwack.

Other than this, the first day of the new term has been acceptable.

In fact until a minute or two ago Taban might have even said it had been a good day.

It unravelled like this →

The bell rings. Taban collects his satchel and leaves the classroom. The day has been nice. No one broke his colouring pencils. No one hit him or called him names. Cowley did not put him in the cupboard. She has not been here to do so. She is absent for reasons the replacement teacher will not say. Sick perhaps? There is a wispy scrap of paper by the windowsill. Taban wonders.

Taban heads towards the parking lot. His mother has to stay late this afternoon to cover Cowley's athletics class – so Eve, their friend and neighbour and Cormack's co-worker, is coming to give him a lift home. Taban likes Eve. Unlike most people, she misunderstands him in a way that is flattering. Around her he feels like his flaws might not actually be flaws.

As he is about to round the corner, a hand touches his shoulder.

It belongs to Daisy.

'Taban, I need to talk to you about something. Could you come with me?'

'Um. Yes?'

Daisy snatches Taban's hand and pulls him toward the tree-shaded area behind the Grade 6 and 7 classrooms. He usually avoids this area. It's where the older kids go to secretly smoke cigarettes. If teachers find you there – they are leery. If bullies find you there – you are dead. None of this is at the forefront of his mind though. It keeps getting pushed aside by another thought: Daisy is holding my hand. A girl is holding my hand. This has never happened before. Other than Hilde, the girls at Taban's school go out of their way to avoid him, and Hilde's interactions are usually limited to calling him an idiot. Caleb says this is because he is creepy – especially his blank-mask face. Scary because no one can see what's under it.

'Where are we going, Daisy?' Taban asks, shock giving way to suspicion.

'Don't worry about it, Taban. I just need to talk to you.'

'Is this about the thing with Cowley and the ants back in Grade 1? Me and Cal already said we were sorry.'

'What? No. It's not about that. Just come with me. Look, we're here already.'

They enter the small clearing by the Balancing Rocks sculpture – three large egg-like stones, one on top of the other, arranged in imitation of the actual Balancing Rocks on the Zimbabwe Dollar. In nature, these precarious formations were formed by slow geological forces over hundreds of years. Highveldt's homage was brute-forced with chisels and slapped together with cement in about a week.

Daisy lets go of his hand and turns to face him.

She smiles.

'So … what is it you need to say?' Taban asks.

'Just a question,' she replies, backing away. 'Why have you peed your pants?'

'What?'

Something slams into Taban's crotch. Icy water pours down his legs. On the ground, by his feet, he sees a scrap of blue plastic. A water balloon?

Daisy starts to chuckle.

'Bullseye,' says a familiar voice.

Hendrick steps out from the shade of a nearby tree, gold hair glinting in the sun. He is wearing a face of joy and triumph – like an athlete collecting a medal.

'Hey Tabby. Why did you piss yourself?'

Taban puts on his neutral mask. He doesn't intend to do this. It just happens. His body has ejected him. He is a pilot out of his plane. He looks down on his physical form as it moves towards collision.

'I didn't pee myself,' says Taban.

Hendrick's proud expression slips. Immediately he is inches from Taban.

'It looks like you did though. And everyone else will think so too.'

'Maybe. But I didn't. You hit me with a water balloon.'

Hendrick shoves him. Taban hits the ground.

'I hate that face you make. Smug. Like you're so much better than everyone.'

In the background Daisy's chuckles turn into hysterical laughter.

Hendrick sits on top of Taban – pinning his arms under hard leather shoes – and punches him.

Then he punches him again.

'That face.' He punches.

'Like you haven't done anything.' He punches.

'You went and whined to Ms Cowley.' He punches.

'Said I was bullying you.' He punches.

'When I was only teasing.' He punches.

'Now I'm being suspended.' He punches.

'Do you know how upset my dad was?' He punches.

'Do you?'

The next punch doesn't come. Taban opens his eyes.

Hendrick is doing that thing the other kids can do – crying.

His fists are scuffed, there is dirt under his nails. His snot and tears dribble onto Taban's uniform. In the background Daisy's laughter has turned low and throaty, punctuated by hoarse gasps for air, like she's in pain, like her body is breaking down.

Hendrick snorts deep – sucking back his phlegm.

'That smug face!'

He raises his fist again.

Taban closes his eyes, braces.

The blow never comes. The weight on Taban's chest lifts as Hendrick slowly stands. He produces a serviette from his front pocket and wipes his face.

'You know what my dad called me, Taban? He called me a thug. I'm not a thug.'

He stares at Taban's face – seemingly searching for something – then grunts, unsatisfied.

'Whatever. Daisy, let's go.'

Daisy clutches her chest, convulsing. Her laughs are more like shrieks now.

'Daisy. Will you cut that out?'

Daisy bites down on her hand. Her eyes water.

'I'm sorry, Henny,' she says, words muffled by her clenched, smiling jaws. 'I can't stop when I get like this.'

Hendrick takes her hand with gentleness that surprises Taban. Like a prince. 'It's okay,' he says. Then he leads her away, further northward, and Hendrick's tear-and-snot-soaked face and Daisy's muffled shriek-laughs are gone, leaving only Taban and the Fake Balancing Rocks.

'I miss him.'

It takes a moment for Taban to realise the words are his. It doesn't take him any time at all to realise the 'him' he's referring to.

Caleb wouldn't have let this happen.

Or maybe he would have? Maybe Caleb would have sided with Hendrick. After all this was nothing like as bad as Saint Vitus.

Taban looks up at the bare blue sky. His body still feels distant, alien. A crashed vehicle he is trying to restart.

I want to die.

The thought is more clear and brilliant than any thought he has ever had. A crystal jutting from the walls of a dismal cave.

I want to die. And I want them to die too. Hendrick, Cowley, Daisy, Caleb, Hilde, my parents, my teachers. Every person who hits me, lets me be hit, or tells me off for not hitting others. I want everything to disappear. Every human, animal, plant. Every speck. I want to go to sleep forever and take everything with me. Take everything into the dark and have it all end.

Taban re-enters his body. He feels a mass of pain where his face should be. Pain. Moisture. There is liquid flowing down his cheeks. Perhaps these are his first tears?

He dabs his finger – inspects the results.

Nope.

Just blood.

<<<

Out in the blackness between
The absence from which all night and shadow springs
Something that has been waiting, listening,
Hears the words it wants to hear

'I want everything to disappear. Every human, animal,
plant. Every speck. I want to go to sleep forever and take
everything with me. Take everything into the dark ...'

It hears these words and says

okay

A Mask Tightens, Squeezes Out The Bad Dreams

Washing his face in the sink, Taban is relieved to find that the damage is less severe than he first thought. Perhaps Hendrick was too emotional to hit him with his usual force and accuracy? Apart from a graze on his cheek that won't stop bleeding, there isn't anything here that can't be explained away with a good story. And explaining it away is exactly what Taban must do. This incident confirms his suspicion. Involving adults simply makes things worse.

They need to disappear. All of them.

The thought enters his head violently. Far more violently than any of Hendrick's punches.

Taban takes a deep breath – sucks everything back in. Eve will be coming to pick him up in a minute. No time to dwell on what happened. He changes into his sports kit from the morning athletics class and packs away his soaked uniform. He takes a wad of tissue paper for his face and then heads out to the parking lot. On the way he wracks his brain trying to make up a story that'll convince Eve that everything is alright. He is so wrapped in this he absent-mindedly steps on a crumbly white dog turd – obscured under dry leaves and ribbon-curled musasa pods.

'Aw yuck.'

From bad to worse. No doubt this landmine was left by Cecil – Headmaster Horlick's geriatric Ridgeback. Despite numerous objections from concerned parents, he pretty much gives the animal free rein of the school. Thankfully the old hunting dog is of an age where it mostly just wants to sleep in Horlick's office and leave 'treasures' for the overworked groundskeepers.

Taban inspects the damage. Mercifully his shoe only clipped it. He scrapes his heel along the grass and is able to get most of it off – though a stubborn white nugget stays lodged in the grip. He'll have to give it a rinse when he gets home.

Taban once asked his mom why dog mess turns white over time. His mom explained that it was to do with too much bonemeal in dogfood. 'Their tummies can't absorb it.'

Taban asked why we kept putting it in their food then?

His mom didn't have an answer.

Taban continues on his way and reaches the parking lot where Eve is waiting by her car. She is a tall, slender woman in her twenties, with black frizzy hair and a red leather jacket. Her skin is a sort of faint brown that reminds Taban of toast. According to his dad this is because her dad was Greek and her mother Shona. One time Taban overheard his uncle joke that Eve and her husband Zahid were a one-couple UN summit. He didn't quite understand what Athel meant by that, but the adults all laughed in that bassy barky ugly way they do when one of them has just said something 'naughty'.

'Oh God! Taban, what happened?'

Eve rushes up and throws her arms around him.

'Sorry I'm late,' Taban says.

'Never mind that! You're all scraped up and this gash on your face looks awful!' She brushes his cheek ever so slightly then brings her hand to rest on his shoulder. Her gaze is intense. 'What happened?'

'Oh I tripped over a bucket by the stairs near Shumba Block and landed on my face. The bucket was full so I got soaked too. It was really embarrassing. All my classmates laughed.'

'They all laughed? I swear kids are so cruel. And who left that bucket out? They ought to be fired.'

'No, no, it was my fault, Eve. I wasn't looking.'

'Really? You sure? You're not fibbing are you? No one pushed you?'

Taban looks directly into her sage-green eyes. 'No,' he says, deploying his neutral-smile. 'It was all an accident.' A lie enters the world. The truth stays burning in Taban's gut. 'Don't be upset.'

Eve pouts. 'Too late. I'm already upset and I refuse to be un-upset-ed. Zahid, could you pass me the first aid kit from under the passenger seat?'

There is a long groan from the back of the car.

'The great Titania does not stoop to gather medicinal supplies from under ... passenger seats ... Urgh. My head.'

'Babe, I know that you're hungover, but Taban's face is bleeding and you are *right there* – so help me out please.'

There is a sigh and a rummaging. Then a dainty hand with long purple nails emerges from the open car window holding a green plastic box. It has 'First Aid' and a cross printed in red on it. Eve fishes out a plaster and some antiseptic cream. Taban feels a sting as she applies the cream and then seals it in with the plaster.

'There we go,' she says, quickly kissing him on the forehead like one might put a full stop at the end of a sentence. 'Now hop in the front. Let's get you home.'

Taban complies. He catches a glimpse of Zahid sprawled face-down across the back seat. He is in a dishevelled white gown decorated with blue and silver feathers. The sight does not surprise Taban. Eve and Zahid work in the theatre.

Eve reverses the car out of the parking lot. Moments later they are driving through the centre of Harare. The open windows let in the scents of the street – petrol, molten tarmac, cigarette smoke, sweat, and jacaranda flowers. After a few minutes Eve speaks. 'Tell us a story, Taban.'

'What?'

'Well I was going to ask about your day, but I know you don't really go in for that sort of small talk. Tell us a story. You're always scribbling on bits of paper. I'm sure you're full of stories.'

'I don't have any good stories.'

'Don't believe you.'

'Really. It's true.'

'Na. Fibs. Tell us one.'

Eve is difficult to dissuade once she gets an idea in her head. Taban thinks for a minute but his mind is still full of fists and can't remember anything from his notebook. He will just have to make something up as he goes along. So he opens his mouth and these words fall out:

'Once two peoples lived in the shadow of a mountain along the bank of a river.

'One lived in the valleys and plains. They tended to be short and brawny and were usually farmers, astronomers, and healers. They were known for their vision. Some were born with silvery eyes that could see for great distances in the day and even further at night. The people had a name that cannot be spoken in our language – for it is more a story than a name, made more with pictures than with words. The best I can do is this – *E*yes. They were *E*yes.

'The other people lived in the hills and caves. They tended to be tall and thin and were usually metal workers, warriors, and musicians. They were known for their height. Some were born with a trait that meant they would never stop growing until they died – and even then they

54

would grow for another year after that. They too had a name that cannot truly be spoken in our tongue. The best I can do is this – Tall. They were Tall.

'These two peoples sometimes fought. More often though they coexisted. They traded with one another. Tall would marry Eyes and vice versa. For, while they saw themselves as two separate peoples, they also saw themselves as two related peoples; two branches of the same family. There was also another idea – popular with a minority – that the two peoples had once been one people. That they had once lived together in a great stone city on top of the mountain. But they angered Heaven with their arrogance and so were punished – split in two, exiled into the bush.

'Most thought this idea was a myth. That the two peoples had always been two. That their alliances were not based on any long forgotten spiritual connection, but on practical earthy concerns. That the two peoples had qualities that were useful to each other. Through Eyes, Tall could get crops and medicine and silver-sighted night-time guides. Through Tall, Eyes could get steel tools and deep-voiced dancing soldiers whose reach with a spear was double their own.

'For a thousand years they bickered, bartered, warred, and loved.

'Two people in the shadow of a mountain they called Parent, along the shore of the river they called Teacher.

'Then one day a third people came up the river and everything changed ...'

Taban feels the source of the words flowing out of him slip away – dwindling into silence. A river dammed.

He realises that at some point Eve parked the car near a petrol station and has been listening intently. Even Zahid has risen from his stupor. The adults stare.

'What in the hell was—'

Zahid fizzles as Eve fixes him with an expression that Taban recognises as her Angry Smile. She turns to Taban – claps quietly in excitement.

'Oh Taban that was wonderful! That voice you spoke with. It was so expressive and deep. And you were using all these big words for someone of your age. It really is as I suspected – you are brimming with all this promise and it's just rotting away in that stupid school. That settles it!' Eve reverses out at great speed. Taban wobbles in his seat. 'I'm going to have a word with your mother. I think you should do after-school drama lessons with Zahid and me. I think it would be good for you. Help you come out of your shell— Oh Christ!'

The car swerves.

Taban's stomach leaps into his mouth.

There is a sharp clunk in the back followed by a groan.

'Bloody hell, Eve!' says a pained Zahid, emerging from the back seat, briefly vertical.

'Oh I'm so sorry, Babe. There was a butterfly. It would've been a tragedy if I killed it.'

'It would've been a tragedy if you killed me!'

Zahid slumps back into his horizontal realm.

'So do you agree with my idea, Babe? Drama lessons for Taban?'

A violet-nailed thumbs up rises from the back seat.

'Oh wonderful! I'm so excited. It was a lovely story. Like

something out of *Lord of the Rings* or the stories Nana used to read me as a child. Did you make it all up yourself Taban?'

Taban does not know what to say. He doesn't know where the words came from – only the texture of them as they emerged. The story had a strange quality. Like an old memory, but one that didn't belong to him. Or maybe it did? For a moment he is standing on the shoulders of *P*arent looking down upon the green foliage petering out into earth-brown and sand-yellow swirls.

'I think so,' he says to Eve, breathing crisp mountain air. 'I think.'

< < <

Prey: Numb

That night Taban cannot sleep. He lies on his back under the mosquito net and thinks about three things – wanting to die, wanting the world to die, and mountain air reaching into his lungs. He rolls on his side and stares at the gap in the curtains. Normally he wouldn't do this. He hates that gap. He always thinks something is about to emerge from it. A demon. A ghost. A monster. Usually he'd bury his face in the pillow or look at the wall or ceiling. Not tonight though. Tonight it doesn't seem so scary. Tonight he almost wants something to come.

No. No 'almost' about it.

He definitely wants something to come.

A glimmer. A wet sheen.

Is he seeing things?

Two familiar lights appear – burning softly from beyond the curtain.

It is himself.

No. Not himself. He is Taban. No, this is the fox from before. It doesn't seem frightening now. Or maybe it's just that *nothing* seems frightening now.

Become conduit.

The fox peeks its moist nose through the mosquito net. It slithers up beside him. Its bones pop and crack as it moves. It brings its face up to Taban.

Taban looks into its eyes. Deep warm hazel. A human's eyes. Taban strokes the animal's head. Grey fibrous fur comes apart in his hands.

The fox snuffles its snout to his neck.

Words ring out in Taban's head like mournful bells.

I hate you more than anything.

I hate you.
I hate you.
Taban can't tell if they are his or the fox's.
Jaws bite down.

< < <

Taban is Solomon. He is Solomon and has always been Solomon. His eyes are silver. He is 5 foot 8 inches. He is all chest and shoulders. His hair is short and black. He is wearing an olive suit. He is walking home after teaching his class, thinking about his student Ibn – a young man on the verge of graduation. Promising, but spends far too much time playing the guitar Father Graham gave him. Worse still he keeps sneaking out from the orphanage to go watch Tall bands play in the township bar. He wonders how he might dissuade him from these frivolous interests.

These small thoughts are pushed aside by a bigger thought –

There is an armoured car outside my house.

It is cream. On the side: a crest. Blue lion on a yellow shield. Four men skulk. They have sand-coloured uniforms and rubber-soled combat boots. Each has an armband with the same crest as the car and a gold badge pinned to their breast pocket. Even though it is dark Solomon can see all of this clearly. This is because he was born with the Eyes gift of vision and also because he has been both expecting and dreading this moment for months – ever since he gave that speech at the church two months back.

Another thought barges in –

Vashti.

Is she still in the house? He and his wife had often discussed what to do if Domestic Protection came. They had carved out a secret compartment under the floorboards in the bedroom. If she had heard that loud vehicle pull up, or spotted it approaching, then she would hide there. If she had not, or if they had found that compartment then ...

Solomon cannot think about this.

He has to trust and hope that she is safe – find safety for himself.

Flashlights. Two of the men fan around the house. Another kicks down the door. The last one walks towards Solomon. Did they hear his footsteps? Or spot him? No. None of them have the gift of vision. The Andrews Government keeps Domestic Protection entirely White Albion to ensure its loyalty.

Regardless, Solomon needs to move. He heads back to the crossroads and breaks south-east into the bush. Fifteen minutes later he reaches the river – one of Teacher's many 'students' where the local Eyes have long caught fish and sifted for flakes of gold and silver that wash down from the mineral-rich mountains. Spotting the old mopani tree across the water, he counts five hundred steps east. There, buried under a thorn bush, he finds the stash he hid two months ago. In it there is a handgun, bullets, rations, a map, and a small tent, all bundled in a bag. Enough supplies to make the trek to the town the Albions call Reedsway, but which the Eyes call Clay Sun. He has contacts there who can smuggle him north to where Isaiah Tatonga Jongwe's revolutionaries have taken power.

Suddenly there is a voice. 'Don't move, Teach,' it says.

Solomon recognises the voice. 'Tanaka?'

'Don't move.'

Solomon puts up his hands. Behind him he hears footsteps, panicked breath, a faint rattle as his former student struggles to hold the rifle steady.

'Why would you do this? I taught you how to read, Tanaka. Got you your job at the factory. I even delivered your child.'

'I'm ... I'm sorry, Teach. You know I have a family ... What the Albions will do.'

Solomon nods. His head understands but his heart still hurts.

'You knew this would happen,' Tanaka continues. 'DP has informants in every city, every township, every reserve.'

Moist sniffles. Is Tanaka crying? That would be in character.

'You idiot!' Tanaka shouts. 'An *E*yes uprising? You can't talk about that sort of thing without there being consequences.'

Solomon stares into the water. The river surges. The wind picks up. A rainstorm is coming in from the west.

'Tanaka, the fact that there have been consequences is exactly why I was right to say what I did. What's the point in talk without consequence?' Solomon turns to Tanaka and smiles.

'I hope for your family's sake you're a good shot.'

Solomon lets himself fall backward into the river.

Bang.

Pain blooms like a flower in his hip. Dark water encloses him. It pulls, tumbles, drags. Solomon loses his body. He's just a mind suspended in a violent churn. Then even his mind dissolves into the river. For a moment he is nothing. Then, abruptly, his body returns – slippery and oozing. He is inside it and it is vomiting – full of mud and muddy sensations, face is scraping against wet stone.

Stone?

Solomon opens his eyes. A cave. But not a cave formed by any natural force he is aware of. The walls are green and translucent – humming with electricity. Veins of light flow through them in pulsating waves further into the cave – slowly fading into the distance like streams of cars on a midnight highway. Behind him there is only the dark swirling pool that spat him out. The river in its tumult must have pushed him into the cave through some underwater entrance.

Solomon tries to stand, but collapses, clutching his side. Water and blood pour out of the hole in his hip. He feels an overwhelming urge to sleep, but knows that if does he will not wake up. He stumbles forward, following the streams of light. Perhaps up ahead there is an exit. He struggles onward step by step – steadying himself against the wall. The path winds. Ascending. Descending. Ascending again. Descending again. There is no discernable pattern to its meandering.

A long time passes.

Solomon slumps to his knees.

He is going to die here.

He lies on the ground – watches his blood spill out onto stone.

Anger. He so rarely allows himself to feel it. Anger so intense it hurts.

This stupid country. We could free ourselves of the Albion in less than a year if we simply stood up and shrugged them off our backs. Instead we betray our bravest brothers and allow ourselves to be emasculated by a waning sickly empire.

This stupid country.

This stupid world.

As darkness engulfs his vision, Solomon imagines the world accompanying him into the peaceful black – snuffing out.

He's disgusted with himself, but can't help but smile.

Vashti. She'd be the only thing I'd spare ...

<<<

okay

A flicker in the dark. Solomon's lids creak half open.

Small. Six wings. Flutter, flutter. Yellow eye. A voice that comes from all around.

'My master has heard your wish sir and has a proposition. Will you come with me and hear him out?'

Solomon's left ear aches. He had an infection when he was young and ever since he has been sensitive to certain frequencies.

'Take this seed,' the creature continues. 'It'll save your life. Consider it an expression of our good intentions.'

Solomon would laugh but he doesn't have the strength.

Why not? At the end of it all, why not be taken in by an illogical dream?

The little winged being, sensing his agreement, places a pebble-sized seed in Solomon's palm. Emerald green. Its interior swirls like a storm cloud's eye. Suddenly, tiny spidery legs unfurl and it scurries up Solomon's arm – pries into his closed mouth.

Gulp.

Panic. Then a burning in his throat that soon gives way to a placid calm. The blackness on the edges of Solomon's vision dissipates. The heavy weight on his eyelids lifts. The pain in his side dulls. He looks down to see his wound has stopped bleeding. Not healed. Simply stopped. Like a faucet someone has twisted shut.

He stands. Never before has such a mundane action felt so magical. He laughs, giddy, confused, intrigued. What a wonderful dream his dying brain is having.

'Follow me,' the little winged being says, gesturing down the path.

Solomon nods – complies.

Eventually the tunnel widens into what looks like the ruins of a grand throne room. Or perhaps a theatre? A church? The vaulted roof certainly gives the space a reverent air. Though it is quite unlike any church, or theatre, or throne room, Solomon has ever seen. The chamber is forged from some metallic substance that throbs with a faint green light. The pulses of electricity surging through the walls terminate here – coiling around a strange ornamental structure in the centre. It looks like a throne, but also the base of a charred tree stump. It is wreathed in gold circuit fibres – spoiled and singed.

It takes Solomon a moment to realise there is something sat on this dark withered thing. A statue? A corpse? It is hard to tell. A human shape melted into the throne. Slivers of bronze peek out from the burnt mass. A suit of ceremonial armour? Around the throne-man there are similar figures hunched in reverence. Some of them are not hunched, but prone on the floor, headless. Hints of silver glint from within their scorched-black forms.

'Behold my King,' the little winged being says, a hint of mourning in its strange voice. 'There is little left of him now – his consciousness hangs on to the edge between life and death. But what remains is still greater than any living lord.'

'I see,' Solomon says, confused by the odd turn his dream has taken. 'And these fellows?' He gestures to the silver-tinged congregation.

The winged creature's voice drops into an unearthly growl. 'Traitors.'

Solomon waits for the creature to elaborate. For a moment it seems like it will not. Then it speaks again – its voice regaining its previous pitch and composure. 'I'm sure you know all about traitors.'

Tanaka at the river.

Solomon feels a rush of anger he quickly suppresses. It's not fair to judge the boy so harshly. *He's not a boy any more. Just a weak man. A weak man who shot you.*

Solomon shakes his head.

'It's hard when you're a man of vision. My master is – *was* – such a person. People who lack that vision will stab you in the back. But maybe you can succeed where my master was dragged down?'

Solomon frowns. He is growing tired of this convoluted fantasy. 'What are you offering? What is this all about?'

Two of the creature's six wings move just a crack. A toothy smile flashes through. 'Take up my master's mantle. Become the ruler he was destined to be. Choose this and you shall be granted the power to realise your vision. Or do not. Simply leave. Your wound is not fully healed yet – only stymied – but maybe you can make it to the north and live out a mundane life.'

For the first time since he encountered the little creature, Solomon begins to wonder if what is happening is actually real. He quickly dismisses it. This is simply some part of his dying brain testing his resolve, his conviction.

'Of course I choose power.'

Solomon laughs. His side aches in time with his chortles. *I'm nothing if not stubborn.*

The creature gestures to the throne-corpse. 'Then step forward and receive your boon, *King* Solomon.'

Solomon approaches the body, at first confidently, then with creeping hesitation. The closer he gets the more he can hear the faintest sound of breath. He can't tell if the breath is excited or fearful. Perhaps it is a bit of both? He stands over the throne-man. He thinks he can spot the vaguest flicker of light in its dead eyes. Beneath the dust and soot, he can just about discern the burnt outlines of thick cables fastening the corpse to its seat, tunnelling into its flesh. On its forehead – a crest. Sickle and a tree.

Solomon is about to ask what comes next when something launches out of the corpse's mouth. Lupin jaws snap around his throat. The air tastes of burnt plastic. A sad, hopeful whisper sounds within his soul, echoes from every dark corner in the room →

... *at last*

At first – nothing.

Then – everything.

Solomon is everything all at once. He is Teacher and also the riverbed beneath Teacher. He is Parent and also the icy trees that crown Parent. He is his father tilling the earth. He is his mother giving birth to him. He is his grandfather marking out the constellations on his sixth birthday. He is the village leader when the Albions relocate them during the Second Dividing. He is the village healer showing him what plants are poisonous. He is the visiting Emet convert showing him a book of human anatomy. He is his grandmother waving goodbye as he is taken by the church to be educated. He is a priest from a time long ago watching a city become an oven – fire and screams filling its stone-walled belly.

He is a king among kings. A king whose kingdom crosses space and time and reaches into other dimensions. A king without equal. A king who still feels inadequate because he is the king of bronze when kings have always been gold or silver. He is a gardener cultivating the tree. He is the tree whose roots, and pollen, and seeds, spread across worlds seeking fertile soil to suckle.

He is a seed of bronze. Or a corpse. Planted in the earth. Waiting to emerge. Waiting. Waiting. Waiting. Emerging. Emerging.

He is a mind in darkness – seeking **silence.**

Then, he is himself again. He is himself in the throne room deep beneath the earth. The little winged creature is gone. Whatever bit his throat is gone. Whatever dim light he thought he saw in the dead king's eyes is still there – barely.

With a heavy sigh, the corpse breaks apart into tiny ashen pieces that float upwards like torn paper before freezing mid-air and disintegrating.

To Solomon everything is at once clear and not clear. It's as if some deep inaccessible chamber of his mind comprehends the meaning of this scene, but does not articulate that meaning to his conscious self.

He feels inexplicable sadness. Inexplicable pleasure.

A thought bubbles up from the inaccessible chamber – *focus on your wound.*

Solomon obliges. He thinks about his hip. Imagines the bullet inside. Imagines the path it took to reach the nook by his spine. He imagines it going backwards – tracing its steps carefully, his flesh closing behind as it leaves his body.

And then it is so.

The bullet is on the floor. Wound: sealed.

A sudden wave of tiredness hits him like an icy gust.

He thinks – I am alive. Actually alive.

This was not a dying man's dream after all.

He staggers towards a recess at the back of the room. It is a thin duct he can barely squeeze into. Whatever has been implanted in his head tells him to press on. He does – even as he longs for sleep. In the tight metal tunnel time flows as in a nightmare – irrationally, imperceptibly fast and incredibly slow at once. Eventually, the chute terminates in a strange cloister. Viridian moss coats the floor. A thick stone door bars what looks like an exit. Above it – a symbol not unlike the one from that distant northern nation across the sea: the serpent that eats its own tail. Only this serpent has no tail, but instead two heads. Or, perhaps, it is two serpents devouring each other in an endless circle – one with the head of a fox, the other with the head of a human.

Before the door there is a throbbing, oily, almost organic receptacle. Some sort of locking mechanism? Solomon looks around the room – spots a large urn in the corner. He inspects it. It is full of skulls preserved in a mysterious ichor. He fishes one out – holds it up to the receptacle. It's the perfect size.

Surely not?

Something deep inside – *surely so.*

He places it in. Like the king's corpse before, it dissolves

– leaving only a faint shimmer. A voice sounds in Solomon's head: **Tribute Acknowledged.**

There is a humming and a whirring and then the door opens. Solomon shields his eyes from the brilliant moonlight pouring into the tomb. He notices that the tips of his fingers have turned white. Did this happen before or after he encountered the winged creature and the dead king? Father Graham once mentioned he had some sort of skin disorder as a child. Perhaps it is coming back? Or perhaps it is a curse? Some sort of price to pay for this power. Solomon is not sure. His head is fat with indigestible alien knowledge. He opens and closes his hand. It doesn't seem like his. Through the gaps in his fingers, he makes out a figure. He can hear the pattering of rain. No. Not rain. It sounds more like a shower. The figure solidifies into a definite silhouette. Vashti?

No. It is Eve.

Wait. Who is *Eve*?

<<<

Curious Souls Entwined Under Pearly-Eyed Night

Taban is himself. He has always been himself. No matter how much he wishes he wasn't.

He is lying on his side on a mound of dirt – slick with fast-evaporating fox fluid. Just like Mana Pools. It is late at night, but he can see clearly – like he has Solomon's silver eyes. He is in Eve's and Zahid's garden – by the lemon trees and the fence that separates his family's property from their neighbour's. A light is on in Eve and Zahid's house. The bathroom. There is a person inside. Eve. Taban knows this because the curtains are apart and there is little in the way other than steam. He also knows this because he can hear the shower running. Even though it is many metres away – muffled by concrete and glass. He can hear water hitting bathroom tiles like it is happening right next to his ear. And the more he thinks about that sound, the more he can sense other things too. The harsh light refracting off the bathroom mirror. The humid air. The water flowing around his aching high-arched feet. No. Not his feet. Her feet. Eve's feet. The dull ache is in Eve's feet. And in her calves. And in her thighs.

Taban recoils, forcing the scene from his mind. He feels nauseated. The idea of himself alone in the dark looking through this window at Eve, remotely experiencing all these sensations, feels instinctively wrong. Even if – according to Caleb – looking at naked women is what he is meant to do now.

A thought enters his head: Could he do what Solomon did? Could he fix that ache in her leg like Solomon fixed the wound in his hip?

Another thought: Could he stop her heart – like Solomon did to that man during the ambush?

Before he has time to consider further, Taban hears muffled footsteps. Someone else is out here in the dark with him. He freezes.

A person sneaks out from behind the lemon tree. It is Justice. Justice is an eighteen-year-old boy who does gardening, cleaning, cooking, and security work for various houses in the neighbourhood. Taban's mother had told him that Justice came here from a remote village and does not know how to read or write, and that his situation is quite sad. Taban asked her why she didn't just get him a place at Highveldt – then he could learn to read and write and his situation would be less sad. She replied to this by mumbling something about it being 'complicated' and then further mumbling about it being, 'too late.' Taban was unconvinced. He remains so. A Solomon thought emerges from his brain: *Learning can never come 'too late' or ever be 'too complicated'.*

Taban tries to think of an excuse in case Justice catches him. Then he realises that Justice cannot see him. Partly because he does not have Solomon's night vision, but also because his eyes are completely fixed on Eve. He is wearing a strange face – like Caleb when he was looking at those magazines, but also like Hendrick when he was hitting him earlier today.

There is a barking. Eve's daft and ineffectual Labrador, Legolas, has dimly sensed something. Justice disappears – around the corner, past the hedgerow, and through one of the many gaps dug under the fence by Legolas. Taban shuffles on his stomach to a similar gap behind him and returns to his family's own garden where, thankfully, he can see the window to his room is wide open. He goes to climb in.

Then – a squirm in his stomach. Something sharp sliding

upward. It is in his chest now. His throat. He quickly covers his mouth – feels something ooze into his hands.

A tooth. Canine. Incisor the size of a fist. Its surface is golden and reflective like a mirror. Taban sees himself in it. Two things have changed. Firstly, his eyes are silver. Secondly, there is a new glowing mark. It is on his neck. White. Cold and chalky to the touch. Long, rectangular. Like one of those Greek pillars he saw in an encyclopaedia once.

Like this →

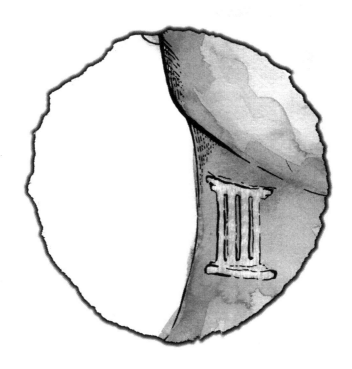

The irony is that – by all the measures by which we have in the past judged our leaders – The Bronze Patriarch is exemplary.

Long ago we celebrated those who expanded the material borders of our empire – no matter how ruthlessly.

And when material borders grew too mundane for us we evangelised those who expanded the breadth of our knowledge – if not the depth. We became a civilisation of babbling essayists and incessant diarists (I recognise the irony in me noting this). We flattered our eyes for seeing and thought little of what we had seen.

The World Tree created by The Bronze Patriarch does everything we did and everything we do better. It accumulates mental and physical territory in an unceasing, unyielding way, that should – and indeed did at first – make our conqueror hearts sing. It turns disorganised wilderness into invisible synaptic libraries.

But The World Tree has a flaw. It does not flatter our frail egos. It views us as it views all other life – as soil, shit, and data, to be mulched and sucked through its roots.

In this way it has expanded the dominion of our knowledge invaluably. We have spent our lives presuming to see.

At last something has looked back.

– Brother Antal of The Bronze Cast,
extract from *The Final History of The Triumvirate of Metals*

Five years later
At the Highveldt
O-Level
Library

Blue Opal Fox Bite

or

*All Your Arrows Dipped In Sweat
And Blood, Aimed Heavenwards,
Ready To Pierce The Moon*

A Lion And A Jackal Look Into The Void

Peering from behind an O-Level Biology book, Taban closes his eyes and imagines the librarian Ms Govera's shinbone – or tibia as the text describes it. He imagines it completely, starting with a full picture of it, then zooming in to observe the tiny details, panning upwards from the base near the ankle until he reaches the knee. Then he envisions a knock. Like a knock on a door. But not too hard. Just a tiny knuckle clack on wood. He doesn't want to cause any real harm. It's just training after all.

'Ewe!' he hears Ms Govera exclaim.

He opens his eyes.

She is rubbing her knee with one hand and with her other hand holding an empty teacup – droplets spilling out onto her long sunflower dress.

'Are you okay, Ms Govera?' Taban asks.

'Aaah it's nothing, Taban. I've just been getting these odd twinges in my knee lately. Getting old I guess.'

'Would you like me to get you another cup of tea?'

'Yes, thank you very much, Taban. That would be lovely.'

He walks to the reception desk, takes the empty cup from her, and goes into the bare-bones staff kitchen at the back of the library. Once there he switches on the kettle – waits for it to boil. Things are going to plan. Solomon's powers are now staying with him for weeks after the fox visitations and have grown strong enough. This weekend he will finally get his revenge on Hendrick and Daisy.

Taban imagines Hendrick, star of the Lion House athletics team, galloping towards victory at the annual cross-country run as he has done every year for as long as he's been a student at Highveldt. He easily overtakes his rivals from

Houses Leopard, Hyena, and Jackal. Everything goes as usual. Then suddenly – not. At the last 50 metres, Hendrick feels a jolt of pain and numbness in his left leg – like someone has punched it right out from beneath him. He trips and falls. His cheek scrapes along dry grass as he slides to a stop. A teacher rushes to his side. Hendrick feels like his bladder is being squeezed in a vice. He resists at first but soon he can no longer hold it. He pisses himself in front of the whole school and all the attending parents. They laugh at his suffering. Such is the way.

The kettle clicks.

Taban puts aside his daydream and makes tea for Ms Govera. Black. One sugar. Then he returns to her reception desk and hands it to her.

'Thank you, Taban,' she says, sipping her tea. 'Perfect. As always.'

'You're welcome, Ms Govera. Thank you for letting me stay in the library all the time.'

'It's no trouble at all. I only wish the rest of the children your age were as respectful and well-behaved. Did I tell you that I found two students the other day getting up to all sorts of indecency behind the History section? And one of them was a prefect! Can you believe it?'

'Yes, Ms Govera. You mentioned it the other day.'

'I swear children just get worse as they get older. They want to be seen as adults but act as irresponsible as ever.' She lets out a short exasperated gasp. 'Anyway, I shouldn't go on.' She eases back into her chair and picks up the book lying open on the desk. The title on the cover is golden and sinuous. It reads: *Tyrant's Heart*.

'What book are you reading?' asks Taban.

'It's history. Well. *Highly dramatised* history. It's about the life of Genghis Khan.'

'I know him. He was in *Age of Empires 2*.'

'What's that?'

'A computer game.'

'Oh. Well I'm glad they're at least putting *some* educational material in those silly games.'

'From what I could tell he was very ruthless. Cruel. Seems odd to romanticise him.'

'Yes. Though really you can say the same of just about every conqueror. Why are Alexander The Great and Julius Caesar lauded – or at the very least viewed with nuance – while Genghis goes down in the history books as a simplistic butcher?'

Taban considers the question. 'I don't think I know,' he says.

Ms Govera sighs. 'Maybe when you're older you might figure it out.'

Taban hovers like a lost balloon tangled up in a bush. 'I like books,' he says, unprompted. 'You can read all their pages and know them inside out. People are harder. You can never read all of their pages and they can never read all of yours. You can't truly know them and they can't truly know you.'

Govera gives him a sad, sympathetic look. 'Oh Taban. But that's the best thing about people. You can finish a book but a person is never finished. There are always new things to discover, new things to share.'

He looks at her blankly, neutrally.

'Never mind.'

Taban nods, puts on his neutral-smile.

Above the entrance to the library the clock ticks. 16:45.

'I better get going, Ms Govera. Mom will nearly be done teaching swimming by now.'

'No worries, Taban. Tell your mom I wish her well.'

'Yes Ms.'

Taban slings his bag over his shoulder and exits the library.

A pebble nicks his ear.

He turns.

Scurrying. Snickers.

Whoever threw the stone is gone. As usual. They don't stick around. When the other students bully him now it is done without direct confrontation. Discreet missiles, whispers. The words 'Creep' and 'Snitch' just barely audible over the whine of flies and mosquitoes. As Taban rounds the corner two girls and a boy walking towards him – chatting, smiling – immediately fall quiet and cut a wide berth. Discreet missiles, whispers, but mostly *silence*. In his presence the lips of a student he has never even met will zip shut. On the rare occasion he tries to talk to one of them they will act like they can't hear or abruptly walk away. But while their voices are mute their expressions are very loud – so loud even Taban can understand them. Disgust. Hatred. Pity.

Oh well. Such is the way.

Actually, the boy is grateful. It makes what he plans to do much easier.

Taban continues north toward his mother's classroom along a narrow green-grass path. A gentle breeze is dragging thin red petals along the ground. Taban recognises them as being from a bougainvillea. His mother taught him the names of all sorts of trees and plants. The petals hover above the grass. To Taban's colour-blind eyes they blend in – becoming shimmering patterns in the sunlight. Absently, he blunders through, squashing the petals beneath his shoes. They are too thin to produce a crunch.

After about five minutes the path comes to an end near the Central Grounds. Nearby is a two-storey building – five classrooms on the bottom, five on the top, with a large adjacent office for Headmaster Horlick on the ground floor. The Shumba Building – as it is officially called – is made of smooth white and grey stone that is cool to the touch. The front veranda stretches out like a yawning tongue. At the very tip of that tongue a grey-blue marble lion is sat sphinx-like – surveying the running field. Taban imagines the school founders must have thought the lion very regal, but he sees its fixed expression differently. There's something off about the way its eyebrows are raised. Behind the image of pride and authority, Taban senses insecurity, a hint of panic. As if the lion is on the cusp of a terrible realisation, but trying to keep up appearances. Or maybe not. Maybe the sculptor was just not very good. Still, Taban feels a sort of kinship with the gaudy cat.

Neutral-smile.

Neutral-pride and authority.

Taban enters the classroom by the stairs. 47A. His mother's. It is empty, but for the dark brown desks and blank chalkboard. Light and cool air pour in through wide oblong windows. In the corner, by his mother's desk, rests a long wire hook for pulling them shut. As Taban takes a seat an image enters his mind. That hook of wire scooping into Hendrick's eye socket. He is pleased. Then displeased with his pleasure. Then displeased with his displeasure at his being pleased. He closes his eyes and tries to do the breathing exercise Dr Green encouraged. Slow inhalations, slower exhalations. Slow. Measured. No thoughts, only breathing. The breath feels warm in his throat. The floor: solid beneath his feet.

Hendrick is not stabbed in the eye.

Hendrick trips and pisses himself at the cross-country run.

No need to go too far.

No need to ...

A vision. Dark orb. His hands wrapped around it. Smooth like glass. Beneath the surface there are glimmers that look like lights, forms that look like people. Taban's hands are enormous – enclosing the orb like an atmosphere around a planet. He feels an urge to squeeze. His hands are squeezing. The sphere resists at first, then cracks, crumbles. Purple liquid pours over his hands.

Warm breath. Not within him this time, but without. A familiar breath on his neck full of earthy smells once unpleasant to him but which have now become alluring. Raw meat. Bone. Matted hair. Sweat. Petroleum. The floor beneath him feels slick with something hot, viscous.

His hands are still squeezing. They won't stop. Shards grind into his palms. His nails dig into the skin between his knuckles, drawing blood. Please stop squeezing. Please stop holding so tight. Please stop. Stop. Stop.

A deafening slam.

Taban feels the sound ripple through him – shattering the image and the spell it had over him. His eyes open. His mother Ann is by the door, cylindrical sports bag dropped by her feet. She is dressed in her usual work clothes – grey trousers, black top, and shoes. Perfectly triangulated between smart and practical. Her auburn hair – still damp from the pool – is cut short, but not so short as to draw attention. Her eyes are the same near-black as Taban's. People often claim they look eerily alike.

'Oops!' says his mother. 'Sorry Taban. I didn't mean to slam.

The janitor repaired the hinge today and I just can't get used to it. So slippery.' She pulls the door open and then closes it again to illustrate.

Taban shrugs. 'Ms Govera says she wishes you well.'

'Oh. That's sweet of her. Rukudzo really is lovely isn't she? Tell her tomorrow that she should come over for dinner again sometime and to give me a call after work so we can sort out the details. Could you pass me my bag? It's just under the desk.'

Taban hands her a satchel filled with folders and papers. Ann slips it around her shoulder and picks up her sports bag. 'Right,' she says. 'Are we all ready to go?'

Taban nods. As he stands up and walks toward her, he reflexively grips the strap of his school bag and feels a grainy substance in his palm.

A shimmering dust.

A familiar warmth on his lip.

'Oh dear,' his mother says, pulling out a tissue from her bag. 'You're having one of your nosebleeds again, Taban.'

Taban stuffs the tissue in his nostril. As he walks to the car with his mother, his mind wanders back to the cross-country run – his plans.

Trip.

Piss.

<<<

Our Flowers Unbloomed, Lodged Tight In Clenched Throats

Outside the car the jacaranda trees that line the road are in full bloom. Their highest branches form a purple-blue canopy which pinprick sunlight sifts through like particles of gold.

The atmosphere in the car is less serene.

Taban stares out the window, avoids making eye contact.

His mother taps her fingers along the steering wheel.

The red light remains red.

'How are things at school?' she asks Taban.

'Fine.'

'Are you making any friends in your class?'

'Not really.'

'You know, I think you should try to spend some time away from the library every now and then. I reckon it'd do you good. Get out and socialise more.'

A nauseous heat rises in his stomach.

'It's just I worry that it's going to be hard for you later in life – you know? As you get older you get less and less chances to make friends.'

'Cool,' Taban hears himself saying. 'I guess that's something to look forward to then.'

'I'm just trying to help, my boy. There's no reason to get sarky with me.'

'I'm not being sarcastic.' He flashes her a neutral-smile. 'I genuinely look forward to it.' Then he turns back to the window – eyes looking empty as they peer out at the world.

Ann remains quiet for a moment. Her brow furrows.

'You know you're not the first person in our family who's struggled to fit in. Your dad had problems. I did too.'

'Oh?'

'It's true. When I was a little younger than you are now I didn't think I was girl.'

Taban listens, considers this. 'What did you think you were? A boy?'

'No, I ... don't know how to explain it. I felt I wasn't really a boy either. I didn't know what I was, but I strongly felt like neither of those words belonged to me and that all the adults in my life were trying to force me to play some sick game of pretend. It's funny to think about it now but I really, really hated them ...' Ann bites her lip. 'I hated them. I would shave my hair off with my dad's razor and wear these ugly dungarees.'

'Oh? So what happened? Did you grow out of it?'

'I wouldn't put it like that. That would suggest it was easy – that I just sat on my backside and waited for the world to come to me. But I didn't. It was painful, but I did my best to compromise – go out there and meet the world halfway. And Taban, really that's all I would like you to try. I think it would do you so much good in the long run. Just go out there and try.'

Taban considers her words. 'So did it?' he asks.

'Did what?'

'Did the world meet you halfway?'

Ann falls silent and remains so for a while.

Then she says, 'I love you my boy.'

Taban is surprised. He can't remember the last time she vocalised such a feeling.

'I ...' he begins. He wants to say, 'I Love You.' Feels he should say, 'I Love You.' Because it is true and something he feels. Despite everything, the boy still loves his mother. But the words stick in his throat – their texture coarse and unfamiliar.

Instead the word, 'Thanks,' comes out.

Ann smiles a disappointed smile.

After several minutes they arrive at a two-storey building with a high wall surrounded by rose bushes. A bronze sign by the bell for the electric gate reads –

'Doctor Chenjerai Green Ndhlovu – Psychologist'

< < <

Dissolving Dreams

Doctor Chenjerai 'Green' Ndhlovu clicks his pen and adjusts his reading glasses.

'July 12, 2000. Session 40.' He smiles. 'My. It's been that long.'

Taban wears his usual comfortable neutral expression.

'So Taban ... how have you been finding the new medication?'

'It's fine. I guess.'

Chenjerai frowns. 'Your mother says you had another sleepwalking incident.'

'Oh. Ja. I did have one last month.'

Truthfully, Taban had a lot more than just one, but after many years of practice he is very good at not getting caught coming back from his night-time journeys.

'That's a shame.' Chenjerai scribbles something down on his notebook. 'I really hoped the Trazodone would put a stop to them.' He puts the pen down, stands up, and walks to a large bookshelf on the left wall. Taban knows that when Chenjerai does this it signals two things – *This will not go in the notebook and I am talking now as a family friend.*

'So how have you been?'

'Fine. Looking forward to the play tomorrow. Eve and Zahid are very excited.'

'Your mom tells me you've got a Gala & Cross-Country event this weekend. Are you looking forward to that too?'

Taban doesn't respond.

Chenjerai smiles, inspects a small framed photo on the shelf. 'You have my sympathies. I hated being forced to do sporting events at school as well. I mean I've never exactly had the build for it.'

'So you were always short?'

'Ouch. You don't have to put it so bluntly, Taban. But yes. Always short. Always a little round as well.' Chenjerai stares at the photo, lost in thought.

'Who's in the picture?' asks Taban.

'Oh. It's myself and an old friend. You can see if you like.'

He passes the picture. The wooden frame has images of baobab trees engraved along its sides. Chenjerai looks younger in the photo – his smile lively while today it is weary. His dress sense is also more vibrant. A multi-coloured jacket, peach shirt, and cream trousers. The man next to Chenjerai is also dressed exuberantly – wearing sunglasses, and a sleeveless vest in the same motley style as Chenjerai's, along with snakeskin boots. He is very tall, maybe even as tall as Uncle Athel. His one hand is clutching a big beer bottle, the other is around Chenjerai's shoulder. He is laughing in the photo. It's an arresting vision. For a moment Taban feels he can even hear the man's laugh – soft, deep, warm. He hands the picture back.

'It's a nice photo.'

'Thank you. Your mother took it actually. We all went to the same university.'

'Who's the other person?'

'Oh. He was someone who was very dear to me. We're not really in touch any more though.' Chenjerai pauses, as if considering whether to say more. 'I ... embarrassed him ... I think. It's hard to explain.'

'Was he dear to you in a way that you weren't dear to him?'

Chenjerai looks surprised. 'Yes. Exactly that. How did you guess?'

Taban remains quiet. *Caleb ...*

'Apologies. I won't pry.' Chenjerai puts the photo back on the shelf, sits at his desk. 'We should get on with what I have planned for today. We're going to be trying something a little different – hypnotherapy.'

Taban looks at Chenjerai sceptically.

'It's okay. I haven't lost my mind. This is something that works for some people. And, given that our regular treatment regime hasn't quite been doing the trick, it's worth a shot. Now I want you to relax and lean forward.' Chenjerai fishes a box out of his desk. In it is a little gemstone on a string. 'I want you to focus on this pendulum.'

Taban complies.

'Watch as it drifts back and forth.'

Taban complies.

'Focus on the breathing technique I taught you. In, slowly. Out, even slower.'

Taban breathes in slow, then out even slower.

'Clear your mind.'

Mind Clearing. Hurt Hendrick. Cross-Country. Swimming Gala. Hendrick Wetting Himself. Hendrick Impaled With Hook. Hendrick Cut With Scissors. Play. Eve. Zahid. Hendrick Hurting. Hendrick Humiliated. Daisy Hurt. Hurt Daisy. Hurt Caleb. Hurt Parents. Shame. Shame. Shame. Alone. Breathing. Breathing. Hurt World. End World. Injury. Wound. Wound. Wound. Hurt Myself. Hurt. Hurt ... Mind Cleared.

After several minutes, Chenjerai instructs, 'Now close your eyes.'

Taban closes his eyes.

'You are going back. It is yesterday. Breakfast. What are you eating?'

'Toast.'

'Good. What is the weather like?'

'Breezy. Mom says there might be rain coming in.'

'Good. We are going back further now. It is a week ago. Breakfast. What are you eating?'

'Sandwich. Mom is watching to make sure I finish it.'

'And what is the weather like?'

'Crisp. It's early morning. I feel the wind picking up.'

'Good. We are going back even further. It is a month ago. Breakfast. What are you eating?'

'Cereal. It tastes like dust.'

'And what is the weather like?'

'Stuffy. Like always.'

'Good. We are going back even further. It is one year ago. Breakfast. What are you eating?'

'Some bit of meat. I don't know what it is. It was stuck between my teeth when I woke.'

'And what is the weather like?'

'It's hot. It's so hot.'

'Good, Taban. Now I want you to go back even further. Back to your earliest memory. Can you go back that far? What is it you see? What is it you feel?'

Taban feels hot. Feels like the whole world is black and burning. 'I am alone. I am dissolving. I am eating … myself. I am dissolving inside myself. I am …'

'Taban, open your eyes now … Taban? … Taban!'

'I am …'

<<<

Let Go?

Taban is Ann. They have always been Ann.

They are twelve years old, sitting near the bank of a river, under a mopani tree. Their short hair is patchy and uneven – the result of a frantic self-administered chop. Their dungarees have blood stains. Their shoulders sting. A devil thorn sticks out, but seems distant. Not in their arm, but the arm of some alien body. The only sensation that feels real and present is the strange itching mark on their hand that everyone else keeps saying isn't there.

I *hate* you, the voice in Ann's head says.

I hate *you*.

I hate you, hate you, hate you, hate you …

Ann cradles their head, plugs fingers in their ears.

'Ann?'

Ann turns to see their brother Joseph approaching. Joseph is Ann's twin and – other than neater hair and broader shoulders – he looks identical. He walks over. His footsteps are absurdly gentle. Athel often jokes that 'Young Jo' has never once broken a twig.

'I'm sorry that Dad lost his cool,' he says, sitting down next to Ann.

'It's not your fault, Jo. And it's not his, or Mom's, or Athel's, or the school's, or anything. I'm a mess.' Ann begins to cry.

Joseph puts an arm around their shoulder, squeezes them close.

'You're not a mess, man. You're fine. It was daft of Mom and Dad to think you were just going to blend in at some kak all-girls boarding school like it was nothing.'

He stands up – offers a hand. 'Come on. Let's go home. Athel and I talked to Dad and he says he'll drop the subject of you going back to Saint Catherine's.' Joseph smiles. 'We'll sort something out.'

Ann wipes their eyes and reaches up, feels the warmth of Joseph's fingers entwined with their own. Mirrored hands – lifting, supporting. As they have always done.

Snap.

A sharp powerful pull.

Screams.

Something leathery is latched around Joseph's leg – dragging him toward the river.

Instinctively, Ann's free arm wraps around a thick mopani branch, holds on.

Heels dig in.

Screams. Clothes ripping. Another ripping – horrifying in its unfamiliarity.

Ann's arms burn. Their joints pop. Shoulders dislocate. Muscles tear. Pain shoots like electricity from the tips of their fingers to the nexus of their temples. Their eyes wince closed for a moment.

Then the screaming stops.

Ann opens their eyes.

Joseph is looking at them. His expression agonised, but with an ambiguous softness – resignation or hope? Trust? A crocodile strains, muddy water splashing around it. He mouths words that Ann can't hear – everything is muted and far away, like it's happening on another planet.

Ann holds on dearly – tightens their grip.

I love you, Jo.

Are the words in their head or on their tongue?

Then, they feel something rend, hear a final rip, and Joseph's fingers slip away.

A distant splash.

The lake is still.

Ann collapses, tries to piece together the words Joseph was saying.

'It's okay. Let go.'

'It's okay. Don't let go.'

Ann's chest burns. They throw up some bloody pulpy substance into the dirt. Across the lake, on the opposite shore, they can see what looks like some enormous, strange, jackal-like animal. Its horrid jaws slowly mouth the words –

'Taban, are you okay?'

'Taban, let go.'

<<<

Loss Whispered To White Petals

Taban is Taban. Taban has always been Taban. He is lying on his side on the floor of an office. There is a small cushion under his cheek. It is yellow and has a blue elephant on it. Above him hazy figures emit muffled sounds. Slowly they solidify into people – his mother Ann and his psychologist Dr Green. The sounds become voices and the voices become words.

'Taban? Taban, are you okay?' asks his mother.

'Taban, can you hear me?' asks the doctor, kneeling beside him. 'I think he's coming around,' he continues, raising a hand. 'Taban, how many fingers am I holding up?'

Taban tries to say, 'Two.' Instead the word, 'Joseph,' comes out.

Ann's eyes widen. 'How … do you?'

'Taban, let's try that again. Taban, how many fingers am I holding up?'

'Two, Dr Green.'

'That's good. What do you remember from before you passed out?'

'You were trying … hypnotherapy I think you called it? Last thing I remember was you asking me to open my eyes. For some reason they wouldn't.'

'Can you stand up?'

'Yes. I think I'm alright.' Taban brings himself to a stand. 'How long was I out for this time?'

'About three minutes. So not the worst episode you've had. But still – Ann, I'm going to get in touch with the hospital and ask them to book another examination.' Chenjerai fishes his notebook from his desk and starts hurriedly scribbling. 'They must've missed something. I simply can't buy that all these episodes and symptoms are purely psychological in nature.'

Ann doesn't respond.

'Ann?'

'Yes. Sorry. I'm just in shock.'

Chenjerai looks at her, eyebrows raised.

'Okay. Well I'll be in touch and let you know when I've heard back from the hospital. Keep me informed of his condition. And let me walk you to your car. I'll just ...'

'It's okay, Green.' She puts a hand on his shoulder, looks him in the eye. 'Please friend.'

Chenjerai nods, a weary smile breaks through. 'Alright, Ann.' He squeezes her hand. 'I understand.'

'Thank you.' She leans in and hugs him. 'This isn't your fault – please don't fret. I'll let you know if anything else happens. Otherwise, we'll see you in a month's time.'

Chenjerai nods. He leads Taban and Ann out the front door and waves goodbye. As they get into the car, Taban feels the weight of his mother's gaze. The click of his seat belt. The wheeze of the chair as he leans back. The ruffling of his shorts and he shuffles his backside into a comfortable position. Every small movement feels minutely, fearfully observed.

Once the car is moving she becomes distant.

After a few minutes they stop at a traffic light. White flowers float down from the bougainvilleas above and spiral-dance across the road.

Taban thinks he spots his mother silently mouth the name, 'Joseph.'

<<<

Prey: Willing

Later that night, Taban lies in bed waiting for the fox. While there is no obvious pattern to its visitations, the boy feels another is due. Moonlight filters through the violet curtains giving the shadows a purplish tint. Ribbons of smoke rise from the mosquito coil on the windowsill. Taban shuffles, impatient, wondering if his hunch is incorrect. Then, he feels the pressure in his skull, the taste of iron in his mouth. Sensations that once brought fear but now only bring excitement. A paw passes through the window without physically disturbing it – like light through glass.

Taban rolls over, shuffles up to the wall – making space.

A voice vibrates in his mind: **I preferred it when you were less eager.**

The bed buckles as the fox slithers up beside him.

'I had a weird experience today,' he says to the fox. 'A sort of dream. Like when I am Solomon. Only this time I was my mother. And they. I mean *she* … her brother was attacked by a crocodile. And you were there.' Taban turns to face the fox. Tonight its eyes are like little black coals, its breath – mint and Olbas oil. 'Do you know what it means?'

Sometimes, during the ritual attaining of a mark, the memories of previous hosts can become lodged in the mind of the present host. Like the taste of a previous hunt mingling with fresh prey.

'Does that mean my mom was also a host?'

The fox remains silent.

'Do you know my mom?'

The fox smiles. **I can't say. You hosts all look the same to me.**

Taban sighs. 'Be coy then. As long as it won't interfere with my plans for Hendrick it's fine.' He moves his hand towards the fox.

You know I still hate you.

Taban forces a neutral-smile. 'That's okay. I hate me too.'

Teeth clamp down on his finger. Then on his wrist. His arm. His shoulder. His body slides into the warm, cramped, fleshy dark.

Then, suddenly, the dark is not cramped or warm.

It is crisp. Airy. The spacious blue-dark of a summer evening – star-pierced and moonlit.

<<<

Taban is Solomon. He has always been Solomon. His blue-grey uniform is in disrepair from the long campaign. His body is changed. His waist is four inches thinner than it was ten months ago – when he began his long envisioned *E*yes uprising at *C*lay *S*un and formed the PRA: People's Revolutionary Army. His face is gaunter than it was four months ago – when they crushed the bulk of President Andrews' army at the battle of *G*rass *C*liff. And in the past three weeks his hands have begun to peel – each disintegrating layer of skin falling away to reveal a more sickly, pallid one beneath. He inspects them, repulsed. Then feels a pressure in his skull – one that has become all too familiar in the past fortnight. On the corner of his makeshift desk sits a small mirror. From it, an unfamiliar reflection gazes back at Solomon. A fox. A strange fox. Snout: long and thin. Body stretched uncannily as if trying to contain something larger. Its expression is fixed, expectant. It has an air of confidence. It is waiting and certain that what it is waiting for will soon arrive. A voice in his head sounds.

Become Nexus.

Solomon's gums begin to bleed.

Then he hears someone approaching his tent.

He lies the little mirror face down on the desk and hurriedly puts on his gloves.

Ibn's hand slips through the entrance – waves. 'Just me,' he says, smile gleaming as he steps inside.

Solomon sighs. There is a new bottle cap pinned to Ibn's uniform. The logo: A tiny bird with zebra-patterned wings, a red and black crest encircled by the words 'Boisterous Hoopoe, Sorghum Malt Beer, 3.2%'. Ibn is a human-shaped magpie.

'What is that on your uniform, Lieutenant General Busani?'

'This?' he gestures to the cap. 'I should think it would be pretty obvious, General Mushonga. It's a bottle cap. From a beer specifically.'

'I know that. I mean what is it doing on your uniform?'

'I thought it looked nice.'

'Where did you get the beer?'

'One of the men found a crate back in the camp we raided last Tuesday. Seemed a shame to let it go to waste. And it was only six bottles. Between the eight of us; it was hardly enough to get drunk or anything.'

'And how exactly, Lieutenant General Busani, would you know how much beer is needed to get drunk when you are only just nineteen years of age?'

'Twenty actually, Sir. Turned twenty last month.'

'Oh. Well. Still. Lieutenant General Busani, please remember your position. Try to keep any extraneous decoration for when we are off the battlefield.'

'Noted, Sir. Though ... you know it is just us in here? You can call me by my first name? Just because we're winning now doesn't mean we've got to pretend we're some kind of uptight "professional" army. We can leave that nonsense for the Albions.'

Solomon nodded. 'I ... I'm aware. It's just. It makes it all a bit easier to process.'

The two men fall silent. For a moment – with the uniforms, the desk, and Ibn's defiantly joyful smirk –

103

Solomon almost feels like he and his former student are back at the school. Almost. But not quite. Ibn is tall. Taller than he used to be. Or maybe not. Maybe the military attire simply makes him look taller. Or maybe he has been this tall for a long while and Solomon has only just realised it. Regardless, Ibn is clearly a man now.

The former teacher feels a pang of guilt.

He should not have come of age here.

Solomon swallows back his emotions. 'Anyway,' he continues. 'What is it you are here to report, Lieutenant General?'

'Two things. Firstly, it is as our scouts predicted – the NRF have stopped their advance. I think there can be no doubt that the intelligence we received was correct.'

Solomon grimaces. 'Yet another predictable disappointment.' He stands and walks to a small portable hob at the back of the tent. He lights it and begins to boil some water in a pot. 'How many times does the Northern Revolutionary Front need to push all the way to the borders of South Sun only for the *wise* and *diplomatic* Isaiah to snatch defeat from the jaws of victory by entering yet another round of fruitless talks with Andrews?'

Ibn shrugs. 'I guess he thinks this is the best way to prevent more bloodshed.'

'If that's the case then he's incompetent. Diplomacy only works if you and the person you're negotiating with share a compatible goal. Isaiah *says* he wants to bring an end to the war and broker an amicable power-sharing agreement with the Albions. But Andrews wants the war to go on forever. Their goals cannot be reconciled.'

'Really, Solomon? I mean Andrews is a bastard, don't get

me wrong, but do you really think he wants the war to go on *forever*?'

'Definitely. Understand this, Ibn – Andrews is a wily, ruthless man whose talents are well suited to this conflict. But if the war were to end – diplomatically or otherwise – do you think the remaining Albions would vote him in again? Even if he won the war do you think those White Albions in their clean houses would look at that man in his blood-soaked khakis and declare, "Yes! This is the fine fellow we want to manage our healthcare system, administer our pensions, meet with foreign dignitaries." No. Absolutely not. Maybe he'd scrape by into another term, but for the most part his political career would be over. He is a creature of his time trying to stretch that time out for as long as possible.'

Ibn smiles. 'Aren't we all, old man?'

Solomon frowns. Then his frown cracks into a chuckle. He puts a hand to his chest as if shot. 'Ouch. Boy, I think you got me.'

He walks over to the now boiling pot. 'Coffee?'

'No thank you. I'm okay.'

'Alright then.' Solomon pours the hot water into a tin cup, then adds a spoonful of brown powder and sticky molasses. 'The best way to end the bloodshed is to bring this war to a swift conclusion.' He sits down at his desk – sips from his tin.

Ibn's smile falls away and his expression becomes serious for the first time since he stepped into the tent. 'So I take it we are going ahead with the operation as planned then?'

Solomon nods. 'Yes. While Isaiah and his forces sit like

obedient dogs on the outskirts of South Sun we will slip in – at night, like we always do – and take the city.'

'Like we always do, Sir.'

Solomon knocks back the last of his coffee. 'Tell the men that tomorrow night we're bringing the war to a close.'

'Will do, Sir.'

'Excellent. Now, Lieutenant General Busani. You did say there was a second piece of news you had for me?'

Ibn's hard expression melts into a warm mischievous grin. 'Yes. Sir, I'm going to need you to stand up.'

Solomon raises an eyebrow. '*Okaaaay,*' he says, obliging. 'Come here.'

Solomon approaches.

Ibn keeps waving. 'Closer. Closer. There.'

Ibn grabs Solomon's hand, shakes it. 'Solomon, you're a father.'

Solomon's knees dip. Ibn's long arms scoop around him – steady him.

'The news came a few hours ago. Vashti and child are both healthy. The child is a girl. Born two o'clock this morning.'

'A girl? Then her name would be Shamira. Oh, I can't … I can't wait to meet her.'

Solomon holds back tears.

Ibn tightens his embrace. 'Congratulations, old friend.'

Solomon nods. Steps back from Ibn's arms, regaining his formal composure.

'Right. Is that everything then?'

'Yes, Sir.'

'Okay. Well then inform the men in the morning and meet me here tomorrow at 1800 hours for deployment.'

'Yes, Sir.'

Ibn salutes, moves to exit.

'Wait,' Solomon calls out, raising his hand.

Ibn pauses, head already halfway outside.

'Thank you, Ibn.'

Solomon catches the gleam of Ibn's smile – half obscured behind the tent flap.

The young man puts up two fingers in a peace sign. 'No worries, Teach,' he says. Then he is gone.

Solomon staggers behind his desk and slumps into his seat, his head full of Shamira and Vashti. Then – after a few minutes – Andrews and the Albions. Warmth, reflection, excitement, freezes into coldness, calculation, purpose. His head starts to hurt.

Then suddenly – blood.

His nose is bleeding. Something hairy and splintery is forcing its way up from his gut – into his throat. He buckles. For a moment he thinks he might suffocate. Then it slips out his mouth and flops on his desk. Something slicked with a black-green oil. Instantly the oil hardens into ash, floats upward, and vanishes – revealing a gnarled paw. A dog's? No. Something within Solomon tells him that this is a fox's paw – even though it is unlike any paw from any fox he has ever seen. Its sparse grey fur is sharp – almost barbed. The claws are brilliant sapphire blue.

Solomon walks to his wardrobe at the back of the tent. From a discreet compartment in one of the drawers, he pulls out the old shoebox – the one that came with the pair of tackies his mom got him. He puts the grey fox paw inside, along with the pearl fox eyes from the last visitation and the golden fox jawbone from the one before that.

Wait. Solomon thinks. I don't have a cupboard in my tent?

What are 'tackies'?

Solomon's head begins to ache. His temples throb. Something is about to burst from his skull. The blood trickling from his nose swells into a ruby-red torrent.

<<<

Bang

Taban is hunched over his box of fox parts. His lips and jaw and throat are caked with dry blood. Closing the box and returning it to its place in the back of the wardrobe, he sneaks out of his room and tiptoes to the bathroom. It is pitch-black in the house but Taban can see perfectly. Solomon's silver eyes still linger with him.

In the cabinet above the sink, Taban rummages for a particular special soap. His mother has an extensive collection of soaps, and creams, and ointments. In her teens she developed a rare chronic skin condition that was painful and unsightly – so she formulated a complex treatment regimen to manage it as well as make-up techniques to disguise it.

Taban finds the soap. It is purple and comes in a plastic bottle with a crane logo. It smells of lavender and mint. Gets blood out like a charm. He puts some in the sink along with some hot water, washes his face and neck, then submerges his pyjama top in the water and leaves it to soak.

A breeze blows through the open window – splitting the curtains, allowing moonlight to spill over Taban's arm. His myriad fox bites reveal themselves. Green, silver, bronze, lilac. All glowing. All pulsing. There is a fresh one now encompassing the tip of his finger. Blue with streaks of golden yellow and marble white.

Like this →

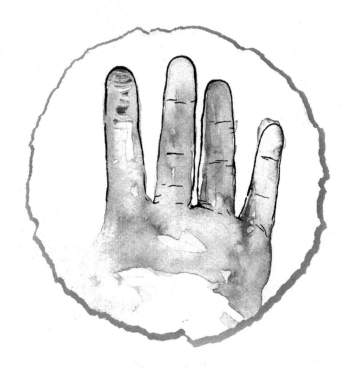

Taban aims his blue opal finger out the window at the near full moon.

'Bang.'

I would be the first to admit I was sceptical that someone hailing from The Bronze Cast would make much of an impact as Patriarch. His appointment felt like a sop to peace-addled weaklings in the senate.

But his creation – this 'World Tree' – is genuinely *transformative*.

Before, extracting knowledge from primitive consciousnesses was a laborious task. But this technology streamlines the entire process.

No longer do we have to rely on cumbersome and inexact conduits of metal and liquid to travel between worlds. The World Tree gets the natives to open the gates for us. And once the gates are open they *stay* open.

No longer do we need to spend years mastering the languages of the primitives. As long as our ambassadors are linked with the tree we can extract the knowledge right from their heads with a simple hand gesture.

This process does have the rather unfortunate effect of destroying their physical forms, but this is an acceptable sacrifice – in both our and our interlocutors' long-term interest.

Better to live forever as a perfect undying parcel of information archived in the shimmering nexus of our World Tree than trapped in a rotting husk of flesh.

– Brother Apollo of The Golden Cast,
extract from *The Final History of The Triumvirate of Metals*

Agate Eyeball Fox Bite

or

*Daggers Held Close, Our
Malachite Roots Search The Sky*

Upside Down: Your Foolish Head Planted In The Earth

The next day. After school. Taban sits on a bench by the Topsy-Turvy Tree waiting for Eve to arrive and take him to the theatre. The Topsy-Turvy Tree stands across the road from the Northern Grounds visitors' car park and is a well-known landmark – at least among Highveldt students and their families. Its name refers to its odd shape – splitting in the middle and unfurling outward in three directions, like a clover. Apparently this deformity was caused when a bolt of lightning hit the tree when it was young. Miraculously it survived and kept on growing – its branches spiralling off in weird directions. Such is the way.

Taban checks his watch. He has changed out of his school uniform and into his costume for the play – a black and red army uniform with white gloves and a prop sabre at his hip. People stare at him as they pass. Taban ignores them. Taking a little mirror and comb out of his satchel, he adjusts his hair. Last week Eve gave him what she described as a 'sort of old-fashioned military-style undercut.' Taban likes it. Both the haircut and the outfit. Which is odd. He thought he'd find the costume's stiff formality a bit of a drag, but it's strangely comfortable. Maybe even comfort*ing.* It all feels somehow uncannily ... *right.*

He hears a honk and looks up to see Eve waving as she pulls into the parking lot. He waves back – puts his mirror and comb away. Eve exits the car and approaches. She is in costume as well. Silver tights and make-up. Hair shaved short and bleached. Shin, shoulder and arm guards – all spray-painted gold. Notionally she is meant to resemble a robot from some

1930s film, but the effect is more like a low-budget, androgynous Tin Man from *The Wizard of Oz* – though Taban would never say this out loud. Regardless, she looks beautiful. To Taban, Eve always looks most beautiful when she's in costume – her happiness somehow even more sincere. Taban would never say this out loud either.

'Hello Taban!' says Eve, seemingly oblivious to the tinsel trail she has left on the tarmac. 'All ready to head out?'

Taban nods, starts to stand. 'Yes. All ready to—' Suddenly it's as if his brain is about to float out the top of his skull. He staggers.

Eve quickly grabs him by the waist and steadies him. 'Woah woah. Are you okay?'

'Yeah … er … I think I need to sit down for a second. Feeling light-headed.'

'Sure thing. There's no rush. Let's rest for a spell.'

She lowers him back onto the bench – takes a seat beside.

Taban does the breathing. Slow inhalations. Slower exhalations. His breath comes out wheezy, thin. For a while the two wait – the sound of air straining through Taban's lungs the only thing passing between them.

Then Eve asks a question – 'Don't you think it's beautiful?'

'Hmmm?'

She points to the Topsy-Turvy Tree. 'After being hit by lightning it should've died. But somehow it survived and grew into this wonderful unique shape. It's uplifting in a way.'

'I guess. I don't think many people think it's wonderful though.'

'Not just wonderful – *beautiful.*'

'I don't think many people think that either.'

'What do *you* reckon *they* think of it then?'

Taban pauses and considers his words.

'I think there's another way to look at it. When this tree was young it survived something terrible – an injury that has come to completely define it – make it grow up all twisted. I think most people don't think it's wonderful *or* beautiful. I think they find it morbid and fascinating. Tragic—'

Eve abruptly hugs him. Taban awkwardly slumps into her shoulder – his neutral-smile slipping into neutral.

'Taban, please stop. I don't want you to think like that. Promise me you'll try not to look at the world that way?'

Taban nods, recomposes himself. 'Okay. I promise,' he says. For a second he wishes he meant it.

'Thank you,' she says, softly raking a hand through his hair – like his head is a lawn being tidied. Beneath the cultivated surface though – the brain knows.

A lie enters the world. The truth stays burning in Taban's gut.

'Are you feeling well enough to stand?' Eve asks.

'Yes,' says Taban.

Eve guides him up onto his feet and they walk to the car together. As he gets into the passenger seat, Taban wonders if the story he told Eve is the grimmest she can imagine. Because it isn't for him. For him the tree's deformed growth being the result of an unstoppable external force is the happiest plausible explanation. There is another possible version of the tree's story, which is far more painful to him. In it everything is the same, but there is no lightning to blame. The tree is simply born a twisted mutant.

<<<

The Dictator & The Stag Beetle

Taban is sitting by himself backstage, nursing a glass of water, when Hilde enters the room. She is dressed in a knee-length black-and-gold cape and a cardboard crown with antler-like protrusions.

'What are you meant to be then?' Taban asks.

'Stag Beetle.'

'Oh. Ja I see it now.'

Taban doesn't know the context for the costume. Hilde is with the Wednesday class who are putting on their own play later in the evening.

'I was told to fetch you. You're on in a minute.' Hilde offers him a hand. 'Eve said you had a fainting spell earlier. Do you need help getting up?'

'Na,' says Taban, standing.

'Okay then. Just try not to fall over. My parents are in the audience – so I'd prefer not to die of embarrassment before I've even got to my scene.'

'I will keep that in mind.'

The two of them walk down the hallway and up some stairs – arriving in a little nook just offstage. Zahid is out in front of the audience – introducing the shows and explaining the format. Taban observes that Hilde is uncharacteristically fidgety – drumming her hands against her thighs and humming to herself.

'So are your parents here tonight as well?' she asks.

'Na. Dad has a late night at the studio. Mom was going to come, but this morning she got a call from Uncle Athel. Apparently some guys came round his farm yesterday and he's really angry and upset – so she took the day off work to go see him. I think she's worried he's going to go do something stupid.'

Hilde gives Taban a concerned look. 'Athel is Caleb's dad right?'

Taban shifts about in his seat, blurts out a 'Ja.'

'Gosh. I hope he's okay. I think I met him once. He seemed … friendly.'

'Big smiley guys always do. He'll be fine probably.'

'And how is Cal?'

Taban looks at his feet for moment. 'No idea. We don't really talk much any more. Only really see him once a year around Christmas. I think he's a goth now.'

'Woah. I can't imagine that. Wouldn't suit him at all. He's super tanned.'

'Ja. Whoever heard of a tan goth?'

Hilde slides into a seated position on the floor. Taban notices she is doing the same breathing technique Dr Green taught him. Slow inhalations. Slower exhalations.

'So what's your play about?'

'A rich jerk.'

'Oh.'

'Yes it's about this prince who gets turned into a bug by a witch and then has to go on a journey of self-discovery and learn a lesson – morals, yadda yadda.'

'And what part do you play?'

'I'm a beetle who eventually befriends the prince and guides him on his journey. Mean on the outside, but kind of sad and broken on the inside.'

'I can see why they cast you for the role then.'

Hilde glowers. 'Are you making fun of me, Taban? Watch yourself. You may have grown a couple of inches taller, but you're still really puny. If I hit you your head would explode like a tomato.' She throws a punch at him but stops short. 'Anyway, what part are you playing?'

'I'm a general.'

'Hmmm?'

'Ja. I give a monologue at the start of the story and then I'm killed off. Then the rest of the play is a murder mystery about who killed me.'

'Did you just give away a big plot twist?'

'Na. It's like in the first few minutes. It's not a big deal.'

'Alright then.'

Silence. For a moment the only sound is Hilde's erratic thigh drumming and Zahid's muffled introduction from the adjacent stage – which Taban isn't paying attention to but can sense is reaching its conclusion.

'Say, Taban, are your parents sending you to Camp Emet this year?'

'Ja. Tried to wriggle out of it, but Mom is convinced it'd be good for my "Social Development". Why? Are you going as well?'

'Yup. Looking forward to it like a root canal. Good to know you're going as well though – so I'll know at least one person at that happy clapper boot camp I guess.'

'I thought you didn't want to be friends with me.'

'I don't.'

At that moment Zahid, dressed in a purple magician's outfit and a top hat emblazoned with a white hummingbird, steps off the stage to a patter of applause. He walks up and taps Taban on the shoulder.

'You're up my man.'

Taban nods. 'Okay, Zahid. Cheers, Hilde.'

'Bye.'

Taban walks out on to the stage. The curtains begin to part. Once his eyes adjust to the bright stage lights Taban is disappointed but not terribly surprised to find the audience small. About eight – maybe ten people. Sad, but expected given how many students from the Friday class have dropped out over the past few months. As things become more 'unstable' in the country, lots of people are moving away. Among the sparse turnout Taban can spot only two people he recognises – Hilde's parents. The most blonde, pale humans he has ever seen – even more so than him. How they have kept their complexions so fair in a country as hot and bright as Zimbabwe is a mystery. Perhaps, being university professors, they had little reason to go out in the day?

Taban steps up to the podium, adjusts the microphone, shuffles the papers in front of him. This is part of the stage directions. He is acting now. Or at least he is more *obviously* acting now. He puts on his neutral-smile.

'Selected members of the press, I have gathered you here today for the first official state address since the Third Unifying Revolution began in earnest earlier this year. I understand that there have been a lot of rumours. Whispers about opposition party members and counter-revolutionaries disappearing in the night. Of rebel towns going silent – found mysteriously *emptied*. I have heard these murmurings – read the cautious scribbles in your papers – and I would like to dispel any misunderstandings the public might have.

'Firstly, the stories are all *true*.

'Every one of them.

'They are true and I see no reason to deny it. I have indeed crushed the opposition. Imprisoned their leaders and financial backers. Had their members beaten. Sent police to break up their meetings. Made organisation impossible for them. Those who have taken up arms – or *talked* about taking up arms –

121

have been met with force. Those who have lent support to the enemy have also been met with force. It is *true*. It is true and I make no apologies for any of it. Some here have written – *poetically* – *daringly* – that I am, "Up to my knees in blood." I am. I am and I make no apologies. I do not wash my hands. I do not disavow. Let the blood dry. Let it dry and seep into my pores. Let it cleanse them. For blood is the medicine that will cure this country and make it whole. For too long we have tolerated division. Division that would crack apart this nation. See us squabble while foreign enemies exploit us – corrupt and supplant our institutions, our traditions, our culture, our society. Division that – under the false mantle of plurality and tolerance – would dissolve this nation. But no more. I will make this nation take its medicine. And I know you will hate me for it. Like the patient loathes the doctor's needle or the child loathes the teacher's switch – you will *hate* me. Like the followers of Moses must have surely hated him when he led them out of the blasphemous Egyptian night into the sanctified heat of the desert – trading the bread of servitude for the hunger of freedom. You will hate me. You will hate my authority. But in time you will see it was for your own *good* and the *good* of this nation.

'We have been sick for too long.

'The time has come to drink the medicine that—'

Suddenly, a masked black-cloaked assassin gallops towards Taban – dagger in hand.

In this moment Taban splits in two.

One half of him hovers above the scene. This observing half is aware that this 'masked assassin' is in fact a thirteen-year-old boy named Jeremy who has misremembered his cue and is now knifing him about five lines too early.

The second half however – the part controlling his body – is in the scene. Panicking as a boy nearly two feet taller sprints toward him – his prop knife all too convincing.

As Jeremy plunges the dagger into the concealed blood pack in Taban's jacket pocket, Taban feels a force in his gut instinctively lash out.

An image flashes in his mind – the assassin's ankle snapping.

A scream of pain.

Taban is not sure if it is coming from himself or Jeremy.

The assassin trips and crashes into him.

Taban's skull shakes as the back of his head slams into the wooden stage floor.

A split second of black. Then …

<<<

Taban is Solomon.

He is Solomon and has always been Solomon. Presently, he is being Solomon on the floor. Specifically the floor of a private room in the newly liberated South Sun State Broadcasting Service. His wife Vashti is standing above – smiling, offering him a hand. She is wearing a long, white, backless dress. Her hair is cut short. Her nails alternate between silver and gold. Her eyes are framed with a light-blue liner that faintly shimmers. A thought enters Solomon's head – I am blessed. I am blessed and unworthy and blessed.

'Are you okay?' she asks.

'No,' he says, taking her hand. 'What happened?'

'You rolled off the couch during your nap.' She grunts and pulls him up to his feet. 'How badly did you hit your head?'

'How would I know? I was asleep when it happened. And why didn't you try to catch me? What good are you?'

'I was busy.'

'Doing what?'

'Reading my book.'

'Tsk.' He puts his arms around her waist – looks into her eyes. 'And here I thought you were a good wife.'

'And here I thought you could sleep properly. I mean honestly, Sol, failing at something so basic. Some Hero of the Revolution you are!' Her expression hardens. 'You were mumbling loudly in your sleep. You sure you're okay?'

'I will be fine, Vash. Probably just a bad dream.'

'You've been having a lot of bad dreams lately.' She kisses him. 'You know you don't have to do this silly TV debate?

You're way ahead in the polls and the election is only a few days away.'

'The battle's not won until it's won. Also, it's the principle of the matter. The "Hero of the Revolution" can hardly run away from a mere debate can he?'

'True. But you don't need to be the Hero of the Revolution either. The revolution is won. The war is over. We could go back home. You could be a teacher again. And I'm sure the old clerk's office would take me back.'

Solomon sighs. 'Please. We've been over this, Vashti. There is nothing I have won that can't be unpicked. I need to *secure* the peace.'

'You can let others secure it. You don't have to do everything.'

Solomon pulls away from Vashti's embrace. He paces. 'Others like Ibn perhaps?'

'Would it be such a disaster? He's smart and charming.'

'Yes. But his ideas are bad.'

'His ideas are different. Which is not the same thing as bad.'

'I know the difference, Vash.'

Vashti frowns. 'How can you be so certain of yourself and yet so uncertain of others? Is your own judgement the only thing that's real to you? If so it must be terribly lonely.' She sits on the couch and turns away.

A long silence passes between them.

Then Solomon sits down beside her, places his hand over hers.

'I'm sorry, Vash. I didn't mean to give you the impression that I don't value your opinion. It's just ... I can't let go. Not yet. My work isn't done.'

'It's okay, Sol,' she says, eyes still averted but hand now entwined with his – squeezing. 'And I guess – in a small way – I'm being selfish too. I mean it's not mine or Ibn's judgement that's important. It's the peoples'. They're the ones who get to decide who the first true president of our nation will be.'

She kisses him, then spots the clock. 'It's nearly eight. I better call Tinashi and find out how Shamira is doing.'

Solomon rolls his silver eyes. 'It's barely been an hour, Vash. I'm sure Shamira is coping just fine.'

There is a knock on the door.

'General Mushonga. The debates will begin shortly. Please come to the studio.'

Solomon smiles, stands. 'I guess I'd better get a move on then.'

Vashti hugs him tightly. 'Do well. Or at least try not to fall on the floor. I understand you're getting very feeble in your old age, but it'd be embarrassing for your daughter and I if the rest of the country were to find out.'

Solomon tries to affect a stern look, but the corners of his mouth curl up in a smirk. 'Your cruelty knows no restraint. Maybe I *will* fall over *deliberately* to spite you.'

'If you do I will run out there and beat you up.' She playfully shakes her fist at him.

'In front of all the cameras?' He strokes his chin theatrically. 'Good. Your bullying will be exposed to the world and I can finally sue you for domestic abuse.'

'The world will side with me when they find out what I put up with.' She winks.

There is another knock at the door – this time more insistent.

'Go! Go! Go!' Vashti shoves him forward. 'Begone!'

Solomon steps through. Immediately a White Albion in a blue suit rushes up and gets uncomfortably close. 'Alright. Okay. Alright,' she says, a calm and cheerful expression failing to mask a cracking anxious voice. 'Come this way, General Mushonga.' She gestures to follow and quickly leads him up a short flight of stairs to some double doors.

'Mr Mushonga will do. I'm not in uniform and the war is over.'

'Alright. Okay. Mr Mushonga then. Please go through. The debate hall is this way.'

Solomon nods, adjusts his tie, and enters. The hall is dim and full of murmurs. A stagehand guides him to a spot in front of a podium. A trumpet blares a regal melody. A string section responds with an equally pompous counter-melody. Lights fade up. Applause sounds off the walls like rain patter pattering. The hall heaves with faces – Tall, Eyes, Black and White Albion. All fashionable and telegenic. Solomon immediately feels underdressed. He'd thought his work clothes would be sufficient, but now feels more conscious than ever that less than a year ago he was just a teacher in a remote township.

On the stage with Solomon – arranged in a semi-circle of podiums facing the audience – are the three other presidential candidates. And standing in front of them is a well-known Black Albion radio presenter whose real name Solomon can't recall, but who everyone has nicknamed 'Handsome Joseph'.

'Ladies, gentlemen, and others. Tonight we at South Sun SBS are honoured to host a very special debate. One of these four people behind me will be the first president of the Democratic Union of Teacherslund.'

Solomon winces at hearing the new Albionised name given to his country. Sadly the old language – which itself varied in spelling and pronunciation between the regions of the *E*yes and *T*all – is no longer spoken fluently across the entire country. So people have taken to using the bastardised 'Teacherslund' in day-to-day conversation rather than the official new name *T*eachers-*S*un – which Solomon finds far more beautiful and poetic. The official new name is represented by the sign for the River *T*eacher (which waters the country's farmlands) and is highlighted with subtle decorations normally reserved for the sign for the mountain *P*arent (which houses the nation's most valuable minerals). This combination sign is then punctuated with the symbol for *S*un – which is itself a play on words. For the symbol *S*un – when modified with certain embellishments – can also be read as *D*escendent or *H*erald. Taken together this suggests that their new nation is not only the light around which the land orbits, but also the child of that land and the herald bringing its light to the rest of the world. 'Teacherslund' captures none of this nuance and falls out of the mouth with the usual hateful, vomitous, 'efficiency' typical of the Albionic language. Though this Albionised name is at least an improvement on its predecessor – Andrewslund. Named for Andrew Chambers – a White Albion whose principal accomplishment was *discovering* the land that would become *T*eachers-*S*un. A man who – while not being a direct relation to the recently deposed President Jack Andrews – was very much his hateful ideological forebear.

Discovering? Really? How can you discover somewhere already home to over a million people? Discovery? Albions have a thousand euphemisms for *conquest*. Perhaps that is where their language's nuance lies?

A stage light blasts into Solomon's eyes – jolting him from his thoughts.

'First of the four candidates,' the presenter begins. 'Solomon Takunda Mushonga of the People's Party. Former General of the People's Revolutionary Army and front runner in all South Sun SBS public polls. The man people are calling the Hero of the Revolution.'

There is a wave of applause and cheers. Solomon smiles at the audience and tries to look relaxed. But below the podium, out of view, he fidgets with his gloves – loosening and tightening the drawstring at the wrist.

A second spotlight illuminates a figure on the opposite side of the semi-circle. He is nearly eight feet tall and wearing a spotless white suit. Pinned to his collar is a silver elephant brooch. Solomon recognises the man immediately and reflexively *tsks*.

'Second of the four candidates,' continues the presenter. 'Isaiah Tatonga Jongwe of the Northern Independence League. Former leader of the Northern Revolutionary Front. The man long hailed as the Father of the Revolution.'

The crowd claps. Isaiah grins ear to ear – pearly maw beaming like a beacon.

Another spotlight comes on, illuminating the podium next to Solomon and revealing Ibn. He is dressed in jeans, snakeskin boots, a cap sewn together from colourful scraps, and a blazer decorated with buttons – half of them fashioned from bottle caps.

'Third of the four candidates – Ibn Jabulani Busani of the New People's Party. Former Lieutenant General of the People's Revolutionary Front – some are calling him the Son of the Revolution.'

Ibn shoots finger-guns at the audience. They laugh. From the front of the crowd there are a few supportive 'woos'. It takes all of Solomon's strength to not hide his face in embarrassment.

The final spotlight comes on – lighting up the podium between Ibn and Isaiah. The person standing behind it is elderly, thin, seemingly hairless. They wear a mint-green snake-pattern robe and gold and blue make-up under their eyes. Solomon recognises this person as a preacher of the old faith – referred to as a Listener in the old language.

'And our fourth and last candidate – Bishop Anah Chitavati Nkosi of the Liberal & Spiritual Unity Party. The only non-male candidate to make the polling threshold for participation in the debates, Bishop Anah is well known for their organisation of non-violent resistance to the Albion Republic's brutal segregation policies. Many say that if Mr Jongwe is to be called the Father of the Revolution then surely Bishop Anah – whose activist work predates the revolution by several years – should be considered its Grandparent.'

Respectful applause sloshes from the audience and the fellow candidates.

Anah gracefully bows their head.

'Now,' continues the presenter. 'Before we begin the debates in earnest we will offer each candidate an opportunity to summarise their party's manifesto and intentions for the presidency. I'd like them each to describe three major policies. Just three though. That should keep things snappy and give us an idea of where their priorities lie. Mr Mushonga – if you may begin?'

Solomon closes his eyes for a moment – imagines he is back at school and that this is just another class he is teaching.

'Thank you, Mr ... I'm sorry, Sir, I've forgotten your last name?'

'Haha. It's Mutsawashe Joseph, Mr Mushonga. I suppose you don't get much TV or radio in your township?'

There are a few derisive chuckles in the audience.

Solomon suppresses a blush.

'Hah. Yes. I'm afraid it's quite far from *South Sun* – so not many programmes reach us. Anyway, if I may continue?'

'Please do.'

Solomon clears his throat. 'Mr Joseph, The People's Party has at its heart one goal – restorative justice. Having won the war we wish to see the greatest crimes of both of Andrews' government and previous Albion regimes undone. To this end we will pursue the following principal policies –

'Firstly, we will complete the dismantlement of all racially discriminatory laws and segregation. This has already begun under the Interim Revolutionary Government. We will continue this important task and enshrine these changes in the country's constitution.

'Secondly, we will begin a wide-reaching and ambitious land redistribution programme. Over their two hundred year misrule the Albion Republic stole vast swathes of *E*yes farmland – forcing many *E*yes onto barren fields. In cases where the labour of Albion farmers has improved the lands' fertility and value they will be compensated, but otherwise Teachers-Sun will *not* pay them. We instead invite the Albion Republic to take responsibility. The Albions are, of course, welcome to buy back the lands should the Eyes farmers resettled onto them wish to sell it.

'Thirdly, and finally, we believe our young nation needs to keep its military strong during this precarious moment in our history. To this end, we will merge both the Northern Revolutionary Front and the People's Revolutionary Army into a single fighting force and begin retraining them into a new professionalised standing army. Thank you.'

The audience applauds, many quite enthusiastically. A few folks very pointedly do not. They look like Tall tribe. Probably Isaiah's lot.

'Thank you very much, Mr Mushonga. And now, Mr Jongwe, if we could hear a similar policy summary from you.'

Isaiah pats his chest to clear his throat. He does this lightly, but his hands are so large and chest so broad that it echoes through the studio with a kick-drum thud. 'Mmmhmm ... Yes. Thank you, Mr Joseph,' he says. 'I'd be happy to summarise the Northern Independence League's priorities.

'Firstly, like the People's Party – and indeed all of the parties here – we will, of course, complete the abolishment of the previous regime's racist policies.

'Secondly, we will also begin an ambitious land reform programme, but one which is more practical and cautious than my good friend Solomon's. We will not take any land by force, but instead buy Albion farms that come available on the market and redistribute them to the most skilled and qualified *Eyes* farmers. It is true, as Solomon says, that the breadbasket of our country has been unfairly monopolised by one group for far too long. But we should be cautious that in sharing the breadbasket we don't accidentally tip out the bread.

'Lastly, as our name suggests, the Northern Independence League believes that the various regions of this country should have greater autonomy going forward. While the *Tall* and the *Eyes* have always coexisted, we did not, before colonisation, share a polity. But, now that we do, we should be careful to construct one that respects our historic independence from one another. To this end we would seek to create a federal system in which the North and South have separate Parliaments that take care of the majority of their affairs – with the joint federal government handling only foreign policy and our interactions with the wider world. Thank you.'

Applause. A few loud cheers from some of the *Tall* tribe members in the audience.

'Thank you, Mr Jongwe.' The presenter turns to Ibn, smiles at him in a knowing way that Solomon finds odd but can't articulate why. 'And now, Mr Busani, if you may follow suit.'

'Oh, Jo, no need to be so formal. Call me Ibn. As to your question – we at the New People's Party prioritise the following three policies. Firstly – finish kicking all those racist laws into the dustbin. Yadda, yadda, etc. No need to go into detail. I mean it's the one thing where we're all on the same page right? If only we could agree on everything else! We could call it a night and go to this nice bar around the corner I know.'

Ibn winks.

Handsome Jo rolls his eyes.

Earthy laughter rumbles through the audience.

'Secondly – our land reform programme. We at the New People's Party believe that the farmlands ought to be collectively owned and managed. We all depend on them. They are simply too important to be monopolised by any one group. We would seek to nationalise at least half of all farmland within a decade – setting up assemblies where farmworkers, agricultural experts, and elected officials can democratically govern the land. Albion landowners with technical knowledge would be invited to stay on and be employed as consultants, but would not be permitted to own the land or extract profit from it.

'Thirdly – we would pursue wide-ranging reforms to empower workers across the country. These would include a minimum wage, a maximum wage, removing the ban on unions, an eight-hour work day, compulsory sick pay, maternity—'

'Ibn!' The presenter tuts. 'You appear to be trying to sneak in a whole smorgasbord of policies when I specifically requested three.'

'Jo, I reject the claim that I was in any way being sneaky.'

More giggles from the crowd. One – an older woman, probably *E*yes but maybe Black Albion – buckles over in her seat, struggling to bottle her laughs.

The presenter sighs theatrically.

'Right. Bishop Anah. If I may ask you to also put forward three policies you think best encapsulate the Liberal & Spiritual Unity Party.'

'Thank you, Mr Joseph. A brief moment – if you will

permit me.' They sip from a glass of water placed next to their podium. 'Aaah. Thanks. Now as the youngest of us so bluntly put it ...' They smile at Ibn. More audience chuckles. 'All us here are in accord when it comes to the urgent need to reform our country's discriminatory laws. So I will instead focus on our two biggest priorities beyond that.

'One – we wish to begin a state-backed, country-wide cultural renaissance focusing on education and spiritual enlightenment. This is urgently needed to repair the damage that two hundred years of violent repression has done to our traditions.

'Two – we wish to enact new laws to protect and nurture the environment which sustains us. The Albion Empire transformed our relationship to these lands from one of cohabitation to one of domination and we need to change course before it is too late.'

There is a pause. The crowd seems uncertain if Anah intends to continue or not. Then a polite, reserved patter – like light drizzle heard from indoors.

'An ominous warning from our fourth candidate there,' concludes the presenter. 'Now it seems to me – judging from those short pitches – that all four of our candidates are approaching Teacherslund's urgent need for land reform quite differently. Beginning the Question & Answer Section, I would like to start by asking The Northern Independence Party candidate about his land reform policy. It seems remarkably conservative in comparison to the other candidates'. One might even say that it appears eerily similar to the proposed land reforms the Liberal Party were suggesting before martial law was declared. Mr

Jongwe, is this not a very meagre offering to bring before a country that has suffered so much?'

Isaiah laughs. It is a deep booming guffaw. Solomon feels like the giant's wet breath is sliming over the top of his head.

'Not at all, Mr Joseph. The Liberals had some nice ideas. They never went quite far enough. And the fact they were always in opposition meant their policies rarely got implemented. But I sometimes wonder if we would've needed a war if they'd been in charge.'

'High praise. Are we to take that as a veiled offer of coalition to the Liberal Party's successors?'

'Now I don't know about that, Mr Joseph. The Liberal & *Spiritual Unity* Party are a very different beast to their predecessor. Merging with Bishop Anah's group has brought in some concepts I am wary of. A lot of it seems a bit "happy clappy" – to be blunt. And some of it strikes me as quite ... *zealous*. Maybe it's a sign of my age, but I think what the country needs right now is moderation. Still, they are certainly less extreme than some of the other parties here.'

The presenter turns to Solomon. 'Mr Mushonga, I think Mr Jongwe just made a veiled criticism of yourself and Mr Busani. Care to comment?'

'Yes, Mr Joseph. And there won't be anything "veiled" about what I have to say. Isaiah has enough veils for us all. Honestly, I've known the man personally for several months – and observed his behaviour as a "revolutionary leader" much longer – and I don't know if he even has a face or if he's just veils all the way down. He says that *now* is the time for "moderation", but he's been saying that for almost the entire revolutionary struggle. And it's nothing to do with his age. It's do with his priorities. Isaiah, frankly, doesn't care if displaced *Eyes* farmers get their land back. He's happy to kick the issue into the long grass to smooth things over with foreign business interests. Really, all he cares about is profiting off the diamond mines he seized during the *Tall* Uprising and securing his little fiefdom in the North.'

Murmurs ripple through the audience. Lips lean towards ears conspiratorially. Isaiah stares at Solomon from across the debate hall. If you didn't know him you'd think his expression was cheerful, relaxed. But Solomon can tell that the old giant is furious. Good, he thinks. If nothing else comes from this, the chance to twist the knife into that pompous, conceited bastard has made this degrading spectacle worth the fuss.

The presenter inhales sharply. 'That's *quite* the scathing series of accusations, Mr Mushonga. But, regardless of your opinions of Mr Jongwe's character, do you not think his policies have some merit?'

'They have merit if your goal is to have the illusion of a land redistribution programme without the actual substance. The problem with only buying up the farms the Albions are willing to sell is that no one is going to sell a farm that is profitable. They will sell us back infertile lands at exorbitant prices and we are meant to accept this? What is the purpose of being so charitable? Why is—'

'Well,' the presenter interrupts. 'I imagine it's because they have the expertise to run the modern industrialised farms our nation has come to depend on. And if they all decide to leave tomorrow that will create a big skill gap and lower agricultural output as a result. We'd be at risk of famine.'

'Our people lived for thousands of years on this land without Albion "expertise".'

'True. But we had a much lower population then, Mr Mushonga. And much lower life expectancy as well. Are we all going to go back to being peasant farmers?'

'No, Mr Joseph. You're extrapolating too much. We shouldn't buy into Albion propaganda. There are no skills they possess which we cannot learn. And much of the expertise they possess is not as "Albion" in nature as they'd have you believe. When I walk through "Albion" fields I don't see many Albions driving the tractors.'

'This is true. We are made of the same stuff and can master the same skills. But can we master those skills in time for the next harvest?'

'It will not be easy by any means. But nothing worth doing ever is.'

The presenter examines Solomon like a suspect dish handed to him by a flustered waiter, then nods. 'Thank you, Mr Mushonga,' he says.

It takes all of Solomon's concentration to not visibly sigh with relief. Didn't this 'Handsome Jo' mainly do lightweight programmes? He had not been expecting such a grilling.

The presenter turns his attention to Ibn. 'Mr Busani,' he begins. 'The farmland nationalisation policy of New People's Party is quite radical. Mr Jongwe and others might even suggest "extreme". What do you say to the criticism that it will result in the government controlling vast swathes of the country? Seems authoritarian.'

'Well, Jo, I think some people don't really get the policy.

The idea is not for the government to control the farms *directly*, but rather to transform them so they can be run cooperatively by the workers. Their labour makes the land productive after all. How the profits generated from the farms are then invested will be decided democratically by assemblies consisting of all interested parties. And, yes, *some* elected representatives from the government will be present. But it will all be very pluralistic and above board.'

'Sounds nice. On paper. But in reality would this not just lead to a lot of meetings in stuffy council halls where not much gets done?'

Ibn laughs. Solomon can tell it's one of the young man's nervous laughs – the sort he'd deploy when asked why he was late for class. 'It's true,' he says. 'That democracy rarely looks pretty. Often it is quite slow and messy.' His voice steadies, takes on a serious tone. 'However it does have the benefit of being the only fair way of doing things.'

A pause. An earnest look cuts through the young man's light-hearted manner. Then he cracks a goofy smile and the mood shifts back. 'Also I feel like my party is getting a raw deal here,' he continues. 'Everyone's saying we're either too bossy or too easy-going. Sometimes at the same time depending on how our critics selectively read our manifesto. Jo, I just wish you'd make up your mind about me.'

More laughter from the audience. Solomon gets the distinct impression there is a joke going on that he is not clued into. The presenter remains unfazed. In fact his expression hardens into granite.

'Mr Busani, have you considered that a lot of people are concerned about your land reform policies because they are complicated – "messy" as you might put it – and you don't always do a good job of explaining them. You joke a lot. People say you have a generous spirit that likes to see the best in everyone. A lot of your policies seem to hinge on that. Everyone trying their best. Working together. Giving each other the benefit of the doubt. Whether it's White Albion farmers staying behind to help run farms that have been repossessed from them or government assemblies where no one bunks off to go to the bar. Isn't this all a bit naive?'

Ibn looks wounded. His voice musters that solemn quality from before. 'Look, Jo, I don't think the Albion farmers would be getting that bad a deal. Sure, they won't be able to profit off the land as they did before. But they can still live on it. Do a similar job. Take home a comfortable salary. Yeah, a lot of them will probably tell us to get stuffed, but enough would accept the offer I reckon. Because, you know, I don't think all of them see the land they live on as just some exploitable asset. I don't think anyone is that basic deep down. At our core we're all creatures of sentiment. We form attachments to the lands we live on and the people we live alongside. I think many Albions will choose that attachment over their pride. And yes – you are right that a lot of our party's policies take for granted that people are capable of working together, acting in good faith, etc. But, to be blunt, that's kind of the premise of having a society to begin with. I'd rather people accuse me of being naive than give in to a cynicism that justifies wallowing in inaction. Or *worse* – a cynicism that justifies *tyrannical* action.'

People clap. Most just politely but a few enthusiastically. Solomon sees some young Black Albion and Eyes people standing up to applaud. A few he recognises from the war. He feels a strange mixture of pride and concern. Pride that his student is now able to speak so well. Concern that his well-meaning but credulous words seem to be resonating. Even the hard-nosed presenter's expression softens – a smile slipping through before he turns to grill the final candidate.

'Bishop Anah. All of the candidates had quite a lot to say on the topic of Land Redistribution, but the Liberal & Spiritual Unity Party barely mentions the matter at all. Case in point – when picking policies to highlight tonight you instead chose to focus on education and environmental conservation. Why is it you don't seem to have a clear stance on the most important issue facing our country?'

Anah sips their water glass, closes their eyes, and emits a soothing, *'Hmmmmm.'*

'Well, Mr Joseph, partly it is a tactical omission. It is no secret that the Liberal & Spiritual Unity Party has been polling fourth for a long while now and the only likely pathway into government for us is in a coalition with one or more of the other parties. It makes sense – given that the other parties feel so strongly about the matter – that we keep our minds open about the subject.'

'I think everyone understands that. But don't you think having a more concrete policy on this issue would give the public a stronger sense of what your negotiating stance would be in such a coalition?'

'We are a pluralistic party and—'

'Well put the party aside then for a minute. You're a presidential candidate after all – not just a party spokesperson. What are *your* opinions on the issue?'

Anah sighs, clasps the bridge of their nose. 'Frankly? As

a preacher of the old faith, I find this whole discussion of land "ownership" entirely wrong-headed. We, the followers of Mouritz, believe that land is not something that should be "owned" any more than a person should be "owned". We believe that our relationship to the land ought to be one of sustainable and peaceful co-existence. For it is our relationship with the land that forms not only the physical but spiritual basis of a nation and its culture. A relationship of "ownership" is a relationship of control and domination. A culture that views such a brutal dynamic as the fundamental way to interact with the world will, in time, come to idolise and spread tyranny. Such cultures end up grasping so hard—' Anah squeezes their palms together, and then pulls them apart in a theatrical jolt. '—their hands break apart. They lose their grip. Mouritz teaches us that this is what befell those who once ruled from the summit of Parent. This is also what has undone the Albion Empire. It will undo us as well if we cannot learn a new way of relating to the world.'

The audience remains quiet for a moment. Some in the crowd seem contemplative – as if digesting a sermon. Others appear confused, but are politely trying to mask their confusion. Solomon feels like there are flies buzzing around his head – little spindly legs brushing the tops of his ears. Before he can stop himself words are coming out of his mouth.

'Lovely speech, Listener Anah, but will it make the potatoes grow?'

The presenter gasps. 'Mr Mushonga!'

'Will a spiritual connection to the land give us more or less mielie-meal this harvest?'

'Mr *Mushonga*! This is *not* the round-table discussion part of the show. I ask the questions for now and if I think your opinions on Bishop Anah's beliefs are pertinent *I* will ask *you*. Otherwise, keep them for the second half. Do I make myself clear?'

Solomon swallows his anger. 'Yes, Mr Joseph. Sorry, I spoke out of turn. Apologies to yourself and to *Listener* Anah.'

'Is it true?' says a voice from the audience. 'That your "daughter" has white skin?'

Solomon's heart goes cold. 'Who said that?'

A man in the front row stands. He is wearing a black, traditional-looking robe, and appears to be an *Eyes* tribe member. 'Is it true that your "daughter's" real father is the devil Amon? That you made a pact with him? Where did you get your powers, Comrade Solomon?'

The presenter gestures, security cautiously moves towards the man. 'Sir. We are not inviting questions from the audience at present. And even if we were – this is not a place to spout vulgar conspiracy theories.'

The man pulls a dagger from his black robes and growls, 'You'll be the doom of this country, you traitor!'

The next few seconds slowly crash in like an avalanche approaching from a far-off mountain summit.

Solomon reaches for the power inside himself – prepares to strike. But the man is quick. He has already leapt onto the stage and is nearly on top of him – his desperate silver eyes so much like Solomon's. So young. Solomon thinks he recognises him. One of his soldiers? There were so many new recruits by the end of the war. Such is the way.

Solomon is just beginning to curl his power around the man's hand – preparing to crush the tendons in his palm – when Ibn steps in front.

Wet ripping.

Steel through cloth. Steel through skin.

Solomon sees Ibn's broad back fall towards him. He braces to catch. His friend's weight hits him and his legs almost collapse as he struggles to hold the man upright.

Damp denim on his chest.

Blood leaking.

Over Ibn's shoulder Solomon can see the security guards dragging the cloaked assassin away. The man holds his hand up, screaming words that are distant, muffled. The hand is a gnarled branch, hanging limply from the end of his arm – purple and red. Snapped bones jut out like thorns. It's as if some force tried to twist it off.

Solomon tries to recall if it was his own power that did that.

He cannot be sure.

I could've sworn I only wanted to break his grip. Make him drop the knife.

Words leak from his mouth uncontrollably.

These words →

'Ibn? Ibn? Ibn? Ibn? ...'

<<<

Three hours later. A hospital waiting room. Solomon sits, hands shaking, clasped together as if in prayer. Vashti paces back and forth – her footsteps the only sound in the large room. Perhaps even the entire floor given the whole section has been cleared by security. PRA guards are positioned at every window and entrance – standing with remarkable stillness. Solomon feels – but does not *notice* – their presence. Like someone might feel – but not really be conscious of – their limbs.

An almost inaudible creak. The guards all turn at once to the door.

A white-coated hand waves – signalling 'friend'. The doctor attached to it slips into the room with the meekness of someone sneaking around a sleeping lion.

'Mr and Mrs Mushonga,' he says. 'Could you come with me please?'

Vashti stops pacing. Solomon nods, stands. One of the soldiers immediately walks up beside him – shadowing his every step. They travel down a narrow hallway with guards dotted in every corner until they reach a door which opens into a clean white room with baby-blue curtains and a window almost the length of the entire wall. It occurs to Solomon that the quality of light in here during the day must be wonderful – dawn cresting over the horizon like a golden wave. It also occurs to him that a window that large is a security risk. He will have to have a word with the hospital and see about moving him into a room without any windows.

On the bed Ibn lies asleep – breathing faint, hooked via

intravenous tubes to a clear bag of saline, antibiotics, and painkillers.

'I am happy to report that Mr Busani's condition has stabilised,' says the doctor. 'A complete recovery will take some time, but he should be conscious again by morning if you'd like to visit him tomorrow.'

A small gasp of relief from Vashti. Her shoulders visibly untense.

'Mr and Mrs Mushonga, I understand that you are both from his village? If it is possible could you please provide us with the details of Mr Busani's next-of-kin so that we can inform them of his condition. Unfortunately we can't find anything in our records.'

'That makes sense,' Solomon says. 'Ibn doesn't have any relatives that I'm aware of. He was separated from them during the Third Dividing – don't even know who they were. He … he chose his surname from a book he liked. Father Graham will want to know he's alright though. I will call him in the morning.'

'Is Father Graham his foster parent? If so, could you provide the hospital with his phone number and address? We will need it for our records and so that we can formally contact him.'

'There's no need. I will speak to him.'

'Mr Mushonga, please understand. It is important we follow procedure—'

Solomon raises his hand – reaches out with his power. The doctor flinches. It's as if a large animal has placed a paw on the base of his neck.

'Doctor. The PRA – I mean *The People's Party* – will *handle* this. Now could you please give us some privacy?'

The doctor nods. 'Okay then,' he says, backing out of the room. 'I will leave you be.'

Solomon slumps in a chair across from the bed. Vashti tenderly squeezes his shoulder. 'Sol, you didn't need to be like that. He was only doing his job.'

'I know, Vash. I ... right now ...' He stares at Ibn's chest gently rising and falling. 'I think I need to be alone for a bit. Please go home without me. You must be shattered.'

'*I* must be shattered? Sol?'

Solomon does not respond.

She bends down and kisses him. 'Alright. I will see you back at the house.'

Vashti forces a smile, walks through the door, and is gone.

Solomon continues to stare at Ibn's chest. Rising. Falling. He reaches out with his power – tries to see if there is something he can do to help his friend's wounded body heal faster.

Nothing.

The doctors have done a good job.

He, however, is useless.

How much more power does he need to stop things like this from happening?

Rising. Falling.

It hurts.

It hurts Solomon to look at the expression on Ibn's face. Neutral. A hint of grimace. Solomon always found his young friend's cheery demeanour overbearing. But now – seeing him like this – he misses it.

Solomon stands, picks up the chair, and hurls it full force into the window.

The glass is reinforced. The chair is flimsy. It bounces off and clatters to the floor – leaving only a tiny crack.

'Fucking idiot,' Solomon shouts.

'Fucking *idiot*,' he whispers.

Solomon is not sure if he is addressing Ibn or himself.

<<<

You: A Silver-Eyed Mind Eater

'Take me to the mansion!' Solomon says, as he and a PRA soldier slide into the back seat of the car. The driver does not respond verbally, but Solomon can sense his instruction has been understood. The vehicle whirs to life. For thirty minutes he, his bodyguard, and the driver sit in complete silence as they glide to their destination – the outside world hidden behind black-tinted, bulletproof glass. Solomon doesn't recognise the man sat next to him. He doesn't recognise most of the PRA soldiers these days. When the revolution first started he knew all of his men by name, but he lost track as the organisation expanded. Their manner around him also changed. They used to be more casual, warm, admiring. But as the victories piled up that mutated into awe, fear, and obedience. A thought briefly crosses his mind – how scary these men might appear, their boots stomping into your village, their jeeps pulling up outside your house late on a cool September evening.

The vehicle stops. Solomon steps out onto gravel. They are parked outside a large three-storey building with a big pool, large fountain, and decorative marble columns and statues. The architectural style is neither Albion, *Eyes*, or *Tall*, but based on ancient Hellenian designs. Solomon sighs – not only at the crass ostentatiousness, but the ignorance. The statues and columns are all white and crisp when it has been well known for over a century that the Ancient Hellenians actually painted their structures in bold sanguine and earthy hues. But, because the Albions first 'discovered' Hellenian artefacts stripped white by time, and that image of them is what is culturally ingrained in the Albion psyche, they make buildings that look like this – like looted ruins.

Solomon walks to the entrance of the mansion – his soldier-shadow right behind him. He rings the bell and is let in by another PRA guard. He is greeted by a gruff bellow.

'Solo Boy? At this hour? What a laugh.'

Grinning from atop an ornate staircase that spills down like a pale tongue into the foyer is former president Arthur Cameron Andrews. Deposed. Dishevelled. Unshaven. Wearing a loose-fitting black-and-gold bathrobe.

'We need to talk,' Solomon says, ascending the stairs.

'Do we? If you think I had anything to do with that little performance tonight you're barking up the wrong tree. What could I know about it? I've been under house arrest for months.'

Solomon glares. 'I'm not here to accuse you of anything. I need information.'

Andrews smiles. 'Oh? Interesting. Shall we talk privately in the rec room?'

Solomon nods – and then gestures for his escort to wait at the top of the stairs.

Andrews leads him into a large room strewn with tasteless objects. A bearskin rug. A pool table with diamond-tipped cues. An elaborate chandelier. Satin curtains with a black trim. And at the centre of the room a gold-framed painting of the country's 'founder' Andrew Chambers hangs above the fireplace.

From a liquor cabinet, Andrews pulls out a bottle of dark rum that is ninety percent empty and missing its lid. 'Drink?' he asks.

'No thank you.'

'Suit yourself.' He pours the remainder into a glass. 'Please. Take a seat.'

The two men sit on opposite armchairs. Solomon finds his stiff – the designers clearly spent more time making the chair look opulent than they did making it comfortable.

'So you want to know my assessment of the debates?' asks Andrews, grinning.

'Not particularly.'

'I think you stuffed it up, chum.' Andrews takes a big sip of rum. 'You came across as a dry, single-minded zealot either unaware or unafraid of the consequences of his actions. Also a bit of a clueless bumpkin. Though that might actually do you some good. Clueless bumpkins form a solid electoral majority in Andrewslund. Oops. I mean *Teachers*lund.'

Another big sip.

'Of course you don't exactly have the strongest competition. Isaiah appeared bloodless as usual. Really your main threat is that Busani Boy. While you seemed like a bit of a bumpkin he seemed like *a lot* of a bumpkin and was funny and charming about it in a way that you weren't. Also heroic. Getting stabbed stopping your dear friend's assassination—' Andrews kisses his fingers. 'Mwah! Magnificent. Before his body even hit the ground I'm sure many plebs switched their votes from People's Party to *New* People's Party. Maybe even enough to split the bumpkin vote down the middle and give Isaiah a narrow path to victory. Wonderful thing First Past The Post. Rewards – loyalty, unity. Punishes – disloyalty, disunity. I hope after the "revolution" you lot will keep the institution going. A relic of a more *enlightened* era.'

Andrews gulps down the last of his rum.

'Though really the Busani Boy getting stabbed *could* be a blessing for you. If he were to die you could easily snap up his grieving supporters. I could see it now, Solo Boy. You, giving a speech at his funeral – nicking a few of his policies. Your road to a massive majority would be literally paved with *woah—*' Andrews slips, nearly drops his glass.

Solomon rolls his eyes. 'You know there is an actual reason I came here tonight. And it's not your barbed commentary.'

'Of course. I know. The "barbed commentary" is complementary.'

Solomon scowls.

Andrews shrugs. 'Give me a break. I haven't had anyone to talk to for weeks.'

'Earlier this year there was a raid on my township by Domestic Protection. I've been trying to find the men who were involved. You handpicked a lot of DP agents yourself so I want some leads on who it could be.'

'Oh.' A smile snakes across Andrews' face. 'I know what this is about. Those rumours finally got under your skin didn't they? I'm surprised it took so long really. Most people would have immediately doubted their wife's words once the child slipped out with the wrong "complexion". No longer buying the "rare skin condition" line?'

Solomon removes his gloves and rolls up his sleeves – revealing the whiteness spreading up his forearms.

Shock and disgust cuts through Andrews' smug demeanour.

Solomon tries not to smile at the old man's discomfort.

'There might be some substance to what the doctors say, actually,' he continues. 'But—'

'You can never know for certain.' Andrews lets his interruption hang silently in the air like a poisonous gas, then walks to the cabinet and refills his glass. 'It's horrible isn't it? We get taught that scepticism – only trusting what our eyes see – is a good thing. But apply it to relationships and then suddenly it's some kind of cruelty – a weakness of character. How could you not trust your wife? Blah, blah. That's why I never pursued marriage. Don't see the point in going after something that denies what's been nurtured in me.' He swallows a mouthful of amber liquid, winces.

'Is it really scepticism that's encouraged?' asks Solomon. 'Or is it *healthy* scepticism?'

'The two are used pretty interchangeably in my experience.'

'Healthy implies that there is also an *unhealthy*.'

'Implies, but does not *spell out*. Where is the line drawn? When do I go see a doctor to get my scepticism checked?'

Solomon frowns.

'Sorry, Solo Boy. I'm rambling. We were talking about your wife weren't we? Not my lack of one.'

Solomon snorts. 'You know in the few months I have known you personally, and in the several years I have been unfortunate enough to have you as my president, this is the first time I have ever heard you say sorry for anything.'

'That's because I've had nothing to apologise for.' Andrews' expression takes on an implacable hardness, like a wall, or a policeman's jackboot. 'I mean it. I have done nothing wrong. It's the world that's wrong. And you will discover that as well – in time. I can tell. We're not that dissimilar really. For all the different masks humanity wears, there are really only two kinds of person – those with the courage to use power and those with the weakness to be used by it. The doers and the done. That simple.'

Solomon smirks. 'Sounds like you've been preparing that speech for a while.'

'Well I do have a lot of spare time at the moment.'

'Have you considered joining a theatre company? You're made for the stage.'

'Look. I mean it, chum. The same crap that's happening to me right now – it'll happen to you too. It's the burden of being a doer. All those done by you resent you. Get another doer who doesn't know any better to come do you. And then you're done.' Andrews' words slur. His legs wobble.

Solomon crumbles into laughter. He wonders why he ever took this man seriously.

Then another wicked grin slices across Andrews' red cheeks. 'Of course with a power like *yours*,' he continues. 'Maybe you *can* avoid getting *done*.'

Solomon stops laughing. 'What did you say?'

'Do you think you're the only one to have ever had a power like that?'

Solomon eyes him up. 'What do you know?'

Andrews wanders over to the portrait of founding president. Andrew Chambers is tall, has a thin orderly moustache and a granite jawline. He is dressed in red and has a sabre strapped to his side. Standing on a rock, sun rising behind him – he looks every bit the cliché of domineering masculine power. Except for the eyes. His eyes have a distant pensiveness. Andrews stares longingly at the painting. When he speaks again his voice has a different quality than before – accent less affected, expressions more formal and reverent.

'My father used to tell me of an encounter he had out in the bush, back when our conquest of this land was new and we were still searching out its boundaries. He was young at the time – a grunt escorting a survey team mapping out the immense mountain your people call Parent. One afternoon, just as the sun was beginning to set, the survey team stumbled upon a small plateau near the summit. It was dotted with the ruins of a stone structure. What sort of structure? They weren't sure. But my father reckoned it looked like a temple. It wasn't exactly a practical location for anything else after all. Anyway, while searching through the area for a place to set up camp they found what looked like a darkly baroque coffin emblazoned with a strange symbol – an eye within an eye. It was oval, but *distorted* somehow. Like the curves didn't quite match up. It gave my father the creeps. He thought they should leave it be. But some of the other men got it in their heads that there might be something valuable inside – some lost pharaoh's treasure. My dad, who had some experience tinkering with machines, kept saying to them, "Look at the mechanism on it. What kind of coffin locks from the inside?"'

A feverish look overtakes Andrews. He starts to shiver – bathrobe barely clinging to his pallid frame – and quickly downs what remains of his second glass. Rum dribbles down his chin, forming honey-coloured rivulets in his exposed grey chest hair. The shivering ceases.

'Wh-What they found in there was a man,' he continues.

'Encased in gold. He looked like a medieval knight. Only *different*. Father thought the armour seemed too ... *sinuous* ... *sculpted* ... like it had been melted on. And the helm ... the eye sockets were just black-green pits.

'One of the men tried to pry the armour off, but immediately fell back – clutching his heart, blood gurgling from his mouth. The man in the armour rose up – like the bloody messiah on Sunday. My father and the rest of the survey team ran. The armoured man pursued.

'What followed was a harrowing three weeks where they were stalked and picked off one by one. It was not just the manner in which the armoured man would kill them that was terrifying – crushing their insides from afar seemingly with his will alone. It was the fact he seemed to know exactly where they were heading – what their fall back plans would be in every eventuality. In time, father figured it out. One night, during an encounter, he hid in a tree and stayed behind to spy on the armoured man. What he witnessed him doing to the corpses – well this is where things get even more *bizarre*. The armoured man would place his hand on the forehead – thumb and pinky on each of the temples.' Andrews puts his hand over his own face to illustrate. 'Then the skull would slide out into his hands, but without ... the skin wouldn't tear or rip. Just fold, deflate. Then the skull would glow and disintegrate. Father didn't know for certain what the armoured man was doing, but his theory was that he was reading his victim's memories. That would explain why he'd been able to track the survey team so effectively. So he and the other survivors hatched a plan based around this – they would lure the armoured man into a pit trap. The thought being that if neither bullets nor running had worked then perhaps ensnaring the monster might do the trick. And you know, it almost did.'

Andrews cradles his empty glass – almost hugging it.

'In the end,' he continues. 'My father was the only one of the Survey Team that survived. Not through any heroism mind you. The armoured man was going to get him too, but then it just ... stopped—' He snaps his fingers. 'Fell over. Like it ran out of batteries or something. Father wondered if it had even been conscious at all, since they unearthed it or if it was just following some sort of mechanical instinct. Like sleepwalking. Or a wet dream. Did you ever get wet dreams as a kid, Solo Boy? Or were you too busy plotting revolutions?'

Andrews bottom-slides off his chair onto the floor – traces circles on the carpet with his finger. 'It must be tempting,' he says. 'Having a power like that. Never have to worry about whether someone was lying to you or not. You could just stick your finger straws right in their brain and—' he makes a guttural slurp. 'Suck the memories right out. And just ... *know*. For once *know* for *certain*. No more doubts.'

'Yes,' replies Solomon. 'But if you doubt someone close ... It's a solution that has the same fatal outcome regardless of whether the person is lying or not.'

'I guess.' Andrews grins. 'But *still* ... very tempting. You could know whether that Busani Boy is up to something.'

'What do you mean?'

'Don't play dumb, Solo Boy. It's all very convenient, isn't it? Why a dagger? Much more effective to just shoot you. Unless of course the Busani Boy planned it all out beforehand. The assassin was former PRA – everyone on the news is already talking about it. Which PRA faction do you think it's more likely he comes from – yours or Ibn's?'

'That all seems very convoluted for Ibn.'

'Really. Come now. You know he's not as simple as he appears.'

Solomon slips into a pensive, contemplative silence.

Andrews throws up. Black and amber pools in his lap.

'Vile,' says Solomon.

'Yeah?' Andrews splutters. 'Well not as vile as my men probably were to your wife.'

Solomon scowls.

'Don't give me that look. You think all your soldiers are angels with squeaky-clean souls? That none of them have ever carried out atrocities in the name of "Revolution"? You can't be that naive. Or maybe you can? Maybe life's blissful when you're an ignorant bumpkin.' He winks. Blows a little vomit-scented kiss.

Solomon's glower splinters into laughter – as if he is remembering a joke. 'I've just realised – if your story is actually true and I have this power to read minds then I don't need to listen to you any more.'

Andrews' eyes widen. He rolls onto his side – gasps.

'If you're wondering what that excruciating burning sensation is – I have just forced open all the sodium-potassium ATPase pumps in your body. Your heart should stop about now.'

The light behind Andrews' eyes goes out. His laboured breathing ceases.

'Sorry to use medical jargon. I so rarely get to show off my education these days, because I had to give up my life to come rescue my country from talentless fucking cretins.'

Solomon bolts up from his chair and kicks Andrews' empty glass. It smashes into the unlit fireplace. He inhales deeply – as if trying to suck in all the air in the world. Then lets out a single muted chuckle – an overheating engine venting a short burst of steam. There is a knock. He heads to the door – opens it a mere crack, keeping his white ungloved hands out of sight.

One of his bodyguards.

'Sir. Just letting you know that we've got details on the assassin. It turns out he was one of Busani's men.'

Solomon sighs. 'I thought that might be the case. Give me five minutes. We're finished up here.'

'Plan B, Sir?'

'Yes. Plan B.'

Solomon closes the door and heads over to Andrews' corpse. He places his white thumb and pinky on the dead man's temples. At first nothing happens and he begins to wonder if Andrews has made one last joke at his expense.

Then – a rumble.

Andrews' face crinkles and distorts like crumpling paper.

Something is emerging.

Suddenly, the white hand is not on Andrews' face but his.

Solomon recognises his father's calloused palm, pocked with soldering-iron scars from years of repairing cables.

Wait. That doesn't seem right.

A voice somehow both alien and familiar speaks.

'Taban, are you awake now?'

<<<

Shadow Pact & Stitch-Lipped Boy Blues

Taban watches his father's hand withdraw from his forehead.

'Just checking your fever,' Cormack says.

'Oh.'

Taban takes in his surroundings. He is in the living room back home, lying on the couch. Still in his costume – though the black blazer has been removed and is folded on the armchair. Across from him the windows facing onto the front garden have been opened. A breeze that smells like fresh rain drifts in.

'Thought you could use some air.'

Cormack is dressed in double denim and a white Alice Cooper T-shirt. This is the archetypical image Taban has of his father – even though there are many occasions where he dresses differently. For a moment this makes him question if this is really his world or a memory he is reliving.

'How are you feeling?'

'Who are you Albion!?'

'Um. What was that son?'

Pain surges behind Taban's eyeballs, then fades. 'Sorry,' he says. 'What happened?'

'There was an accident at the theatre. From what Eve described it sounds like one of the other guys tumbled into you and your head got a nasty knock.'

'Oh. Ja. I remember. That twit got his cue wrong. Did the play end up continuing?'

'For the most part. There had to be an intermission and some "improvisation" according to Eve. Had to shuffle some parts around because the guy who ran you over also got injured and he was meant to play another character later in the story. Also, remind Mom to get something sweet for Justice.

Poor guy had to help carry you from the car and you know what Eve's like when she's freaking out. Screamed his bloody head off at one point just because he slipped and nearly dropped you.'

Cormack goes quiet for a moment – as if gathering up the courage to say something. 'Are you still sure you want to do the sports day thing tomorrow?' he asks. 'I know we've already argued about it to the moon and back, but Mom and I still aren't sure it's a good idea given how your health has been.'

'Dad, like I've said before, this … *stuff* … I've been dealing with doesn't follow any logic. It happens regardless of what I'm doing. So there isn't any point trying to pre-empt it. Also, you and Mom are always trying to get me to do "normal healthy teen" stuff. Now I'm finally doing that and all of a sudden you're reluctant.'

Cormack looks at Taban forlornly. He reaches out. Taban wonders if he is going to check his temperature again or if he is about to hug him. Before he can find out which, his father falters, pulls back. 'Okay,' he says. 'But try not to push yourself. If you're not feeling well just walk right off the track. If any of the teachers or prefects give you hassle I will march over from the stands and yell at them.'

Taban wants to say, 'No you won't.'

Instead he forces his neutral-smile and says, 'Thank you, Dad.'

Cormack nods. Then his cellphone squawks a descending digital melody. 'Ah. I think I know who that is.' He hits answer. 'Yup. Ja cool he's awake now. I'll pass you over.' Cormack hands Taban his blocky Nokia. 'Son, if you're feeling up to it there is someone special on the phone.'

Taban takes it warily.

Cormack gives a thumbs up, walks into the adjacent dining room, and then into the kitchen – closing the door behind him.

Taban hellos into the plastic brick.

'Whatsup?' replies a familiar voice.

'Caleb?'

'Hey Tab. Sorry I missed your birthday. I know I promised to give you a call. Thought I would try and make it up with a call today. Was going to try and ring before the show to wish you luck, but things are a bit hectic on the farm at the moment. Lost track of time.'

'It's no problem. No problem at all.' Truth be told Taban had little expectation of actually receiving a call. This might be the first time Caleb has followed through on the promise of a phone call.

'You say you're at the farm? Isn't it term time at Saint Vitus?'

'Um. Ja. They kicked me out.'

'Oh.'

'Ja. I thumped someone who was spreading rumours about me. Mom is negotiating with the school to get me readmitted. In the meantime I'm helping Dad run the farm. Lot of tension here. Have you been following the news?'

'Nah. Not really. Something about war veterans?'

Caleb laughs. 'Aw shucks Taban. Please never change. You're probably the one person in the country clueless about what's going on. Honestly, I hope it stays that way. You know sometimes I think back to Highveldt and …' Silence. An awkward breath, as if he is about to say something more – quickly swallowed. 'Ah, never mind. So how are things with you?'

Taban stares out the window. As moonlight trickles through the glass pane, his fox bites begin to throb.

'Things are fine,' he lies. 'Play went okay. Apparently. Despite everything. Suppose Dad told you about it all already. Looking forward to the cross-country run tomorrow.'

'Really? You always *dreaded* the cross-country run in junior school.'

'I guess I've warmed up to it. And it's not really the competition I'm looking forward to.'

A small flicker inside the boy wants to tell Caleb everything. He smothers it.

'That makes sense,' says Caleb. 'I always hated the running, but I enjoyed going to the ice-cream stand by the Topsy-Turvy Tree with you and Hilde afterwards. How is she by the way?'

'We don't talk much these days. But I saw her before the show. She seems fine. She's going to Camp Emet this year.'

'Aw sike! Same here. Mom's making me go as penance. Says a few weeks with the god botherers will set me straight. Or at least bore me into submission. But it might actually be fun now. When we're there we should all meet up and hang out like old times.'

Taban's hand clenches around the phone. The words clatter in his mind like dropped cutlery. *Like old times? You're the one who pushed me away and now you want to just reset everything? What a joke. I'll end you. I'll end all of this.*

'Anyway,' Caleb says with big cartoonish yawn. 'I should say goodbye. Better go check up on Dad. I don't like leaving him on his own too long at the moment. Take care, Tab.'

'Goodbye Cal.'

Taban hangs up.

Through the window opposite he can see a familiar set of eyes in the front garden.

'I was Solomon for a lot longer than normal this time,' he says to the eyes.

The eyes speak back –

Yes.

'Also, I didn't realise that could just happen whenever. I thought you had to bite me.'

Who's to say I didn't? We're far enough along now that I don't need to *bite* you to bite you. From your perspective – increasingly – the bites will just start appearing on their own.

'Will I be myself long enough to even enjoy my revenge?'

Hard to say.

'Well … I guess it doesn't matter. The outcome is what matters.'

A loud kitchen door creak. The eyes disappear.

Cormack arrives with a large unwieldy glass of water. Taban can't imagine drinking it all – even over the course of an entire day.

'I thought you might like some water. Did you enjoy catching up with Caleb?'

'Ja,' Taban lies.

'I'm glad.' Cormack shivers. 'Yeesh. Should probably shut these. The temperature is starting to dip.' He closes the windows tight.

'Dad. Is it okay if I rest my eyes here for a bit? My head hurts.'

'Sure thing. Do you want me to pop the light off?'

'Ja. That'd be great.'

'Cool. No problem.'

Cormack's forlorn, shy smile pops up from beneath his bushy moustache. He looks like he's about to say something more. He *always* looks like he's about to say something more. He never does. He flicks the switch and leaves.

In the moonlight, Taban sees his own reflection in the glass.

Sure enough there is a new glowing mark – this time on his cheek. An unnaturally perfect sphere, with rings of translucent white and pink. Like this →

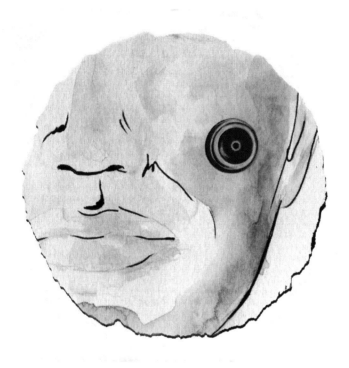

Gold Cast Emissaries linked to the tree have been reporting strange 'visions'.

Adjuncts assigned to them have noted uncharacteristic mood swings and heightened psychic fluctuations during sleep.

Probably just a case of brothers going stir crazy from being out among the primitives too long.

Regardless, I have ordered our finest medical psychics to begin to pilot treatments.

They have already theorised a severing ritual which will allow them to break an emissarie's connection with the tree.

I have given the order to keep this matter quiet. I don't want to give those cowards in the Senate an excuse to shelve this amazing technology.

– Brother Apollo of The Gold Cast,
extract from *The Final History of The Triumvirate of Metals*

Turquoise Prism Fox Bite

or

Bleeding Out On A Chair Of Viridian Wires

Prey: On The Run

It's the day. Taban has made it. He stands on the starting line in his black and yellow Jackal House T-shirt, bumping shoulders with a Hyena House boy on his left and a Leopard House girl on his right. A mess of teens has assembled for the Highveldt Junior High Mixed-Sex Cross-Country. Through the crowd he can spot Hendrick in his white and yellow Lion House colours – jogging in place.

The cross-country route is structured like this →

The students start at the North Field track. They loop round this track twice then veer west down a narrow corridor by the tennis court where they must leap over the Water Jump – a metre-deep trench, filled with water, with a tarpaulin stretched over the bottom to prevent it from getting too muddy (note: the tarpaulin does not prevent it from getting too muddy).

After leaping over – or more likely *into* – the Water Jump, the students then veer onto the Central Field. This is another 500-metre track that they must also loop twice before exiting east into a corridor of pine trees called the Obstacle Forest. They must snake around these trees in a strict right-left pattern heading north – returning to the starting field to repeat the entire route. On the second time round – instead of going on to the Obstacle Forest – students stop at the finish line on the Central Field track.

Taban has a different plan though. Instead of repeating the course he will slip away in the Obstacle Forest, blend in with the audience by the finishing line, and wait for Hendrick's arrival.

Taban notices that Hendrick is looking back at him now – as if sensing his stare. Hendrick has always had this odd intuition. He just seems to know when Taban is nearby – no matter how inconspicuous Taban tries to make himself. Like a predator sensing prey.

Hendrick scowls, turns away.

Good, Taban thinks. I want you to know I'm here. I want you to know I'm watching when it all goes wrong for you. When you eat dirt and piss yourself just before the finish line I want you to know that frail, sickly, disgusting Taban is there, shoulder to shoulder with the whole world, laughing at you.

A teacher shouts for the runners to squash into position.

Taban rocks back and forth on his feet at the starting line.

'Ready. Set. Go.'

A loud bang.

Taban stumbles into a brisk jog – a middling pace he has calculated will be just fast enough to get him near the finish line in time for Hendrick's arrival. Half of the runners pull ahead. Then a select ten or twelve pull ahead of that half. That group is about a third of the way into their second loop of the North Field track when Hendrick breaks away and takes a comfortable lead.

Initially Taban doesn't feel too exerted, but, as he approaches the end of his second 500-metre loop, he feels his throat start to burn. Trying to maintain even half of Hendrick's pace is a stretch.

As he swerves towards the Water Jump he feels his high-arch feet judder on the rocks and patchy grass – running shoes slipping on the shallow incline. He spots another student buckled over, wheezing. An older prefect orbits – provides 'encouragement'. This is realised as a series of aggressive taunts. The prefect advises that the wheezing boy is letting down Leopard House. 'Come on!' he instructs over and over in exasperated tones. Eventually, he calls the younger student a 'Pussy'. 'Come on, you pussy,' he taunts.

Such is the way.

Taban reaches the Water Jump. As usual it's a chaotic scene – evocative of the Bosch paintings the art teacher, Mrs Fauré, showed the other week. On the far side of the trench the tarpaulin has already come unfastened exposing a muddy ledge which is gradually collapsing into mush as children attempt to scale it. A prefect is reluctantly hauling up a sodden runner too short to manage the climb on their own, while other runners scramble past like desperate wildebeest trying to cross a river during migration. On the opposite side of the trench an injured girl howls while an irritable teacher holds a blue plastic freezer block – fresh from a cooler bag – to her swollen ankle and tells her to stop being such a 'big baby'. The runner in front of Taban clears the jump but slips and falls butt first into damp soil. Not wanting to get tangled in the carnage Taban waits a second for him to get up, then attempts to clear the jump himself. The remaining runner in the trench ducks his head. Taban just about makes it, but tumbles over and lands on his elbows – grazing his arms. A big splash in the trench behind him sends water spraying. Taban does not look back to see who or what caused it. He rises to his feet and continues running towards the Central Track.

Suddenly – pain.

Pain in his chest.

Pain like paper thorns if paper thorns grew in your blood, clogged veins flowered out of your skin. Taban stops to catch his breath. He must have pulled a muscle or something when he fell. Already a prefect is bee-lining towards him. Taban reaches inside for Solomon's power – sends it coursing through his chest. He doesn't have the time to heal, but can suppress the agony for a time. He continues running. Behind him the prefect yells, 'Go! Go! Go! Famba! Famba!'

Taban keeps moving. As he completes his first lap around the Central Field, the teachers, students, and student families clustered around the finish line cheer – presumably for other students. Their words melt together into a cacophonous stream of syllables – *golioleogojackjimmufwopardfambago* … and so on.

He finishes his second lap and continues on to the Obstacle Forest. Once there Taban stops, buckles, breathes hard. Other runners shoot by – weaving right-to-left through the row of sun-scorched anachronistic pines marked with chalk. One runner mistakenly starts going left-to-right and immediately a prefect stops and orders her to start over.

Picking himself up, Taban weaves between the trees – looking for the moment he can escape. Eventually his opportunity comes. A gap by some hibiscus bushes – their red trumpet flowers sagging under the sun. Surveillance is light. He slows, waits for the other students to overtake, then slips away. Sneaking down a narrow path, he finds himself by the Topsy-Turvy Tree and begins doubling back towards the Central Field when a familiar voice calls out.

'Taban?'

It's the librarian Ms Govera. She is sitting on the bench overlooking the parking lot – part way into a sandwich still half-wrapped in cling film. She stands and approaches.

'Are you okay?' she asks.

'Um. Na. Ms, I'm not feeling so great. Is it okay if I bail?'

She looks him up and down. 'Well part of the reason they stationed me here was to catch pupils trying to skive. But I know about your condition.'

Taban exhales, relieved.

'Come. I will take you to the nurse's office.'

Taban inhales – sucking his relief back in. 'Uh, no need for that,' he blurts. 'I just need to catch my breath—'

'Taban, we need to take this seriously!' She moves closer, blocking his path. 'If you're not feeling well I can't just let you wander off. What if you have a fainting spell and no one's around? Now come with me.'

Taban shuts his eyes and reaches out with his power. He imagines the carotid arteries below Ms Govera's jaw closing then counts to ten.

One. Two. Three. Four. Five.

He hears Ms Govera fall to her knees, mumble a sleepy, 'Huh?'

Six. Seven. Eight. Nine. Ten.

A muffled thud.

Taban opens his eyes to see Ms Govera passed out on the ground.

'I'm sorry. I didn't want to do that,' he says. He rolls her onto her side – sliding her head beneath her palm. She should only be knocked out for a minute or two.

It was necessary. I can't stop now. I'm so close.

He heads south down the small stone steps that connect the Northern Grounds parking lot to the Central Field. There he slips into the crowd by the finish line. Many students of different ages – those who have already run and those set to run next – mingle about in their house uniforms with their parents. Everyone is distracted. Taban blends in easily. He takes his spot about 50 metres from the finish. Next to him a large man in a Hawaiian shirt eats an ice-cream cone with incredible precision – almost none of it ending up in his sandy-blonde beard. Taban thinks he might recognise him, but before he can remember from where a loud shout startles him.

'Come on, Hendrick!'

Taban turns to see Hendrick fly past – a flock of other runners trailing after. For a moment his heart plummets – thinking he's missed his chance. But Hendrick keeps running. He's on his first loop – not his last.

Taban centres himself. He focuses on Hendrick's left leg. Envisions his veins. Saphenous. Femoral. Iliac. Tibial. Pumping. Squeezing blood around the body. Feels muscles stretching and compacting as feet hit the ground. Tibialis Anterior. Soleus. Extensor Hallucis Longus. Extensor Digitorum Longus. Peroneus Longus. Peroneus Brevis. And finally, his target, the Gastrocnemius. As Hendrick nears the final stretch and is about to pass directly in front, just before his foot touches track, Taban wills the Gastrocnemius muscle in Hendrick's knee to instantly, painfully, contract.

Hendrick crashes face first. His cheek drags along thin patchy grass and rust-coloured earth. Skin scrapes off in thin strips – revealing little fissures of blood. He clutches his knee. It is locked at a right angle – a fleshy protractor. He howls like a dog – raising it into the air.

A teacher runs to his side.

So far so good, Taban thinks.

Then the man in the Hawaiian T-shirt also rushes to Hendrick, his foot slightly limping. Taban realises the man is Hendrick's father.

Not exactly in the plan. But not really a problem either. In fact it might be better. Hendrick's dad is distraught – calling him 'Henny my dear' as he and the teacher help him up. Exactly the sort of thing that Hendrick would find embarrassing.

It's about to get more embarrassing though.

Taban reaches out with his power, locates Hendrick's

bladder, and starts to squeeze. Hendrick squirms. Taban can sense all his muscles straining to hold it in. He keeps squeezing.

A trickle.

Then a gush.

Yellow pours down from the centre of Hendrick's white shorts in full view of most of the audience. Taban waits for the snickering. Waits for his fellow Highveldt students to point and gossip like they always do. To turn on him like animals.

Nothing.

Taban keeps waiting.

Nothing.

Hendrick is taken off the pitch. For a brief instant his glaring eyes meet Taban's.

Nothing.

Hendrick is guided through the crowd in the direction of the nurse's office and disappears from Taban's sight. The crowd's expressions are a mixture of concern – some genuine, some merely polite. No snickering. No cruel comments. In fact no comments at all. Nothing.

When someone finally does say something it's this – 'I hope he's okay.'

All at once Taban's mind arrives at three conclusions. They stab like needles.

ONE: His plan to humiliate Hendrick was never going to work. The reason the other students laugh when he gets beaten up is because of what he *is*. Not what is being *done* to him. He is a freak. His brain doesn't work. His body doesn't work. When horrible things happen to him it's funny. When they happen to Hendrick – whose body is perfect, whose brain is broken in admirable rather than pitiful ways – then it's a tragedy.

TWO: There is nothing he *can* do. There is nothing he *can ever* do. It's not about what he does. It's about what he *is*. To be born a freak is a tragedy. To keep living as one is a farce.

THREE: There is nothing that can happen to him that is so horrible that people will not laugh at or use it as evidence of his irredeemable freakishness. Even killing himself would only reaffirm people's view of him. The only way it will ever stop is if the world that sees him this way disappears.

It *should* disappear.

FOUR: Martial law must be re-imposed until such time as the dissident New People's Party and NRF Rebels are suppressed.

Taban flinches. What on earth was that? It's as if someone's just raked frigid fingernails across the top of his skull. His head aches. He closes his eyes and does the breathing technique Dr Green taught him.

Slow inhale.

Slower exhale.

Slow inhale.

Taban is at the swimming pool.

How did he get here? He doesn't remember walking. He is sitting on one of the benches that were set up so people could watch the swimming gala. Is it that time already? Wasn't the gala much later in the afternoon? Taban feels something cool on his scalp. He runs his hands through it. Damp like morning grass. His hair. Has he already swum? Nearly every student has to swim in the gala. The teachers make sure that there are many races and relays at varying ages and skill levels so that everyone gets the 'opportunity' to be 'included' and 'show team spirit'.

A voice like wet static. An announcer introducing the next

race. The Form 2 Girls 100m Backstroke. Wasn't there something he was meant to do at this race? His mind feels clogged – like it's coming up for air after nearly drowning. He sees Daisy stepping up to the edge of the pool along with seven other contenders all in dark blue swimming costumes and colourful caps representing their houses.

Taban remembers.

He was going to get revenge on Daisy wasn't he? Doesn't really make any sense does it? Going after the accomplice after the main villain has already been punished? But it had to be in that order – with the Gala scheduled after the cross-country run like it was.

Did it?

Does it?

Did it really make sense to plan some elaborate punishment for her too?

Does it really make sense to go through with it now?

No. Not really. If the pain inside him couldn't be eased by Hendrick's suffering then what good would Daisy's do him?

Daisy stands at the edge of the pool, twitching (a thing which no one talks about), biting her bleeding pinky (another thing no one talks about). Her eyes are tired. She is skinnier than Taban remembers. No longer admirable "healthy" thin, but pitiable "unhealthy" thin (no one talks about how one relates to the other).

He gets up to leave.

A voice: **Oh no you don't.**

Taban's body freezes. His legs bend back – returning him to his seat.

You don't get to change your mind.

You can't take back how you felt – say you want the

world to end and then just take it back like it's nothing. The world has ears. It _heard_ you ...

Taban feels Solomon's power whirring inside his guts. Before it has always flown _from_ him – like an invisible limb stretching in the direction he wills. Now it flows _through_ him – breaking out in an uncontrollable torrent toward Daisy. He closes his eyes, hunches, strains, wills the power to halt – _please stop, please stop, please stop ..._

The squeal of a whistle. Water splashing.

... please stop, please stop, please stop ...

Faintly, through Solomon's phantom limb, Taban feels something like a soft warm bag.

... now it answers _back_.

Squeezing. Crushing. Screaming. Gasps from the people next to him.

The whistle again. A teacher yells orders.

The force flowing through Taban vanishes – retreating through some hole deep inside, leaving him empty, spent, nauseous. He opens his eyes to see a teacher dragging a figure from the pool – which is now evacuated, swimmers encircling its edges in hushed reverence. As the figure is pulled it leaves behind a faint trail of brown red. Once on land it coughs up water and what looks like stomach lining. Then something connects in Taban's brain. The figure becomes Daisy. It's Daisy. Daisy is crying. Daisy is coughing up fluids. He averts his gaze – darts towards the exit gate. As he passes the horrid scene, his nostrils catch scents. Blood. Shit. Vomit. A small part of him wonders if he looks suspicious – or even guilty. But it has no sway over his body which moves instinctively to flee. Once beyond the gate, it is running. Where? He's not sure. His legs – still aching from the cross-country run – seem to be taking him to the Southern Grounds Library. It's as if he is going to go hide from a bully. He can't help but find it funny. A weird barking laugh. It's coming from his lips.

He feels eyes on the back of his head. Something is pursuing. He turns. The fox smiles. Bares teeth. Drools. Body twisting and contorting like it is breaking down then reforming with every lolloping stride. His fox bites start glowing – even though it's daytime and they never glow in the day. More bark-laughs. Are they his or the fox's? Gunshots in the distance.

You don't get to run away.

Paws slam against Taban's back.

His chin hits dirt.

'Taban? Taban!'

Hilde looks at him with a fearful expression.

'Huh? Ja. What? Where am—'

Taban is sat on the floor of the assembly hall, packed tight with knee-hugging students. One in the corner is having an 'episode' – mucus and tears coat the collar of his uniform. 'I need to get out. I need to get out,' he screams. Teachers hold him down. A nurse administers a sedative. Echoes of his voice refract off the chill stone surfaces of the hall – fading into silence.

Headmaster Horlick steps up to the podium. Taban has never once seen the man sweat. His tousled hair is slick with sweat today though – a semi-circle of grey algid seaweed strands.

'Students. You must all remain quiet and seated until Mr Knight returns to confirm that it is safe.' Horlick wipes his brow, speaks a beat faster than usual. 'I understand some of you may be disturbed. But please understand this is only a precautionary measure to keep you all safe until the commotion out in the streets has passed.'

A muffled bang.

Followed by another.

Gunshots. They sound like popcorn.

A lot of things Taban has overheard and largely ignored over the past several months click together like puzzle pieces on a lazy afternoon. A failed referendum. Zanu PF. Zanu PF Youth. War Veterans. MDC – Movement For Democratic Change. Farm invasions. Spiralling Inflation. Protests. Counter Protests.

Ah.

There it is.

You don't get to run away.

Some of Taban's fellow students start crying. Mr Horlick backs away until he blends in with the curtains. Taban thinks he can see him consulting the little cross hung round his neck. Perhaps the old man is praying for some sort of intervention?

Above the stage, framed in gold, a portrait of President Robert Gabriel Mugabe looks down on the weeping children through thick-rimmed aviator spectacles – neutral smile giving nothing away.

A much louder bang.

A din of angry voices and political chants that Taban doesn't understand.

Another adult wobbles up to the podium. It takes Taban's addled brain a moment to recognise Ms Govera. There is a graze on her knee. One hand rests on her forehead – gently massaging her temples.

'Rukudzo? You should rest,' says a voice. Taban thinks it might be his mother. He's not sure. His head hurts. Wasn't he running from something a moment ago? His head hurts. The back of his neck feels wet. His head hurts. He thinks about asking Ms Govera for a painkiller. Wasn't she taking him to the nurse's office?

Then a gentle familiar song whispers through her lips.

'*Simudzai mureza wedu weZimbabwe ...*'

The students around Taban solidify – tears mending into reverent silence.

Govera repeats. The children repeat with her.

'*Simudzai mureza wedu weZimbabwe ...*'

The other teachers regain their composure, stand side by side with Ms Govera at the podium and join in. Soon everyone packed into the tiny hall is singing the national anthem. Much softer than usual though. Normally it sounds brash and brassy to Taban's ears, but in this hushed tone it is pleading, mournful, but still assertive.

Taban, swept up, tries to join in.

'*Yakazvarwa nemoto wechimurenga ...*'

And that's it. He can't remember the rest. He tries to mumble along to the melody but he can't quite keep up. During assembly he would normally just pretend to sing. Or bunk off. Pompously, he never thought he would want to know the words to the national anthem. He wanted the world to end after all.

Eventually, the anthem reaches its conclusion. The other children look to each other – still disturbed, but calmer, a shared sense of relief among them.

The boy wonders – was he excluded from this moment or did he exclude himself?

Outside the threatening din subsides and disappears.

The double doors to the assembly hall grumble open.

Mr Knight stands in the entrance with a cricket bat.

'It's all sorted everyone. They've moved on. Mind where you step. Some stray debris got chucked over the fence.'

The teachers try to lead the children out of the assembly hall in an orderly fashion, but it soon devolves into a disorganised crush. Taban's head *hurts*. He closes his eyes.

When they open he's alone in the hall – just him and the portrait of Robert Mugabe.

He steps out into the courtyard by Central Field, rubbing his temples.

Fire and glass. There are rocks, broken bottles, a few smashed windows, a burning plastic bottle filled with paraffin. The fence between the road and the school is slightly buckled inwards.

Overall the damage is quite minimal – the result of some glancing blow intended for another recipient.

So why does he feel so sad?

Why does his head hurt?

Why does his neck feel wet with *breath*?

His chin is in the dirt again.

A voice vibrates from all around.

You can't escape the fact that this is what you wished for. You wanted this world to end.

'Please. I want this to stop.'

Don't worry. It *will*. Everything is going to stop very soon.

Taban's fox bites burn like branding irons.

Canines sink in.

Gunshots in the distance.

<<<

Gunshots in the distance. A metal heartbeat deep beneath the earth. A tree. A tree that is also a throne. A throne that is also a garden. A garden that is also a poison drip.

Drip. Drip. Drip.

Become Nexus.

Solomon's eyes open.

'Sir, are you awake?' asks the man next to him. 'We've arrived at the hospital.'

'Yes. Thank you, Lieutenant.' Solomon rises from the back seat of the car – puts on the blazer that, moments before, formed a crumpled pillow beneath his head. 'Could you give me an update on the situation?'

'We've rounded up the remaining rebel PRA officers affiliated with Lieutenant General Busani's New People's Party. There are a few pockets of resistance in the city, but we don't think they will hold out much longer.'

'And the NRF?'

'We haven't found any real evidence that they were involved in the assassination attempt. Isaiah's faction seems to have been caught flat-footed.'

Solomon looks down, pinches the bridge of his nose. 'Lieutenant, I told you to *find* evidence. Not *look* for evidence. Do you understand?'

'Yes ... Yes, Sir.'

'Good. You and your men are smart. You'll know where to *find* the evidence.'

Solomon steps out of the vehicle. Immediately, swarming from the darkness, a hundred soldiers form a protective cocoon. One hands him a neatly folded uniform.

Solomon takes it. 'Thank you,' he says. Then he walks towards the hospital. The soldiers spread into thin army-ant lines that flank his path.

More gunshots in the distance. Red and yellow flickers atop the burning ring of Athelsway Sports Stadium where people – Rebels? Rioters? Protesters? Who Knows? – are being 'quelled.' Red and yellow flame lilies pressed into calm by the black boot of night. Such is the way.

Once inside the hospital, Solomon goes straight to the bathroom to change. Partly because – having spent the whole night in it – the outfit from the debate is now sweaty and dishevelled. But also because it feels ... *appropriate*. The city is a battleground. He should dress like a general.

Solomon unfolds the uniform. It's one of the new black ones with the red trim. A pair of white gloves have been included. Thoughtful. An ironic choice of colour though. He chuckles. When did the blue-grey uniforms become black and red? Hell, when did they even get uniforms to begin with? Was it just before or just after they finished capturing Clay Sun? He can't remember.

He changes and steps outside.

A man salutes. 'Lieutenant General Busani is in a secure room below ground. As you instructed, Sir.'

'Good. Thank you, Second Lieutenant. Please show me the way.'

The man nods and leads him through corridors lined with statue-still soldiers. The hospital has probably never been so packed with humans – every wall propped with guards. And yet to Solomon it feels eerily empty. This entire section of the hospital has been made off limits to all but the most essential staff – and even those chosen few are keeping out of sight. Whenever he and the Second Lieutenant enter a room there is an immediate hush – so quiet Solomon can hear the dawn chorus filtering in from outside. Broadbill purrs and bee-eater whistles accompany the percussive creaking of rifles held too tight against tense chests.

Eventually, they step into an elevator, which takes them down.

'It was hard to find somewhere in the hospital that wouldn't be vulnerable,' states the Second. 'So I had a storage room in the basement converted. It's not ideal, but it's the safest option.'

'Thank you, Second Lieutenant. Lieutenant General Busani's safety takes priority.'

Solomon spots the man's shoulders ease slightly – hears a whisper-breath of relief.

The elevator opens into a dark hallway littered with dusty medical carts, IV poles, gurneys, bedpans, and other equipment in various states of disrepair. It terminates into a cross-shaped junction with three doors.

'He's in the one on the left, Sir.'

'Thank you. Please wait here.'

The man salutes and stands by the elevator.

Solomon adjusts his collar – walks to the indicated door. He steps through into pitch-black. He flicks a switch. A harsh fluorescent light comes on. Then off. Then on again. Slowly, it settles into an unstable flicker that feels ready to plunge back into total darkness at any time.

The room is bare but for a bed, an IV, and a saline bag. On the bed a figure lies curled in a foetal crumple of sheets and clothes unconsciously pulled off in the night. Ibn always was a restless sleeper.

'Ibn, are you awake?'

'Urgh. Yes. Who wouldn't be? So bright ... like a bloody torch being shined in your face.' He rolls upward into a seated position – takes in his surroundings seemingly for the first time. 'What is this place? Teach? The debates!' Ibn attempts to stand but immediately falls back – clutching his side. 'Ow, ow, ow.'

'You were stabbed,' says Solomon. 'While trying to stop a man attempting to assassinate me. The wound was bad. But not fatal. Very *not* fatal. Almost *calculated* to not be fatal.'

Ibn looks at him – raises an eyebrow. 'Solomon, you don't sound like yourself?'

'Ibn, the man who stabbed you – who tried to stab me – was one of yours.'

'One of mine?'

'A New People's Party member.'

'What?' A new look. Surprise. A hint of fear. 'I can't believe it!'

'Is that the truth?'

'Solomon, what on earth are you trying to hint at?'

'Was it a setup? Did you plot the whole thing? Is it part of a plan with Isaiah to split the Eyes vote – let the NRF win? What did he promise you in return? Money? Rank? Some kind of power-sharing arrangement?'

'Solomon, can you even hear yourself right now? You sound crazy. Who'd execute such a convoluted scheme which involves themselves getting *stabbed*?'

'*Heroically* stabbed. *Non-fatally* stabbed.'

Ibn laughs.

Solomon thinks he spots a glint in his young friend's eyes. Desperation?

'Solomon, have you slept since the debates? When did the debates even happen? How long have I been out?'

'About eight hours.'

'Then it's Election Day? Oh god. I've got to get in touch with Farai to make sure everything is in order – put out a statement.'

'You misunderstand the situation, Ibn. There won't be any elections today.'

'What?'

'I have suspended them. Until such time as the seditious elements plotting to subvert our democracy have been quashed.'

New look. Anger. 'Have you lost your mind?'

'New People's Party members were found to be involved in an assassination plot. In time I suspect we will find links to the NRF as well. Now, Ibn, I need to know your level of involvement.'

New look. Horror. 'You really think I'm involved?' Ibn asks. 'You've known me my whole life, Teach. You really think I would—'

'No. But then I didn't think Tanaka would either.'

'That's not fair. You know I am not Tanaka. I wouldn't betray you.'

'You already betrayed me when you ran off to start your own party. You were meant to be at my side. My right hand. My successor.'

'Oh come on! Listen to yourself, old man. You know me, Solomon.'

'I don't *know* anything!'

Solomon hears his words reverberate – coloured dark and brittle by the room's bleak acoustics.

Ibn edges back. New look. Fear. Deep fear. The fear an animal shows in the presence of a predator.

Solomon grimaces, removes his right glove. 'I'm sorry, Ibn.' He approaches – pale hand outstretched.

'What are you doing?' Ibn edges further and further back.

'I have to *know*,' says Solomon.

'Please, Teach. Whatever you're doing ... don't ...'

Solomon puts his hand on Ibn's forehead. His thumb and finger jab like fangs into each temple. The man's skull folds. A rush of information floods into Solomon – too fast for him to comprehend in any orderly narrative sense. Trying to pick out threads in the stream of data is like trying to tease out singular fibres in taut muscle tissue. Instead fragmentary images and sensations linger like morning residue on a windowpane.

Ibn as a child sitting outside the church. Dawn rays heat the porch. Father Graham whistles a gospel tune – pulls up the shutters.

Ibn as a young man on a stool at the township bar. The triumphant strum of a freshly tuned guitar. The hiss of a bottle cap. That first fizzy sip of cold beer. The smile and knowing look of the woman a few tables away. The fleeting thought that the man next to her looks good as well.

Ibn a few weeks ago in bed. The coolness as the covers lift. Joseph's beautiful bare arm as he reaches into the bedside drawer to pull out a packet of smokes. His amusing murmurs of indignance as he slips and falls. A duvet-muffled thump.

Ibn holding Solomon when he tells him the news of his child. Strong and tender. Solomon feels for the first time the depth of Ibn's love and appreciation from the other side. Nothing he's given him has ever gone to waste. No bit of wisdom or kindness has slipped through. His clear heart has contained it all. Cherished and added to it. Reflected it back out to the world with a simple, honest brightness he himself could never muster.

Ibn's smile. Ibn's laughter. Ibn's warmth. It's all there.

Then it's gone. And it is just data in Solomon's head. Filed in among his own memories with the same disjointed inscrutable logic. Why *that* moment on the porch? Why not any of the other moments on the porch?

What is not there is any evidence of an assassination plot or coup attempt.

Of course there isn't. You knew there wouldn't be. But you did it anyway. Because you don't have any faith – not even in yourself.

Solomon can feel it. Deep in the earth. Something growing, rising to meet him. Roots clawing their way to the surface. Or are they claws?

So many claws and teeth.

Become Nexus. You've delayed your part of the bargain long enough.

'Shut up, Fox.'

Solomon catches sight of something vanishing into the shadows.

There is a muted thud as Ibn's empty husk slumps onto the bed.

'You really did think everyone could just get along?' Solomon asks – half speaking to the corpse, half probing the stolen memories now inside his head. 'Either you were a bad pupil or I was a bad teacher.'

A knock at the door.

'I told you to wait!'

'General Mushonga, it's urgent. Your wife has left the safe house.'

Pain. Exhaustion. Solomon scrunches up his face. 'I will be there momentarily.'

He looks one last time at Ibn's body as it breaks down into cold black ash.

Solomon growls, 'You stupid child.'

<<<

The car pulls up outside a cream-walled bungalow on the outskirts of the city. Soldiers stalk the perimeter – machine guns pointed out at the blue-grey morning. This is the place the bodyguards tracked Vashti to.

Solomon does not recognise the house. His men have yet to finish combing the records to find out who it belongs to. As he steps out onto the driveway Solomon wonders who the owner is and what connection his wife has to them. He walks to the door – enters. He hangs up his coat and gloves on the hooks by the landing. Then he wonders why. It felt right, didn't it? The layout is so similar to his and Vashti's. For a moment it felt like he was coming home.

He walks through to the kitchen. There, sat at a small plastic table, cradling a cup of tea, still in her clothes from the night before, is Vashti. She looks up at him – tired eyes narrow and angry.

'Sol, what the hell is going on?'

Solomon does not respond. He takes a seat opposite. 'Why did you leave the safe house? You know it's dangerous out right now.' Rage bubbles in his gut. 'Who did you come here to meet?'

Vashti looks away. 'Something has come over you, Sol. The whole city. Violence everywhere. They say you've cancelled the election.'

'Postponed. Until we get the situation under control.'

'It doesn't look like you're getting it "under control". Looks like a coup. Like a new civil war. I thought the reason you started the revolution was to fix the injustices in our country – bring all the madness and the killing to an end?'

Silence. Solomon stares at Vashti trying to puzzle out the meaning behind her expression. Fear? Desperation? Anger? Exhaustion? Then he notices an absence – a hole in this domestic scene.

'Where is Shamira?'

Vashti averts her eyes. Solomon is about to ask again when she says, 'Someone is taking her some place safe.'

Solomon snorts. 'Her real father perhaps?'

Vashti's jaw drops. Disgust.

'Sol, what the fuck are you talking about?'

'Or perhaps not. Perhaps her father is one of the Albion soldiers who raided our house back when this all started?'

Vashti reaches across the table and slaps him. 'I can't believe you'd think I'd keep something like that from you.'

'Her skin is white, Vash.'

'In patches. She has a condition. Have you looked at your own hands?'

'Every day with horror.'

'Then why don't you believe?'

'I don't know!' Solomon hunches down – covers the top of his head as if shielding it from invisible blows. Or trying to contain something within.

Vashti kneels beside him. Places her smooth palms on his face – cradles it. Guides it up to meet her gaze. 'Sol, there are some things you just can't know for certain. Or at least know *absolutely*. At some point you need to place your trust in something.' She brings one of his pale hands to her cheek. 'Even if it's just your eyes. If not me then at least trust your eyes. Please.'

Solomon looks at Vashti. He wonders how he must appear to her. Do his eyes glint translucent and silver? Or are they marble white and opaque – giving no hint of anything beyond.

'Vashti, that's where you're wrong,' he says. 'I *can* know everything.' He raises his hand to her forehead and reaches out with his power. Her face crumples. She begins to disintegrate.

A rush of memories.

Her mother washing herself in a bucket of lime-green river water – scars on her shoulders from when the Albions beat her for taking a mielie from the storehouse – thrashed flesh textured like old wood grain. A hymn of the old faith whisper-sung. Contralto. Resonant. *Come Oh Blessed Wind From The Mountain Top. Come And Blow Away My Sin.*

Standing outside the secretarial school in Clay Sun, drinking a cold coke in the afternoon heat – watching students leave the university opposite. A lone black face emerging from the white crowd. Silver-white eyes. A brilliant smile.

Sol driving her home at night after picking her up from her bosses' office in Clay Sun. The stupid boy blurting, 'Would you like to get married?' Her reply – 'You call that a proposal?' Followed shortly by, 'I'll think about it.'

The inside of a cupboard. Her terrified heart rattling like a faulty engine – doof, doof, doof. Footsteps. Growing louder. Doof. Doof. Doof. Then softer – *doof, doof* ... Then gone. The sound of vehicles driving away.

Hugging Shamira one last time. Handing her over to Tinashi – telling them to get her as far away from the capital as possible. Tinashi crying. Nodding.

Alone in Tinashi's house – waiting. Resolute. The same prayer sung like a lullaby. Mezzo-soprano. *Come Oh Blessed Wind.*

Alone in Tinashi's house – waiting. Fearful. Leg twitching up and down like a frightened animal. Steadying it like one. Her faith is being tested. Her love is being tested. Let my heart be a steadfast flame. Let it guide him out of the dark.

Come Oh Blessed Wind ...

Then it is done. All her love is only memories. All her strength is only memories. All her trust is only memories. And all of her memories are now Solomon's.

As Vashti's body dissolves into ash, he feels several incompatible emotions.

Relief that she did not lie.

Horror that she did not lie.

Anger that she did not lie.

Despair that she did not lie.

Despair that he could not believe like she believed.

His eyes crack. Tears. His face rolls into a painful ball. He reaches out to Vashti's remains. But – as if they were recoiling from his touch – a gust carries the ash through a nearby window where it flutters moth-like into the night and disappears.

Come Oh Blessed Wind ...

'Wait,' begs Solomon. 'Please wait.' He runs after, barging through a door onto the veranda, snatching at air – catching nothing. His power surges in every direction – hunting. The ground shakes. Something in his stomach stirs, swells. The moon hangs precariously like a teardrop threatening to drip down. Yet Solomon's silver eyes are fixed only on the black – searching for Vashti's ashen wisp. Then malachite branches splinter out of his throat and something rises out of the ground to cradle him, lift him, entomb him. A throne of fleshy wires and humming steel. His vision dims.

Then suddenly: lights.

A car at the gate? Who could be coming here at this hour of the morning? Did the guards not ward them away? Where's Justice? Shouldn't he be watching the gate? Christ what do we pay that young man for? A figure steps out.

It's Eve.

< < <

Justice?

Solomon is Justice.

Solomon has always been Justice.

Solomon was Justice aged five – when the strange dog bit his ankle. His first memory. The wound never fully healed. When he told his mother it glowed at night she told him not to make up stories.

Solomon was Justice aged six – when his father came back from the war on crutches without a left leg. He lost it in an explosion while fighting for independence in the bush. He remembers being held in his father's arms and the sight of his father's face when he asked when his leg would grow back.

Solomon was Justice aged twelve – when his father went to the shop and did not come home. He had thought at the time he was just off to get some beer. His father had never been an abusive drunk. Just a sad, quiet one who tried and failed to make himself useful. He was no good at chores and his disability meant he was of little help in the fields. After independence it had been expected that the new government would look after him. They didn't.

Solomon was Justice aged fifteen – arriving at the house of the aunt who, after years of disagreements between his mother and father's family, had begrudgingly agreed to take him. Her expression – embarrassment, pity, irritation. It did not change for the three years he stayed with her.

Solomon was Justice aged eighteen – arriving at the house of Mr and Mrs Kokkinos-Tilke to become their gardener and assist the maid – a distant relative. He remembers the sight of Mrs Tilke – who insisted he just call her 'Eve' – emerging to greet him. Her immaculate skin – not quite black or white or even a definitive midpoint between. Just an ethereal foreign haze of wealth he could not recognise as part of the same world he lived in. Even her surname was opulent – a double-barrel of her and her husband's. Not one, or the other, or something in between. Both. She got *both*.

He got nothing.

Yes. Solomon was Justice then – with nothing.

And he is Justice now – still with nothing as Mrs Tilke honks the horn and waves at him from her silver Hyundai. He pushes the button. The electric gate yawns open. As Mrs Tilke parks on the gravel drive, Justice wonders how many cars her and her husband have gone through since he started working for them. It feels like every year they get a new one – even if the old one works just fine.

Mrs Tilke steps out of the car. Her nail polish is slightly chipped. Her black frizzy hair – normally artfully dishevelled – just looks messy tonight. She has a relaxed air. A slightly glazed expression.

'You're home awfully late, Ms,' he says.

'Yeah. Sorry, Justice.' She sighs. 'Car ran out of petrol suddenly. I think the fuel gauge is buggered. Had to get someone to help push me to the nearest petrol station. There was a queue, but thank God they actually had some fuel for once. Did Cormack not call? I tried ringing home, but it just rung and rung. So I texted him to tell you and Zahid I was going to be late.'

Justice shakes his head.

'Oh. I'm so sorry. I guess he must have been pre-occupied.

Zahid's really got to get his cellphone fixed. We can't keep relying on Cormack to play secretary. Anyway, someone at the petrol station mentioned something about riots in the city? Scary stuff. I hope you and Zahid weren't too worried?'

'Not too much, Ms. You come home late quite often.'

'Yeah.' She awkwardly bounces on her heel – clearly uncomfortable with the silence between them. 'You know lately you've got to queue for everything. Did I tell you the other day that I ended up queuing for two hours just to get groceries?'

'Yes, Ms. You did mention that.'

'Ridiculous isn't it? And now there are riots. Things have just got way out of hand. You know me and some of the other people at the theatre are organising a march in a few days – a protest against the rising division and unrest in the country. You should come along. Also, what have I told you about calling me "Ms", young man? You've known for me for how many years now? Call me Eve.'

She smiles her pretty half-moon smile.

Justice can't decide if it is intended to be sarcastic or seductive or something else entirely. He can't read her but suspects an ulterior motive. Then she lets out a big affected sigh – indicating the end of small talk and the beginning of another task. 'God I'm beat. Cormack asked me to hold on to this speaker for him. Could you help me shift it out of the boot?'

As she strolls round to the back of the car, Justice thinks about all the times Eve has come home late and Mr Grayson from next door – 'Cormack' as everyone calls him though his first name is actually *William* – has been involved in some small way. How blatant their affair is and yet no one seems to notice. Or perhaps people do notice, but just let it slide. Because it is *this* woman.

This beautiful woman with her easy pretty half-moon smile who has *everything*.

This beautiful kind intelligent woman who has **stood by his side** through everything – despite his plain appearance, meagre income, melancholic demeanour, and his **revolutionary ambitions** which endanger both their lives. Who could blame her for having an affair or concealing an **unspeakable truth?** Did she really hide in the cupboard? Did they find her? **I have to know.**

This woman he'd known since he was child who he looked up to. Who saw only good in him, despite there not being anything redeemable – just a meekness she mistook for gentleness. Deep down he is rotten, rotten, **rotten**.

This young girl who **betrayed him**, laughed at him, helped Hendrick humiliate him when he'd already lost everything – **Why did Caleb have to move away?**

This spoiled, oblivious woman who has *everything*. Did my father lose *everything* just so people like her can live in luxury while my family suffered? You'd think we'd never even won the war!

'Justice? Are you okay?'

Hands hold a shovel in the air.

Eve looks up. Eyes widen.

A shadow casts over a half-moon smile.

A mouth speaks, 'Taban is Solomon is Justice is Taban is

Solomon. Eve is Vashti is Daisy is Eve is Vashti. Taban is Solomon is ...'

Before Eve can dodge the shovel comes down and connects with her head.

She falls over and is still.

Justice realises the hands on the shovel are his. The mouth speaking is his. Or at least they are both connected to him.

He realises that Eve is dead and soon his life will be over too.

Out in the darkness a familiar animal bares its teeth.

It looks like a fox.

<<<

Leftovers

Taban wakes in bed soggy with hot sweat. His bedroom is pitch-black, but he can see every detail of the off-white ceiling and the giraffe-print hexagonal lightshade with a crispness that is *sharp*. Too sharp. Jagged. Like it might cut his eyes if he lets his gaze rest on any one detail too long. His brain oozes as he moves his head. He feels like he's been asleep for days. His belly burns. Something is melting his insides. He rolls over and throws up on the floor. In the vomit – slicked with undigested food – he can see an emerald fox skull with a crest of matted hair. It glows – emits a high-pitched hum. The cupboard opens. It rolls inside and into the hidden shoebox with all the other fox parts. There is a rattling, a scratching, a writhing – like a small animal struggling to be born. Then something – an amalgamation of bits – emerges and scuttles out of the nearby window.

Taban hears a chuckle that makes his left ear throb. A little figure hovers in mid-air. Six gold wings conceal a face – revealing only a single lidless eye. 'Seraph?' Taban asks. 'What happened? What happened to Eve …'

'I'm sure you have many questions. If you'd like answers – simply imagine the worst. What you imagine will not be far from the truth.'

'Was Justice… Was he also a host . . ?'

'Do you remember every meal you've eaten?'

'His. Mine. Solomon's. It was all jumbled together. But he seemed *awake*. It's only ever been memories before. Was he *awake*. Did that just happen? Was I in control? Was Solomon in control? Did Justice?'

'Last night at dinner did the food on your plate slosh

together? Did you mix and match bits on your fork? Did you put one flavour in your mouth, then add another, and another? Merge them on your tongue? Or was it only fused together when your stomach boiled it all into mulch? Do you follow my analogy? My master does not keep track of the myriad strands of thought that flow through him – he makes no special effort to keep them separate. In the end it all comes out as shit just the same.'

Taban buries his face in his hands. 'I don't want any of this. Not any more.'

'I'm sure you don't. But you *did* want this. And you *did* wish for this. And perhaps some part of you even now *still* wants this all to happen. And it is happening. Six weeks from now – under the auspice of an unnatural moon – you'll become a conduit through which the Tree of Solomon will enter this world and bring everything into his dominion. You know, you've been an excellent host. That's why I felt the need to come say goodbye. I had my doubts. But over the years you've really blossomed into the most exquisite vessel. Goodnight and *thank you*.'

The Seraph slips through the closed door as if it had no substance.

'Wait.'

Taban stumbles into the hallway. It is empty. The oval clock on the wall ticks. Ten o'clock at night. For a moment he forgets why he is there and then he remembers. Seraph. *Seraph!* He holds tight to the memory.

Muffled voices in the living room.

Taban walks towards them.

The door is slightly ajar.

'Fucking bastards!'

The air-raid-siren screech causes Taban to recoil – eardrums stinging. Once they settle he peers through the crack. A man is bleeding on his old dimetrodon sleeping bag. In the middle of his foot a juicy star-shaped gash oozes. He sweats, trembles. Taban recognises him from the theatre. Gondai? Wasn't his name something like that? His purple braids – normally held in a neat ponytail – are splayed out like damp seaweed. Sitting next to him, holding his hand, is Zahid. He looks numb, bleary. They are both wearing haggard T-shirts – slogans and peace signs obscured by dirt and dry blood. Cormack sits on the couch in his blue and red bulldog-patterned boxers, hands pray-clapped together, a week's stubble encroaching around his bushy moustache. Ann stands in a black silky nightie by the window massaging her temples, head bowed, auburn hair flopped in front of her face.

'Fuck, it hurts,' the man possibly named Gondai rasps. 'We were unarmed. Unarmed!'

'Please try to calm down!' Zahid begs, wincing as fingernails dig into his wrist. 'I can't think with you screaming your head off.'

'Calm down? Calm down! They attacked us. In broad daylight. That man's head got split open like a fucking watermelon. A fucking watermelon!'

'I know! I was there too! This is why I said I didn't want us to get involved in the stupid "peace" march. But you and E—' Zahid chokes on a name he cannot utter. Something echoes in Taban's heart. A flash of pain. *Could it be?*

'Look,' Cormack interrupts. 'We have to take him to a hospital.'

Zahid rolls his eyes. 'We can't do that.'

'It'll get infected. He'll lose his foot.'

'We can't take him to a hospital! Every hospital in the city is going to be crawling with ZANU PF Youth and cops. He'll lose a fuck-sight more than a foot—'

'Would you two please stop bellowing!'

The men go silent.

Ann lets out a long exhausted breath. 'Better. Cormack, could you please go to the bathroom and get the first aid kit. Zahid, by the door, next to the phone, you'll find my address book. I'll give Chenjerai a call. He lives in the area. He will help.'

Taban watches in quiet awe as his mother takes control of the situation. In the span of a few minutes Dr Green is on the way and the rowdy men are banished to the kitchen while she cleans and bandages the possible-Gondai's wound. In the dark of early morning, his mother assumes a powerful aspect. One which the boy has not noticed before, but begins to suspect has always been there. A silent seabed beneath roaring waves.

Eve.

Taban's mind drifts to the name Zahid could not say.

He creeps to the kitchen door to listen in on the men's conversation.

Cormack opens the fridge. 'Well I guess we were told. Drink Zahid?'

'Actually. Cormack.' Zahid leans against the wall – as far from Cormack as he can be while still being in the same room. 'Now that we're alone I need ... I need to ask something.'

Cormack freezes, hand gripped on the fridge door handle.

'Were you and Eve ...' Zahid fizzles. 'Please? Tell me.'

'Were we what?' Cormack glares at Zahid. It's the first time Taban has seen his father mad. His anger has a sort of unpractised, childish quality. Sulky. Bitter. Unsure of itself.

'Were you having an affair?' Zahid asks.

'Are you actually taking the insane crap that came out of that murderer's mouth seriously? Boy could hardly get through a sentence without rambling some delirious nonsense.'

Zahid's lips quiver. 'Please just answer the question.'

'No! Of course not, Zahid! How could you think that?'

Zahid's face erupts into snotty tears. He slides down the wall until he is sitting hunched – hugging his knees. He croaks, 'I just can't believe she's dead. Eve. God!'

'Can you two please keep it down?' begs a voice.

Taban takes a moment to realise it belongs to his mother Ann – who has entered through the door on the opposite of the kitchen.

'We haven't told Taban yet, Zahid. He's been in bed with a fever since athletics day.'

The kitchen goes quiet. Only the sound of Zahid's muffled crying can be heard. Then, after a few minutes, he stops, stands, and walks out the door.

'Wait!' says Cormack. 'Zahid! Stay the night. Don't … I didn't mean …'

It's too late. Zahid is gone.

Cormack does not chase after him. Instead he grabs a bottle of lager from the fridge. It has a lion on it. From Taban's low-crouched perspective, the lion's face looks long. Pensive. Remorseful.

'Well?' asks Ann.

'Well what?' replies Cormack, looking for a bottle opener in the sink.

'Did you?'

'No.'

'But you would have.' Ann's voice contains no malice. It is wistful and sad. She fidgets with the red-hemmed pocket of her nightie. Stares into the blood stain down the front – as if trying to divine something in the blotchy shape.

Cormack faces away – head bowed like a scolded schoolboy. He hugs his lager close to his chest. Gasps – as if coming up for air.

'I loved her.'

The words hang in the air for what feels like forever.

'I know,' says Ann. 'I always knew. It makes sense. She had a really good heart. It must have pained you to be lumbered with someone so wholly her opposite.'

For a moment it looks like Cormack might turn and face her – say something. Instead, he puts the unopened bottle back in the fridge, opens the door Taban is crouched behind, and strides past – appearing not to notice him. His footsteps down the hall are surprisingly soft and delicate. *Paff, paff, paff* – fading into nothing as he marches away.

Silence.

Ann seems calm, composed.

Then her fidgeting hand shakes uncontrollably. She rips the pocket off her nightie and stamps her feet.

A single agonised howl.

A face buried in shaking bloodied palms.

Taban feels the weight of his arms pull down on his shoulders. The weight of his torso bear down on his legs. His body has never felt so heavy. He lies on his belly and crawls around the corner into the little nook where the phone is kept. A single window overlooks the garden. Outside he can see the moon. It seems eerily large.

As if approaching.

<<<

His Eyes On Empty Space, Your Eyes On The Moon

A week later. Taban and Ann are driving to Uncle Athel's farm. The official reason for the visit is to pick up Caleb and Gertrude for a family trip to Kariba. The unofficial reason – which Taban has gleaned from hushed words whispered into telephone receivers – is that his mother is desperate to convince Athel to sell the farm. Since the invasions started happening Athel has received a number of threats, offers, and threatening offers. He's ignored every one of them. The other unofficial reason for the trip – which the adults won't even dare address – is that Ann and Cormack have barely exchanged a word since the night of the peace march. Such is the way.

Through the car window Taban can see the moon. Just like a week ago it is unnervingly big and hanging in the sky far longer than it should. It is well past lunch and yet it hovers next to the sun like a big clenched toothy mouth. When Taban asks people if the moon seems at all odd they just give him strange looks.

The Dehannas farmhouse looms into view. All around the land is flat and drab. Chalky, dusty soil. Patchy fields of muted yellow grass. Tin-roofed sheds. Taban doesn't really know what crops his uncle actually farms or if the land is even used for farming. Something related to tobacco curing or irrigation? For all the khaki-coloured machismo and broad-brimmed hats he seems to spend an awful lot of time on a computer – managing spreadsheets.

Caleb runs up and opens the gate. They park beneath an avocado tree – the only thing taller than the house for kilometres.

'Hey Ann. Hey Taban.' Caleb waves a hand tipped with black

nail polish. He is wearing a purple T-shirt with 'KoRn' printed in yellow on it. Apparently it's his favourite band. His unkempt hair is nearly down to his shoulders. You can just about catch the ear piercings glimmering through his mane.

'Do you need help with your bags?'

'Na, we're good my boy. But come here.' Ann pulls him into a hug. Caleb feigns resistance.

'Cut it out Aunty.'

'Na.'

Wriggling free, Caleb points to the large book Taban is carrying. 'What's with the book?'

'Oh. It's just something I borrowed from Hilde,' Taban says, clutching it tightly to his chest. 'Nothing special.'

A lie. It is special. One of only three copies in the country – a fact Hilde has been keen to reiterate at every opportunity. He'd gone to her asking if her parents – who were experts on mythology – had anything on Seraphs and Foxes and Ancient Kings. She'd lent this book to him – seemingly incurious as to why he wanted it. She promised to extract a high price for lending it at a later time. Two pages in and he knew it was worth whatever she'd ask.

Caleb gestures for Taban to give over the book. Taban reluctantly complies. Caleb traces his thumb over the title. '*Psychopomps & Heavenly Portals: What We Know of the Zambezi River Fragment and its Related Mythologies*? Quite the fucking mouthful.'

'Caleb!' Ann slaps his wrist. 'Language!'

'I know. There's too much of it. Couldn't some of that title be on the back or something?'

Ann stifles a smirk. 'You know what I was talking about, young man. Where's your mom?'

'She drove to town to fetch some groceries. You know that

when you Graysons visit we always need three times as much tea? You bloody well drink us out of house and home.'

'Is that so?' Ann tickles him.

'Sut! Aunty, cut it out.' Caleb again wriggles free. 'I'm not a kid any more. You can't do this.'

'Oh. Big now are we?'

'Ja. Biggest.'

'Is that so?' Ann's smile melts into a frown. 'Speaking of "big men" where's your father? I'd like to have a word with him.'

Caleb winces. 'He's out back.' He hands the book back to Taban. 'How about you go settle into the spare room and I go get him? He's in a bit of a mood.'

Ann squeezes Caleb's shoulder. 'Sure thing, Cal. See you in a minute.'

Caleb nods and marches off.

She starts to collect their bags from the car boot. Taban assists. There's not much to carry. Within a few minutes they have made their way to the guest room. It has an odd quality. The walls seem lopsided – the ceiling slanted. Like its construction was improvised rather than planned. There are two beds, a desk, a wardrobe, and a tiny window. Objectively, it's quite spacious, but its off-kilter dimensions make it feel cramped and unwelcoming.

After waiting for a while, Ann pulls a towel and a change of clothes from her suitcase. 'Taban, if Caleb or Athel pop by tell them I've just gone for a quick shower.'

Taban nods.

Ann leaves.

A few minutes go by.

Taban decides to go get something to drink from the fridge. As he walks into the dining room and heads toward the kitchen he hears raised voices from the veranda.

'For Christ's sake, Dad. Can't you keep it together for one day? How much have you had?'

'Only like four or five beers.'

'Ja and it's not even three o'clock yet.'

Taban tiptoes towards them – peers through the mesh screen door. Athel is sat on a wooden bench that faces out over an empty horizon. Nothing but grass and dirt and the odd scrap of bush or the broad leafy umbrella of an acacia tree. Up close you can see the bumps and cracks and thorns and curled seed pods that set apart one spot from another. But from this distance all those subtle creases appear ironed flat. A still sea in which the Dehannas household stands alone. An island cut off from the mainland – evolving down its own separate path into something strange and unrecognisable.

Athel is dressed in his usual – white polo shirt, beige shorts, flip-flops. He faces out across the blank terrain. Sips his can. Places it by his feet on wooden decking punched full of insect holes. It's a scene Taban's seen a hundred times. The only difference is what's at his uncle's side – a shotgun.

'Dad, for the last time please put that thing away.'

'Caleb, stop being such a fairy. I got to keep this near. I swear if those ZANU bastards come again I'll— Oh. Hi Taban.' Athel raises his can. Taban waves.

Caleb flushes hot red. 'Whatever Dad. Just please go say hi to Ann. See you at dinner.'

Caleb brushes past Taban and heads back inside.

Athel frowns. Then his frown slowly strains into smile. 'Don't know what's got into him.'

He burps.

<<<

209

The Flame Out Yearning Heart Boy Blues

Taban finds Caleb in the garage scowling at a battered Honda motorcycle. The boy dimly recalls Caleb mentioning something about getting a 'starter bike' earlier in the year. Judging from the flaky sky-blue paint and wobbly seat, Taban decides the vehicle must have been a 'starter bike' for quite some time.

Taban opens his mouth to speak. Then closes it. After seeing Caleb and his father argue, he'd felt the need to say *something* to him. Now he'd found him, he was paralysed. What was he meant to say? Why was he here? He should be reading the book Hilde lent him – figuring out a way to stop whatever calamity was set to befall the world in six weeks. But *something* in him moved him here. He felt if he didn't listen to it he'd somehow lose *something* far more important than the world.

In the end Caleb breaks the silence. 'Hey Taban. Do you want to go for a ride?'

'Isn't that thing falling apart? And isn't fuel super hard to get at the moment?'

'Yes. But – and this is *crucial* – Fuck. It.'

Taban nodded. In that moment, even he understood.

Ten minutes later they are belting down a narrow dirt track, wind ripping through their hair as they snake around the perimeter of the farm. 'Fucking It,' in Caleb's words.

Taban clings to his cousin's chest. The bike sways – barely able to hold up the weight of one teenager, let alone two.

'Are you sure this is safe Cal?'

'I never said it was safe.'

'Oh. I guess you never did.'

'We'll be fine. Bugger all out here. Not like there's much we can hit.'

'Aren't there like armed guys who want to take the farm?'

'Oh. Ja. They're parked like ages away though. It's all show. For the moment. There's this guy who used to work with my dad back in Harare. He's "mediating". Has government connections. I think there is going to be a buyout before things get violent. Hopefully.'

Taban hugs Caleb a little tighter. Sparse fields and the occasional withered tree zip past his vision. They probably aren't going more than 40 kilometres. But it feels faster.

'You know I saw Dad slap a man the other day?'

'What?'

'Ja. I don't know if you ever met Tendai? Guy's been working for us for as long as I can remember. He came on behalf of the other workers to say they're quitting. They'd heard about labourers getting beaten up in the other farm invasions. Beaten up or *worse*. So he came to say they were bailing. Smart move. Smart people.' Caleb digs his hands into the bike handles. The little Honda growls – accelerates. 'Dad slapped him. He slapped him and called him a "stupid munt". Tendai took the slap like it was nothing. In fact he laughed in my dad's face. Called him a foolish old man. Still had the grace to wish him well as he left. Dad didn't even have the composure to look him in the eye. I felt embarrassed for him.'

Taban remains quiet. He doesn't know what to say. All of this sounds like an Athel who is completely alien to him. A different man walking around in the old giant's skin.

Caleb takes a breath. The bike decelerates. He continues. 'Tendai needed his job way more than Dad needs this farm. Dad has contacts. He can go back to a desk job at the firm any day. Fuck we could even move to SA. Oupa would be over the moon. Tendai hasn't got anything like that. But he still has the good sense to leave. He's way shorter than Dad, but holy shit did he look taller than him that day. Reminded me of what this guy from school, Zander, said about the Shona's strategy for dealing with Matabele raids. Basically – don't. If you see them – book it. Take your livestock. Go live elsewhere. No heroics. No macho bullshit. Smoke dacha. Raise cattle. Keep walking. Now fuck if that isn't some wisdom to live by. Take it with a grain of salt mind. Zander is *full* of shit. Once tried to convince me his half-Japanese uncle was a ninja who could stab someone without harming their organs – used his skills to stage fake hit-jobs for the Yugoslavian mob. Also, that you can tell a chick is Russian because she'll have a third nipple.'

'How do you know that's not true?'

Caleb emits a froggish '*uuuuuuuuh!*' The bike leans left – bumping over clumps of dry grass – before he regains his train of thought and straightens course. 'Not important. What I mean to say is there is no shame in living, Taban. No shame in looking death in the eye and saying, "Sorry man. Another time." Don't let anyone convince you otherwise.'

Abruptly, the motorbike slows and comes to a stop. Caleb sighs. 'Guess the fuel ran out.'

The boys hop off.

The machine has sprung a leak. Clear fluid trickles. Gas fumes stink up the air.

'So are we walking it back?'

'Na. I have a more fun idea.'

Caleb kicks the bike over. He fishes some matches from his pocket. Strikes one – chucks it.

The boys quickly back up several metres – expecting some Hollywood explosion. The motorbike catches alight. It is a dim, pitiful fire. The silvery Honda H singes grey, then drops off with muted *pffft*. Caleb looks disappointed. Then laughs. 'Even in death you manage to be shit and unimpressive. Can't believe I worked two weeks at Mr Pierce's to save up for you.'

He leans in and lights a cigarette off the dismal flame.

'Those are bad for you,' says Taban.

'Ja. So's school. At least this looks cool and calms your nerves.'

He sits down in the middle of the dirt track and watches the flames. Taban sits next to him. The fire casts shadows on Caleb's tanned face. He suddenly looks much much older to Taban. When did Caleb start smoking? Who is Mr Pierce? When did he get the bike? When did his jaw become so well defined? He looks almost nothing like the boy he grew up admiring.

Two thoughts at once:

I barely know my cousin now.

All this time I've both resented – and pined for the company of – someone who isn't even really there any more.

Caleb takes a drag. Stifles a cough. 'You know Tab. When we were kids ...' He sputters out. 'Never mind. Why don't you talk instead? I feel like I do all the talking.'

Taban looks up at the sky. 'Can you see the moon?'

'Er. Ja?'

'Don't you think it's a bit big? Like bigger than usual?'

Caleb scratches his cheek. 'Na.'

'Okay.'

In the distance the sun leans below the horizon. It's starting to get dim. The world smells of petrol, tobacco, and cattle shit and it seems absurd that in six weeks it will all end.

<<<

... it claims in unexpected ways

'Where have you been?' Gertrude asks the two boys as they slip through the front gate.

'Went for a walk,' Caleb lies.

'A walk huh? Well you stink of cigarettes.'

Caleb grits his teeth into a grimace-smile.

She groans. 'Whatever. I don't have time for this. I've got to get dinner ready. Could you get your dad from the veranda. He's been sat out there all afternoon and it's getting dark out.'

'Aw for Pete's sake. I told him to come in hours ago.'

Caleb marches through to the veranda where, sure enough, Athel is still slumped on the bench – eight cans deep and half-asleep. Taban hangs by the backdoor – observes.

Caleb prods his father. 'Wake up old man.'

Athel's eyes snap three-quarters open. 'I'm awake. What's the issue?'

'The "issue" is I told you to go in and say hi to Aunty Ann and yet you're still out here dossing, pissed as a fart, clinging to that bloody gun.'

'I told you *boy* that I am *keeping watch*. If those bastards come again I'll—'

'You'll fucking what? Chunder on them? Do you even know how to use that thing?'

'I shot plenty during the war.'

'Ja? Actually hit anything?'

'God what did I do to deserve getting such a faggot for a son?'

'Fuck you. Not like you're even really my dad.'

Athel's mouth forms a little 'o', which it holds for several awkward seconds before sputtering out, 'Wh-what the fuck are you saying boy?'

'You heard me. You aren't my dad. You're just some piece of shit who married my mom. And if you wanted to keep that kind of thing secret perhaps you two should have your shouting matches at a lower volume next time. Hopeless fucking drunks.'

Athel lurches up and throws a sloppy punch.

Caleb dodges.

The two stare at each other. It's hard to tell who is more surprised.

'Cal. I'm sor—' Athel's words dribble away as Caleb runs off – rounding the corner towards the front garden and disappearing. He scowls at the offending hand. 'Fuck's sake. You idiot.'

Athel notices Taban looming by the backdoor – wearing his neutral mask.

'Taban? You saw?' He stumbles back – kicking over his can. Amber liquid floods the decking. 'I'm sorry my boy. I can't believe I nearly … I would never … have never. I love …' Athel approaches slowly – as if Taban were a twitchy farm animal – then pulls him into a hug. It is a desperate, awkward, sincere hug. Taban keeps his arms at his sides.

'Why are we even here, Taban?' Athel relinquishes him – gestures to the mute wilderness beyond the fence at the edge of the garden. 'Why did I go through so much crap to bring my family to this place? Some nostalgia for where I grew up? No. I *never* grew up. Not after J—' He chokes back tears. 'I *just* … I'm sorry. I've been selfish. Your mom is right about everything. Tomorrow I'll give up the farm. Get whatever I can still get and move on.'

Taban's gut burns. Fire billows into his nostrils. Words erupt from his mouth.

'Just like that? You think it's that easy? You think you can just

215

apologise, walk away, take it all back? You messed him up. You messed me up. You took away my only friend. The only one who understood me. All for some miserable strip of earth you don't even need?!'

Athel's eyes widen. 'Taban, I—'

He stops, clutches his chest, buckles.

For a moment Taban is confused.

Then: panic. Panic as he realises what is happening. The power given to him by Solomon has reached out – gripped around the arteries of Athel's heart.

He wills it to release.

It ignores him.

He wills it again.

Like a rabid dog it sinks its teeth in deeper.

Again.

I will not be restrained.

He begs.

'Let go!'

Finally, it lets go.

Taban rushes to the vacant-eyed giant on the grass.

He gently pushes a shoulder.

Athel does not wake.

He shoves a shoulder.

Athel does not wake.

'No.'

Taban remembers the time Athel took him fishing by Lake Kariba. Helped him reel in, then release, a baby tiger fish.

'Wait.'

The time Athel brought down an old Meccano set from the attic – used vinegar to clear off the rust. Eyes full of childish wonder.

'Come back.'

The time Athel shyly showed him his childhood paintings – which he hid in a box in a cupboard. Tender strokes of purple and brown. He was also colour-blind.

'I didn't want this. I'm sorry. I love you.'

All the times Athel carried him on his shoulders.

'I'm sorry. I'm sorry.'

Taban's tone remains neutral. His mask remains neutral. Inside though everything shakes with pain. Pain all the more unbearable because it cannot escape. Instead it pools. In time it will turn cold, freeze, and become part of him. Like all the pain before it.

The moon, massive in the midday sky, looks down impassively.

Taban notices that his fox bites are glowing – visible despite the sun still shining. In the centre of his palm a new mark has appeared. He hears a faint sound emanating from it. He moves his hand close to his ear to better make it out.

A high-pitched hum.

Glassy. Dissonant.

The bite looks like a triangle from which lines of greenish grey surge outward.

Like this →

The creation of the World Tree has inspired a truly vile technological boom.

Engineers of the Bronze Cast have made 'Feeding Bowls' which allow knowledge to be directly transmitted to the tree for archiving without a linked psychic even needing to be present. As we speak they are setting up temples in various dimensions for enthralled peoples to offer up skulls.

The Gold Cast meanwhile have created special suspension vats that contain the consciousnesses of so-called 'primitives' – preserving their bodies while allowing us access to their minds. Brother Apollo assures me that in time this will allow us to get around the 'bottleneck' of locating ideal host candidates. With these vats anyone – given enough time – could be turned into a conduit for the Great World Tree. The machines are in their infancy though and processing times are not ideal.

I asked him if he'd thought to try out this wonderful technology on any citizens of the Triumvirate. That seemed to hit a nerve. I will need to be more guarded about my distaste for his 'innovations' in future.

Truth be told, we of the Silver Cast are secretly engaged in our own research. We are developing a back-up archive based on prior tech – in case the World Tree turns out to be unviable in the long term.

We are also preparing contingencies should the tree turn out to be a threat to us. Though I dare not write any more on the matter.

I begin to suspect our people's best days are long past us now.

– Brother Glycon of The Silver Cast,
extract from *The Final History of the Triumvirate of Metals*

One month after
Athel's funeral
On the second night
At Camp Emet

Emerald Vein Fox Bite

or

Holding Hands In A Whirlpool
Of Strange Metals

Our Frail Constructs, Pull Tight Each Other's Seams

Taban checks his watch. Twelve o'clock. Even the most adventurous Camp Supervisors will be in bed by now. Regardless of how it markets itself to unwitting parents, Camp Emet is a religious institution and the supervisors are selected for piety and sobriety. Their primary job is to play the role of Cool Older Sibling, win your trust, then explain how condoms are a trick by Satan to make people more promiscuous and how the only way to avoid AIDS is to wait until marriage, be baptised by the Church of Emet, give them your money, recruit your family, etc.

Despite the pitch of a fun week of outdoor activities, games, and wildlife watching with maybe a *bit* of Jesus on the side, the camp has turned out to be a whole lot of Jesus and very little of anything else. Jesus in the morning. Jesus in the afternoon. Jesus in the evening. Oh Lord! Jesus in the evening. Taban shudders. Jesus in the evening had been particularly torturous tonight. Two hours of the same weasel-faced man burbling away in a cold concrete building. Air thick as syrup with forced solemnity. Dead spiders raining down from cobwebs in the thatched roof – as if they too were asphyxiating on tedium. Barely thirty minutes into the first sermon he, Hilde, and Caleb had already created a game around guessing which banal slogan the sparkly-suited weasel-man would repeat next. It was named, 'And that's when Jesus comes into the picture!' After the phrase he would use over and over again – as if trying to chisel it into their skulls.

Taban rolls out of his sleeping bag and puts on his clothes. Jeans. An old blue tracksuit top. Cheap running shoes. Nothing he'd mind getting messy. None of the nine other boys in the barracks-like dorm stir. He looks to where Caleb is sleeping. Seeing no movement he whispers, 'Caleb?'

No response. Fast asleep. He grabs his satchel and tiptoes out.

The air is crisp. The moon fills the sky. If Taban really focuses he thinks he can hear a low whirring from within. In the moonlight his fox bites glow even brighter than in the day – emitting their sounds and scents. So far no one has acknowledged his bites or that the moon is drawing closer every day. Taban isn't sure if people simply cannot see or if they are *choosing* not to see.

Taban heads north. Once he thinks he's far enough out of the camp that he won't be spotted, he pulls a map out from his bag. Still possessing Solomon's eyes he can read perfectly in the dark. The abandoned quarry he's identified as a likely site for the ritual should be about forty minutes away.

A torch shines on him.

'Taban, what are you doing here?'

It's Hilde. Wearing a thick canvas jumpsuit and sturdy shoes, and carrying a satchel. All very practical for a moonlit wilderness walk.

'Hilde?' Taban blurts.

'Well what's all this then?' says another voice.

Hilde blasts torchlight in its direction.

Caleb winces at the brightness. He's not dressed practically at all. Leather jacket. Ripped jeans. Combat boots. A T-shirt that says 'Napalm Death' on the front. No eyeliner, earrings, or nail polish though. The camp supervisors had confiscated all that for being 'deviant goods'. They tolerated the 'blasphemous' and 'violent' T-shirts only because Caleb had packed nothing else and being topless would be even worse.

'What are you doing here?' Hilde asks.

'I saw Taban sneaking out and wanted to make sure he was okay. He's been acting weird.'

Hilde raises an eyebrow.

Taban's neutral mask does not permit that level of expressiveness, but, internally, he raises one too.

'Okay – *more* – weird. Anyway why are you both here? Are you two like running away together? How romantic.'

Hilde scowls. 'Real funny, Cal. I was just on my way to go do something and I happened to bump into you both.'

'Ja? And what do you need to do?'

Hilde grimaces, blows out a sigh. 'I think this quarry might be where they found me.'

Taban and Caleb are silent. Hilde told them many years before the story of how she'd been found as a baby in a derelict quarry. It was at the very end of the Gukurahundi massacres and this area of the country was in turmoil. No one knew exactly what had happened – if her biological parents had been killed or if she'd been abandoned in the chaos.

'I think … I think I would like to see it,' she says.

Caleb nods. 'Okay. We'll keep you company, Hilde.'

'Shall we get going then?' asks Taban.

He starts moving northward, but Caleb grabs him by the shoulder. 'Wait, wait, wait,' he says. 'You haven't told us why *you're* out here yet.'

Taban stops, thinks about how much he can reasonably explain to Caleb and Hilde without them hauling him back to camp and then off to some psychiatric institution.

'I've been having strange dreams for a while now.'

He pauses. Gauges their reactions – attentive. Curious.

'In these dreams I'm another person.'

Their expressions remain unchanged.

'When I am this other person I have these abilities. These abilities stay with me when I wake up. I thought I had mastered them. But recently I seem to be losing control.'

Their masks crack – concern leaks through furrowed brows and downturned lips.

'I think I made some sort of pact without meaning to and now I'm under a curse.'

Expressions – indecipherable. Has he shared too much? Who cares? The world is about to end. He needs help. Before Taban can think, the rest comes tumbling out in a breathless hurry.

'Also there is a fox who brings me into the dreams and he leaves these bites that glow and the moon is getting bigger every day and I think I might have doomed the world.'

Caleb and Hilde exchange awkward smiles.

'Is this why you asked for those mythology books?' Hilde asks.

'Ja. I didn't know where else to find info on something like this. I think what I've been experiencing is similar to a story in the Zambezi River Fragment.'

'The strange one about the King of the Underworld who lures people to their doom?'

'Yes. It's not exact, but there are a lot of similarities. The fragment talks about a temple where you can perform a cleansing ritual to remove the curse. But it can only be reached through something the book describes as an "elemental medium combining water and metal." Not sure *exactly* what they mean by that, but maybe something like a—'

'A flooded quarry?' Hilde interjects.

'*Exactly* … Water and metal combined – you get it? Do you guys believe me?'

Caleb rolls his eyes. 'Taban, I think you're penga man. Mad as fuck. But I've always thought that.' Then he says something Taban never thought he'd hear from him. 'I love you.' He hugs Taban. It is a warm, sincere, desperate embrace. Like Caleb is trying to hold him together – trying to hold *himself* together. Taban has always thought of his friend as a single, solid, unbroken form. Now he feels all the parts that make him up. His long thin limbs and knobbly joints. The whole construction he calls 'Caleb' seems so fragile and small. Taban wants to say, 'I love you too.' But the words fizzle on his tongue. He's a fish. His mouth opens, shuts – wordless.

Hilde clears her throat. Caleb, suddenly self-conscious, releases Taban and steps back.

'If it's any consolation, Taban,' Hilde says. 'I have also always thought you were insane and nothing you've said tonight has changed that opinion. Also I'm going to the quarry anyway so we might as well all go together.'

'I think she likes you, Taban.'

Hilde punches Caleb in the arm.

'Ow!' Caleb looks at her sarcastically aghast.

She stares, points at her eyes, then points at him – the universal gesture for, 'I'm watching you, you naughty shit.'

Caleb sticks his tongue out. 'Anyway,' he continues. 'Let's go find this temple or whatever. Don't want to be out too late or we'll get caught by the Happy Clappers.'

The three of them follow the map north towards the quarry. Taban feels oddly nostalgic. Like they're back on the playground in Highveldt – which seemed so vast when they were kids.

'Now.' Caleb takes a deep breath – as if knowing that what he's about to say next is going to invite a lengthy exhaustive response. 'Tell me about these dreams, Taban.'

Taban echoes his big breath. Where do I even begin? he thinks.

< < <

Paper Chain Into Darkness

'This Solomon guy sounds like a dickhead,' says Caleb, as they near the flooded quarry. 'Like just a total bastard. Killing your best friend and your wife because of your own paranoia? Christ. What a two-faced piece of shit.'

Internally, Taban winces at this simplistic judgement. Neutral-smile slips to neutral. 'Well I wouldn't put it that way exactly.'

'Ja? You're too delicate. That's why. Sometimes you've got to be blunt.'

Hilde snort-chuckles.

The three come to a ledge overlooking the quarry. The oblong gap in the earth is broad and deep. Water shimmers in the moonlight. There seems to be only one eroded path below – barely wide enough for a single person. Otherwise it is all sheer seven-to-ten-metre drops

'I'm going to go change into my costume,' says Hilde.

'What? We're getting in?' asks Caleb.

'Well yeah. At least *I* want to get in and have a look around. You and Taban do whatever.'

'I'm getting in too,' Taban says. 'The temple is meant to be where the water and metal meets. So I think it'll be in the quarry itself – not near or around it.'

Hilde nods. 'Logical. Well. Sort of. Anyway, no peeking while I get changed.'

'How the hell are me and Taban meant to peek? It's practically pitch-black out.'

'You weren't paying attention to Taban's story. He can see in the dark now. Also I need the flashlight on to see what I'm doing. So just look away, okay? No gross pranks.'

Hilde pops behind a wizened marula tree.

The boys turn and face the quarry. For a minute or two they stand together in shared silence – Caleb restlessly tapping his foot. Then Caleb abruptly throws off his coat, strips to his underpants, and dive bombs into the water with a loud splash. Hilde rushes out from behind the tree – hurriedly straightening out the straps of her costume as she runs.

'Christ, Caleb!'

Caleb emerges gasping for air. 'What?' he replies, pinky squishing water out of his ear.

'You could've hurt yourself!'

'Oh come on,' he says, grinning. 'The diving board at school is higher.'

'But you didn't know how deep the water was you fucking dolt.'

'Oh.' Caleb pauses. Taban can picture the little hourglass turning in his head. 'Ja. You're right. That was kind of dumb.'

'Kind of!? I swear I've had more headaches in the past two days than I've had in the past five years and you are the cause of *all* of them.'

'Glad to be of service.' Caleb winks. Taban is not sure if Hilde can see this in the deep indigo moonlight, but intuits she must be able to sense it because she is now intently checking and re-checking her bag – just like she would back in junior school when trying to ignore Caleb's attempts to rile her.

'I better get changed too,' Taban says.

'No peeking, Hilde!' Caleb yells from the water below. 'Tabby is an innocent soul.'

'Piss off!'

Taban slips behind the marula and rummages through his satchel. The costume he has packed is different from his school one. Red trunks with grey sharks on them. His mom picked them out two years ago. Never worn. No occasion to swim recreationally. He puts them on. They fit. Just about. He packs away his clothes, leaves his satchel by Hilde's, and heads toward the narrow downward slope.

As Taban checks his angle of approach – he spots Hilde slide toe-first into the water.

'Brrrr. You didn't warn me it was cold, Cal.'

'It's a quarry filled with rainwater and it's like twelve degrees out. Of course it's cold. Also is it smart to bring that torch in here?'

'It's waterproof. I plan ahead you know.'

'Ja? And was the idea that water might be cold in winter part of your plan?'

'Shut up.'

Taban tunes out their bickering and focuses on keeping his footing secure. The two of them really are acting like they're back in primary. A few minutes later he reaches the bottom.

'Aw come on man.' Caleb winces in disgust. 'Those trunks are a *disaster*, Taban. The chicks are going to be laughing at you when the supervisors take us swimming tomorrow.'

'Says the boy currently bobbing up and down in his pants.'

'Hey! I didn't plan on coming on an adventure tonight. Also, you're in no position to make fun of anyone, Hilde. Your costume is pretty much just a school one with a few stripes. Lame.'

She rolls her eyes. 'It's a costume for competitive swimming. Adidas.'

'Whatever.' He sticks his tongue out.

Taban drops in and paddles over. For a moment they all quietly bob up and down together. Tiny waves of metallic blue and green radiate out from them like pings on a radar. Apart from this the water is incredibly still. The moon above feels like it's right on top – silver reflection encircling them.

'So … now what?' Caleb asks.

'I'm not sure,' Taban admits. 'The book was a bit vague. Does anyone else seriously not think the moon is really, really big right now?'

'Jasis! You've asked this question like fifty times, Tab. The moon looks *fine.*'

There is a loud creak like a great door opening. A brilliant shaft – white with hints of carmine – spotlights the centre of the quarry pool. The air whiffs of charcoal.

The three teens stare at the mysterious light.

'What the hell is that?' asks Caleb.

Before Taban can even begin to guess at an answer there is a strong pulling sensation.

Hilde's eyes widen.

A whirlpool forms beneath the circle of light. Taban has just enough time to suck in a desperate breath before he is dragged under. His body twists, turns, spirals. Then – hands. One grabbing his arm, another his leg. Wind on his face. He breathes, opens his eyes. Hilde is wrapped around his shoulder – Caleb curled around his foot. They spin around the vortex eye. It pulls them down into unknown depths. Down, down, down – until everything is so dark that even Solomon's eyes cannot see.

Then – an upwards jolt into stale air.

They land with a wet slump on the shores of a lightless underground place.

Caleb spits water, retches.

Hilde gasps. 'Guys, I'm afraid I lost the torch.'

'Be quiet,' Taban says.

'Huh?'

'Crocs.'

Leathery forms lie along the water's edge. Still. Slumbering or waiting in ambush? Taban can't tell – even with his new night vision. He recalls a fact from a wildlife documentary. How crocodiles can burrow into riverbeds – go into trance-like hibernations for months. He spots an exit at the far side of the den. It's almost a metre up off the ground – accessible by a narrow causeway of loosely piled rocks. Crocodiles cover nearly every surface.

'Follow me,' Taban whispers. He takes Hilde's hand. 'Cal, you hold Hilde's other hand. Stick close. I'll lead us out.'

'What? You can see? Even in here?' Caleb asks.

'Did you pay *any* attention to my story?'

'It was long. And I didn't think it was really true. Christ was all that other shit true as well?'

Shuffles. Coarse hides shifting against wet earth. Pebbles dislodging. Click. Tock. Schlick.

The boys fall quiet.

Taban starts to tiptoe towards the exit – guiding his two friends. Every step forward feels agonisingly slow and deliberate. He weaves between the unnervingly static reptiles. Hilde grips his hand so tight it starts to go numb. He does the breathing exercise Chenjerai taught him. Slow inhale. Slower exhale. Focus. Focus. Focus. The wet, sandy textures squelching between his toes eventually give way to rock and mud as he moves up the incline, to the base of the causeway.

A huge croc blocks their path.

Taban turns to Hilde and whispers, 'There's a big one. We're going to have to step over him. Big step. Really stretch.'

Hilde stifles a squeak behind gritted teeth – relays the message to Caleb who whimpers.

Taban goes first.

Big step. Really stretch.

His foot clears the reptile and lands on stone.

He slowly arcs the other foot over.

Big step. Really stretch.

Stone. Safety.

'Okay Hilde,' he whispers. 'Your turn.'

Still holding his hand, she nods and follows his lead.

Big step. Really stretch.

Big step. Really stretch.

She clears the crocodile. Taban lets out a tiny relieved breath.

'Right, you're up,' Hilde whispers to Caleb.

Caleb sucks in a huge mouthful of air. Raises his leg. An impressive ballerina stretch.

Slips.

The step – big but not big enough. Destination ever so slightly misjudged. The sole of his foot briefly brushes the crocodile's mud-soaked back before slipping forward onto stone. He hurriedly lifts his other leg over.

The three stand at the base of the arch and remain perfectly still.

The croc does not rouse.

Holding their breath, the three make their way along the rocky arch – holding hands as Taban leads. As they reach the middle, the causeway narrows further and they have to turn sideways and edge along step by step. For a moment, looking at his friends and himself stretched out hand in hand, Taban is reminded of those repeating paper doll chains Ms Cowley would make in art class. Then he catches himself thinking that word – *friends.* He feels a cold sensation, painful but soothing, filling up his chest, flowing upwards, on the verge of spilling out.

'Why have we stopped?' Caleb asks.

The feeling quickly subsides.

'Sorry,' says Taban. 'I was just catching my breath.'

Taban continues towards the exit. He reaches the other side of the causeway and tentatively steps onto a flat surface. Smooth. Dry. Secure. Exhale. Looking back from this vantage he gets a different impression of the cramped space they've just traversed. Rather than some naturally occurring underwater cave – it appears man-made. A basement? Or perhaps a *dungeon*? At the very least the platform beneath his feet feels more like a stairway landing than the stony outcropping it did from the shore.

Hilde follows Taban up onto the landing.

Caleb is about to follow suit when the rocks beneath his feet give way.

'Shit,' says Caleb.

Hilde, still holding on to his hand tightly, buckles to her knees. 'Taban! Help!'

Taban scrambles, grabs Caleb's other arm – pulls.

'Guys. I think they are waking up!'

Splashing. Writhing.

Taban wheezes – pulls with all his strength. They barely manage to heave Caleb's torso up onto the ledge when he screams, 'My foot!'

Suddenly, everything is in slow motion. Taban feels Solomon's power reaching out from him in every direction. The beating hearts and pulsing synapses of every living creature in this room are in his hands. The word, 'Stop,' goes through his mind.

Caleb goes limp – his legs dangle over the edge.

Hilde slumps – hand still gripped tight around Caleb's forearm.

There is a splash as something heavy falls over.

Silence.

'Hilde, wake up!' Taban shouts.

Her eyes twitch open. 'What was … Ahhh!' She winces.

'Help me get Caleb up!' Taban orders.

Slow blinks. She nods – eyes dazed and unfocused.

Together they drag the unconscious Caleb fully onto the landing.

'Cal, are you okay?' Taban jostles his cousin awake.

'What? Huh? Fuck!? My head. *Yeowch!* I feel like someone just split my skull in half.'

'Same,' says Hilde. 'It's like my brains have been scrambled.'

Caleb stands up and paces in a circle like a goldfish in a tiny bowl. 'Before we continue,' he begins, circling faster and faster, 'I would just like to say – sut, fuck no, na, fuck that, fuck this, fuck whatever is down there. When we get out of here I would like you to go over that story again, Taban, because I didn't catch all of it, but clearly some of it was true, and you mentioned something about the end of the world, and I would like the world to stay *unended* because I *fucking live* on it. I go to a kak all-boys boarding school and have not even touched a tit yet. I've got a lot to live for. Jasis.' He flops like a deflating balloon.

'Are you done freaking out yet?' Hilde chides, her voice cracking, hands shaking.

'Don't worry guys,' Taban says. 'I'll get us through this and explain everything again when we're out of here.' The boy is unsure if this is a lie.

Caleb frowns, slaps his cheeks as if trying to wake himself. 'God I've fucked up. I shouldn't need reassurance from you, Tab.' He rises up, jogs on the spot like a boxer. 'Right. Lead the way, you're the one with the superpowers or whatever. We'll have a good long freak out about all this when we're back at camp.'

Taban forces a neutral-smile.

The three exit the reptilian abyss and enter a narrow tunnel – Taban guiding them with Solomon's eyes. The tunnel curves and twists in chaotic and disorientating ways. Then, eventually the shadows lift and the air freshens.

'I think there is some kind of light up ahead,' says Taban. 'Only a little further to go.'

'How do you know that?' asks Caleb.

'I have a feeling.'

Caleb groans, steps forward, and falls over.

'You klutz!' Hilde says as she reaches down to help him up. 'It's not my fault. Can't see shit in here. Tripped over a weird rock.'

Caleb presents a brownish lump.

Taban takes a moment to recognise what it is – 'That's a skull.'

'What! Eugh!' Caleb gags and lobs it further into the tunnel.

'What did you do that for?' Hilde shouts.

'It was a gross skull!' He wiggles his hands as if trying to shake off invisible skull particles.

'That *gross skull* was once a person! It could've been—' She stumbles over her words. 'You know I didn't come here tonight for the insane Taban and Caleb bugger-around adventure hour.

This was meant to be … I was *meant* … I *wanted* … my parents.' She stumbles again. Taban thinks he sees Hilde reach up to wipe away tears, but in this dark, even with Solomon's eyes, it is unclear. 'Whatever,' she says. 'I'm going to go find it.'

She marches about two or three metres deeper into the tunnel before stopping, turning around, and coming back. She grabs Taban by the wrist and drags him. 'I can't see anything in this light so you're going to have to help me find it.'

'Hey!' Caleb yells. 'Don't leave me behind. I can't see anything either you know.' He snatches Taban's other hand. For a moment Taban is reminded of when the substitute art teacher, Ms Chelsea, would bring her two dogs to school. Her arms flailing like magnetised compasses as the Dobermann and the Ridgeback pulled their leashes in different directions.

<<<

Promises Whispered To Midnight

Eventually, after retrieving the skull and what feels like at least an hour of walking, the tunnel spits them out into a large circular chamber that looks eerily familiar – like a distorted mirror of the chamber where Solomon made his pact. The moss-covered walls appear metallic, rusted, etched with intricate patterns halfway between runes and electronic diagrams. In the middle of the room there is a waist-high pedestal about a metre in diameter. Carved into its centre is a silvery receptacle which resembles a basin. It glitters with a pinkish luminance.

'That looks like the light from just before we got pulled under,' says Hilde.

Caleb makes a throaty grumbling noise. 'Thank Christ we can finally see again. I thought that tunnel was never going to end.' He scouts the perimeter. 'I'm not seeing an exit.'

'There must be one,' says Hilde. 'That fresh air has to be coming from somewhere.'

'Sut. You can't say that for sure. Nothing is for sure in this weird place.'

'This inscription on the ceiling. Looks almost like Viking runes.'

'Great,' says Caleb. 'Can they tell us how to get out of here?'

'I can't make it out clearly, but it seems to say something about passing on the will of the "Silver Ones".'

'I guess it would be too convenient for it to be, like, directions or something.'

Taban inspects the basin. Along its oval boundary there are hand imprints in the metal with little circuit-like patterns flowing toward the centre. He traces his finger along one of the circuits. As he does he begins to hear a low electrical hum – feels a tingle in his teeth. He pulls his hand away. Both sensations subside as he does. 'I think this is what we're looking for,' he says. 'The book talked about how an "offering" must be made to complete the ritual. It was vague. The latter sections of the story are incomplete. But I wonder if this is where we place the offering?'

'What do you suppose the offering is?' asks Hilde, as she waves her hand up and down above the basin – like you might near a nervous animal to test out the extent of its aggression.

'The texts don't say. But I wonder if it's to do with the skull we found. In the dreams Solomon had the power to absorb people's memories – their knowledge – from their skulls. The skull was destroyed in the process though. I wonder if this operates in a similar way?'

'So put the skull in the thingy?' asks Caleb.

Taban nods.

'Okay then.' Caleb smiles sadly. 'Hilde, it's up to you.'

Hilde hugs the skull close. For a moment Taban wonders if she is going to reject the idea. Then she says, 'Alright. But I want to be the one to do it.'

'That's fair,' says Taban. 'Thank you, Hilde.'

He puts on a neutral-smile that he hopes is reassuring.

Hilde slowly, tenderly, places the skull in the basin.

The pinkish hue turns coral then blood red.

A low grinding sound – like machinery starting up.

Nothing more happens.

'I think we might need to put our hands into these palm prints,' says Taban. He inserts his hand into the indentation in front of him.

Hilde follows suit – putting her hand into the one next to his.

241

Caleb whines like a dog, before sighing, 'Okay then,' and placing his in the one opposite.

For a moment nothing happens.

Then, suddenly, the light envelops the chamber.

A pulse zaps through Taban's temples and within an instant the world warps and cracks as if it were paper folding in on itself.

Quiet.

Then he is Tinashi.

No? No. No '*he*.'

They are Tinashi.

They have always been Tinashi and Tinashi has always been a 'They.'

They were Tinashi as a child barefoot beneath the kigelia tree – heavy sausage-like fruits dangling above their head as Teacher Baruti recited the parables of the Elders.

They were Tinashi many years later at the Temple of Mouritz – the taking the oath to become a Listener. The Temple was little more than a riverside shack with a corrugated tin roof. The only indication of its sanctity – an ornate stone altar with a serpent and dagger engraved into it. But as Teacher Baruti says – any house is a temple if you walk into it with love and wisdom. They take the oath – vow to revere life, memorise the stories of the elders, and abstain from meat (Tinashi quips that as long as they don't need to keep eating Baruti's Sadza this can be managed. Baruti frowns, but the joke goes down well among the witnesses).

They were Tinashi almost half a decade ago when the cloaked figure came by their house – argent outline glimmering vividly in the dead of night. They claimed to represent The Silver Guard – an order of Mouritz followers whispered about only in the oldest and most secret of tongues. Tinashi had been chosen to take up the edict and receive the Will of The Silver Ones – who long ago thwarted an apocalyptic curse. But now that curse was being reborn. A 'host' was being groomed – world events manipulated to aid in their cultivation, obstacles culled. Tinashi had no interest. They were spiritual not superstitious. But then they heard the harsh guttural cough, saw crimson splash across the figure's pearly raiments, and resolved to provide a small mercy to the mystic. That night, in a temple beneath the temple, the Ritual of Succession was performed and Tinashi was named Purifier. In that moment, knowledge of the curse filled Tinashi's skull to the brim and they knew it all to be true.

They were Tinashi searching all these years – searching for the Host. Investigating every lead. Aching in the morning from long nights spent walking to remote villages – tracking the source of dark rumours. Peering into other dimensions with the abilities passed to them by their predecessor – cautiously so as to not risk crossing over. Looking everywhere for the signs. Then not liking where they pointed. *Solomon. How could it be that he is the host?*

They are Tinashi now. Running through the bush – cradling Vashti's daughter in their arms. The car ran out of fuel about two kilometres back and they had no other option but to continue on foot. In the distance the city of South Sun – normally a sea of electrical lights – is illuminated only by sparse patches of flame. A shape looms above the city, just barely visible against the black horizon. A spire shooting spires into the sky.

Tinashi cannot dither. In the ground they sense his presence stretching out – seeking like serpents hunting through the long grass.

Any hope of getting to the border and seeking refuge in Maalai has long since been dashed. Would there even be a point if they reached it? The curse is all-consuming. Just as the warnings said it would be. A parasite stretching out from its host to envelop the world. Only the Dagger of Cleansing can avert the end now and it has been lost for centuries. Misplaced in another world by a forebear far too partial to dimensional wanderings and dipping into different streams of time – before the practice was banned.

Tinashi has to find a medium – a place where metals and water meet. Substantial enough to enable a gateway. Doctrinal prohibitions be damned.

Tinashi trips over a fallen branch. They catch themselves – hands planting on the earth with a muted thud. The baby is not hurt, but is jostled awake and begins to wail. They gently rock – make soothing coos until the child is quiet and sleeping once more. It takes barely a minute.

'You're such a good a girl,' Tinashi says. They don't know if they are saying this to calm the baby or simply observing a truth deserving of acknowledgement. They scramble to their feet. Being part Eyes tribe and gifted with limited night vision, they spot a lump of iron glinting faintly in the grass. In fact looking around they can see all sorts of metallic detritus and up ahead a steep drop into a pit.

Of course. This is the opencast mine outside of South Sun that was trashed and abandoned a few months back. As the PRA forces approached, the Andrews government adopted a so-called 'Limited Scorched Earth' policy to make sure the revolutionaries would struggle to utilise any of the resources they captured.

A voice: **Tinashi. Return. My. Child.**

The voice does not emanate from any specific direction, but rather from within Tinashi's own skull where it echoes like an ill-tuned gong. They run to the edge of the pit, find a ladder, take off their shirt, use it to secure the child to their back, then – as quickly and carefully as possible – descend. At the bottom they locate a heavy barrel filled with rainwater.

They try to push it over.

It does not budge.

They try *again*.

Again it does not budge.

'Please Lord. Please Lord.'

Above the pit, looking down on them, glowing eyes materialise in great number – like hateful little stars pricking through the sky as twilight gives way to blackest midnight.

Tinashi rams their body against the barrel.

'Please. Please. Please.'

It topples. A shallow puddle pools around their feet.

The eyes approach. Grow larger. The wet glistening of saliva and teeth become visible.

Tinashi kneels in prayer and recites the incantation from memory – phrases that sound like something between poetry, coordinates, and code. Internally though they think only one thing. *Please, Lord, just spare this child. Just give her a chance.*

Tinashi shuts their eyes.

Then – cool wind on their face.

Their lids open. Rocky ground rushes towards them. A quarry? They spread out their arms to absorb as much of the impact as possible – to shield the tiny life on their back as best they can. For a split second it looks as though they are trying to embrace the entire earth. Just like their faith always taught. They smile and feel an overwhelming sense of gratitude. They close their eyes one last time.

'Thank you,' Tinashi says.

And then Tinashi is Taban.

They have always been Taban.

And Hilde.

And Caleb.

Each individually and yet all at once.

They all say, 'Thank you.'

Then are back in the chamber – hands pressed against glowing steel.

Caleb recoils. 'What just happened!'

Taban squeezes his forehead. A heavy ache behind his eyes is forming.

Hilde has a shell-shocked look. Eyes wide. Red lightning-crack veins pulsing through the white like a distant storm. She mutters something. Taban thinks it might be, 'It was me.'

Suddenly, the room shakes. The skull in the central bowl dissolves into black ash and then the black ash blinks out of existence. Red light fades back to pinkish white.

Silence.

Caleb speaks, 'Do you think—'

'Ritual complete,' booms a voice that comes from all around. 'Candidate selected. Take up the Final Will of the Silver Cast.'

Harsh scrapes. Metal on stone. The receptacle splits – parts like an Egyptian sea. The teenagers jump out of the way as an egg-shaped, coffin-sized, metallic object emerges from the floor. Then there is a hiss. A crack forms along the egg-coffin. Purple gas emits from within, turns transparent and dissipates – leaving the air smelling slightly of battery acid.

'Nah. Sut. Sut. Sut.'

The lid of the egg-coffin slides up – revealing what looks like a suit of silver armour. It is hard to tell if there's a person inside. The face of the helm forms a smile. A neutral-smile by Taban's estimation. The gauntleted hands hold a dagger like a cross over the chest. It is made of chiselled greenish stone. Blunt. Ornamental perhaps?

Hilde steps forward and picks it up.

'Hilde! What are you …'

Hilde looks at Caleb with empty half-open eyes. 'What?' she groans. Her finger traces an engraving along the blade – something between picture and script. 'The End of Kings,' she mumbles – speaking as if in a dream.

Taban feels a roiling in the pit of his stomach. Like something is squirming to get away. He cups his mouth – retches. Hilde stares at him, approaches as if sleepwalking – swaying the dagger like a dowsing rod.

'Please Hilde,' Caleb begs. 'You're freaking me out.'

Hilde lunges. The tip of the dagger stops centimetres away from Taban's gurgling stomach – like it has struck some unseen thing in the air. Slowly she guides it upward. As she does Taban feels something rising from his gut. His throat burns.

Then it emerges. A seed the size of a small egg. Glimmering. Metallic. Little branches of steel jut from its core. It splats to the floor in a pool of blood, saliva, and bile. Its branches drag its oozing body along the floor like little malformed limbs.

247

Hilde brings the dagger down.

A tearing like tinfoil being cut. A deflating hiss. Flames. Putrid ash billows up like a cloud of flies then disappears.

The seed is gone.

Taban stands up. He experiences an intense clarity – everything sharp and vivid where it was once muffled and blurry. His head feels lighter than it has for years.

The air pressure in the chamber fluctuates. The voice from all around sounds again. 'Purge complete. Autopilot disengaged.'

Caleb groans. 'Jasis. I just want this shit to be over now.'

There is a buzz. A small hatch at the opposite side of the chamber slides open. Caleb runs over and sticks his head in. 'It's some kind of shaft or duct,' he says. 'I think I can see a way to the surface. Bit tight but should be fine.'

'Should I lead?' Taban asks.

'Na. It's not that dark in there. Let me go in front this time. I want to see the outside world as soon as possible. Unless you'd like to go first, Hil …' Caleb glances over to Hilde. She is staring at the drenched dagger – eyes half open – tracing her finger over it again and again. He approaches slowly, each step soft and deliberate – kneels beside her.

'Hilde. Are you there? I don't know what's come over you but please come back to us.' He puts a hand on her shoulder, gently rocks it. 'We've got to go.'

'Huh!' Hilde's eyes snap fully open. 'Where was I just now?'

'You don't remember?'

'This?' She looks at the dagger. Her eyelids start to shut but she shakes her head. 'I think. I think I know.' Hilde flinches from Caleb's hand – as if only now noticing his proximity.

'Um,' she declares.

'Do you need to take a breather before we move on?' Caleb asks.

'What? No. I'm fine. Just wiped all of a sudden. Like, did you all see it as well? The dream? Where we were Tinashi? I think I might have ... I can't make sense of it right now. Let's just get out of here.'

'That's the most sensible thing you've said all evening.'

'Stuff you, Caleb.'

Caleb laughs. 'Okay, now I can tell you're back with us. I'm ... I'm glad.'

Caleb quickly clambers into the hatch. Taban enters after. The inside is like Caleb described. A sort of shaft – perhaps for venting exhaust or circulating air? Large enough to crouch-walk through, but not large enough to stand up in. It gently inclines towards a distant light. The metallic walls are jade-coloured and slightly reflective. All around Taban sees his distorted reflection. He's muddy. Bug-eyed. Looks like shit. Before pressing on he yells over his shoulder.

'Do you need a hand getting in, Hilde?'

'No thanks, Taban.' She pulls herself up into the shaft – one hand still gripped tight around the dagger's hilt. 'Sorry. I'm just ... No need to worry.'

Taban nods, continues forward – occasionally glancing back to make sure Hilde is still there. For a while the three of them move towards the light in silent, shocked exhaustion – the only sound in the shaft being the paff paff of bare feet on the cold metal. Then Taban notices something red. Caleb is leaking a thin trail from his foot.

'Caleb, you're bleeding.'

'Oh? Ja. I guess that croc nicked me. It's not painful. Could've been worse.'

Taban grimaces internally. Guilt flushes through him like adrenaline through veins. 'Thank you, Caleb.'

'What do you mean?'

'Thank you for coming out here and helping me with this … *thing*.'

'You dork. As if I would ever say no. Besides – I owe you.'

'For what?'

'You were there.'

Caleb goes quiet.

Paff paff. Paff paff.

Then, just when Taban is about to ask him to clarify, he continues.

'You were there for me when Dad died. Despite everything.' He stops again – a faulty engine struggling to spark. 'Taban, I'm sorry I pushed you away when we were kids. When we moved to the farm and I got sent off to Saint Vitus. I didn't take it well. I got caught up for a while in trying to fit in. Lost sight of what matters. I was … I was unkind to you.'

Taban feels like he's been stabbed. Or – rather – like he's stabbed himself. Only instead of bloody and warm the pain inside is cold, numbing.

Regret. Shame.

'Caleb,' he begins to confess.

'Ja?'

Taban can't do it. The words stick to his tongue and slowly slide back down his throat like disgusting medicine – a tablet half-dissolved and mulchy. How could he even explain? That Solomon's power killed Caleb's father? No! That *he* killed Caleb's father. That in a moment of anger *he* lost control, reached out unconsciously, and … It simply cannot be verbalised. It simply cannot be believed. Did I kill him? **You killed him.** Did I kill him?

'Taban? What was it?'

'Sorry Cal. I forgot what I was going to say.'

Taban almost wishes Caleb would see through him. Demand to know what he is hiding. Instead he shrugs and says, 'Okay then.'

The moment passes. A lie enters the world. The truth stays burning in Taban's gut. If only the dagger could cut that out as well.

*Something **else**. Something **leftover** squirms in Taban's stomach ...*

They continue in silence and in time arrive at an exit to the surface – a narrow hole lined with a mysterious silvery material that feels rubbery and scaly.

Caleb squeezes through to the other side.

'Oh thank Christ!' He yells. 'Fresh air!'

Taban follows after. Being smaller than Caleb he slides through easier. His hands grab chunks of dry earth as he pulls himself out and up to his feet. Above, a dim lapis sky heralds early morning. Taban is relieved to see the moon looking smaller. It seems like Solomon's power is slowly draining out from him like it used to. His fox bites still look the same though. He begins to wonder if they'll always glow. He wonders if anyone else will ever see them.

... squirm ...

'Aw sweet,' says Caleb, pointing to a tree. 'We're right by where we left our clothes.'

Hilde's torso emerges from the hole. 'Taban, could you help me? My hips are stuck.' Taban offers a hand and, with a little straining, she pops out with a vaguely oily schlick. The tunnel immediately shuts behind her and blends into the scenery so seamlessly that even if you knew exactly where to look you'd struggle to find it.

'Thank you, Taban,' says Hilde.

Caleb appears from behind the tree dressed in all his clothes – save for one crucial item.

'Hey Hilde – catch!' He chucks his muddy underpants towards her.

'Jesus!' Hilde ducks behind Taban. The underpants land with a limp flop on the ground.

'Caleb, you are *vile!*'

'It's not like I kakked myself. Though I did come close when we were in the room with those crocs.'

'Ugh.' Hilde groans.

'Oh come on. Just trying to lighten the mood. Anyway, you both better get changed. We've been gone a l-o-o-o-n-g time. Better rush back before someone notices.'

'I wouldn't bother,' says a voice.

Harsh yellow light.

Taban, Caleb, and Hilde wince as their eyes adjust. It's Hendrick. Holding a torch. Looking smug. Leg all healed up with only faint scars – despite it being barely six weeks since his injury. Standing at his side, as usual, is Daisy. She has jam stuck to the corner of her mouth and is holding an empty lunchbox. They are both dressed in khaki shorts and white tees emblazoned with Camp Emet's logo – a sunflower with a crooked smile (a print error with this year's batch).

'Oh God.' Hilde buries her face in her hands. 'I do not have any patience for this right now. Why are you here, Hen?'

'I'm here to catch three truants in the act of breaking curfew.'

'Christ. Did you like sit here for hours by our stuff waiting for us to come back?'

'Yes. Though I must confess sometimes I was tempted to just throw all your stuff in the quarry and call it a night.'

'Jesus. Why do you even care?' Hilde asks.

'Because that little shit is with you and I would love to see the supervisors make him scrub toilets for the rest of the week.' Hendrick inches closer – barely displaying a slight limp. Given how he looked after the sports day it's a miracle he's standing at all let alone walking unaided. *No. Not a miracle. At least not one granted by a loving God.*

You know how much hate can propel someone.

Taban's head starts to ache. Above the moon fluctuates and starts to emit that strange hum again.

… squirm …

'Taban?' Hilde groans. 'What did Taban ever do to you? I've never understood why you give him so much hell. It's weird.'

'He did something at the cross-country run. I don't know what exactly, but he definitely did *something*. I saw him there staring daggers at me – muttering to himself like a creep.'

Caleb squints at Hendrick, scratches a bit of dry mud off his cheek. 'Wait a minute. Don't I know you? Weren't we in the same class or something?'

Taban feels like hands are gripped around his skull – squeezing. In the morning gloom he can barely make out the wounded look on Hendrick's face. 'Huh? We were more than just in the same class, Cal. We were friends? Sat next to each other? Don't you remember?'

Caleb stares into space – his brain visibly straining, poring over its memory banks. 'Oh. Ja!' He punctuates his discovery with a finger click. 'I think I remember. Man. You grew up to be really lame.'

Hendrick lurches forward.

Punch.

Caleb drops. Blood pours from a freshly split lip.

'Can't believe you turned into some limp-wristed goth who can't take a hit,' Hendrick growls. 'You used to be cool. It's not your fault though. You have a bad influence in your life.'

He glares at Taban.

Strained guttural laughs bubble up from Daisy. Hendrick passes her the torch.

Hilde spreads her arms out like a goalkeeper in front of him.

'Hendrick. You need to calm down.'

Hendrick shoves her out of the way effortlessly – despite being almost a foot shorter. He is a compact little wrecking ball. His eyes remain locked on Taban. They don't even seem to blink.

'People are always asking, "Hen, he's just a little retarded creep – why does he get under your skin so much?" And the answer is … *I don't know.* Something about you makes me more angry than I can understand or contain. The way you carry yourself. Like you're above it all. That *expression.* I just can't let it pass. I've just got to put you in your place. Whatever is inside you. Whatever gives you those airs. I've *got* to break it.'

Daisy's cackle grows louder. The torchlight trembles in her shaky hands.

Taban's headache is an echoing thump now. DUM, dum, dum. DUM, dum, dum. He covers his mouth. He feels like he's about to vomit again. Red and black trickles from his left nostril.

… *squirm* …

'I hate you,' Hendrick continues. 'I hate that someone as pathetic as you is able to inspire such incredible bloody anger in me. But if you think I feel even a hint of remorse you're *wrong.* Because the only moral difference between you and me is you're *weak* and I'm *strong.* Everyone thinks you're this passive little victim. But I know the real you. You're cruel. Scheming. Like a jackal hiding in the bush. God knows what sick shit you'd do if you had an ounce of *my* strength.'

Caleb grabs Hendrick's leg. 'Taban. Run.'

Hendrick remains standing, staring directly at Taban – rigid like a corpse. He kicks Caleb in the head almost absent-mindedly. Caleb keeps clinging. Hilde scrambles to her feet and latches onto Hendrick's arm. Hendrick drags both of them forward then wriggles free. He barks. 'You're full of shit, Taban!'

Taban can't hold it in any longer. Something inside makes him step forward.

'So. Are. You.'

A moment: Breathless. Silent. Weightless.

It's as if all the air has been sucked out. The world is a sealed vacuum chamber. The world is a prison in space. After finally returning to normal – the moon is right on top again. No. Not just the moon. The whole sky. Distorting. Bending downwards – like something on the other side is forcing its way through.

It's all coming out. Taban vomits chunks of iron, fur, gold, silver, teeth, claws. Finally, a lupin face. Small. Hairless. Eyeless. Skull-less. An oozing mask of skin and muscle tissue. It plops to the ground – bringing with it an entire boneless saliva-coated body. It lets out a newborn rasp. Then things emerge from the surrounding bush. Mash-ups of flesh, stone, metal. They crawl to the mewling creature, merge into a familiar form – a familiar *toothy smile*. Taban buckles over as he hears a voice – No, *feels*, a voice – that he knows too well.

You stupid child. Thinking you could just spit out the seed and be done with us. Contracts with King Solomon aren't broken so lightly.

Caleb quickly stands up and holds up a hand in front of the

creature – as if trying to ward off a simple animal. 'Taban, get out of here!'

You'll make adequate soil.

The giant fox distends it jaws like a python and swallows Caleb whole. Its stomach engorges like an amniotic sac. Its skin is thin, furless, almost transparent. It pulses with light. Caleb's silhouette thrashes inside for a moment before going still. Then the fox spits him out. No. Spits *something* out. Something which looks like Caleb but immediately seems *off*. Like some essential part has been drained.

The fox leaps into the air and floats towards the bulging moon which appears to be reaching down to catch it.

If you want him back you'll have to come to us, boy. Renew your vow. Renew your commitment to this world's consumption. Ingest the seed. Become Conduit.

Or don't. It makes little difference. We could try using this one instead. Though a willing host is quicker to turn. More fertile. Less likely to break.

An incision opens in the moon.

Meet us at the House of Foxes. I'm sure you'll figure out what that means.

We'll be waiting.

And with that the fox slips through the cut and disappears.

Hendrick stares at the moon. Falls to his knees. Fingernails dig trenches into his cheeks – almost breaking the skin.

Daisy's laughter turns into deep hoarse panting.

Hilde tenderly prods the Caleb-like husk. 'Come on now,' she says. 'Get up.'

The husk looks at nothing – its eyes still, glassy, empty. It breathes, but does not move.

Hilde screams.

Taban collapses to the ground. His gut aches. It feels empty for the first time in years.

The sun rises.

The moon retreats into space.

A new bite has formed. Or perhaps it formed long before and now is simply the first time he is noticing it. A splintered channel of green. From the tip of his thumb down to his elbow.

Like this →

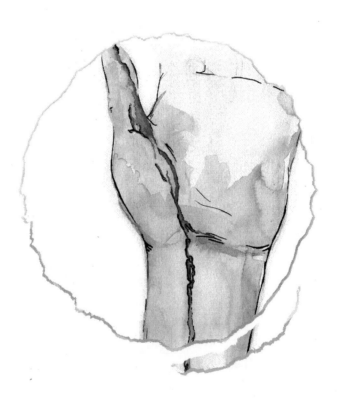

Here is the truth I dare not speak.

The World Tree is not my invention.

It is true as I claimed that it came to me in a dream.

But not as a schematic to be synthesised in an orgone vat.

It whispered to me from the darkness.

Within me and without.

It offered me power.

True power.

Not the flimsy power of political appointment, but the power to truly change the universe.

To break an unjust cosmos.

Remake it just.

To bring to heel those who have wronged it.

Those who have wronged *me*.

I wanted that power.

I make no apologies.

But that power also wanted *me*.

And it has terrifying designs – far removed from my own.

Perhaps all power does.

When we first experimented with using primitives as hosts for the World Tree's seeds they would rant and rave about seeing strange and horrid 'foxes'. We dismissed this as a side effect of the incredible psychic energies contained within the seeds. When some of our own began to have the same visions we dismissed them as well – locked them up in wards for the mentally ill.

But the truth is – *I can see them too.*

In fact I saw them that very first night – when those roots reached out tenderly from the shadows and offered me the ur-seed from which all this disaster sprung.

I saw it. An immense black tree. Bough teeming with glowing lupin eyes.

For a second I felt its incredible hatred. Its yearning for a silent peaceful mechanical universe – devoid of thought. A sleeping cosmos.

I felt its mind reach into my heart – pick out echoes of its own desires.

And then, with a single world of approval, take all that buried sadness in me and cultivate it into a blossoming I could not halt.

I said I wanted the world to end.

And, before I could go on to say I wanted to restart it better.

It interrupted.

okay

– *Confession of The First Patriarch of Bronze*

Ochre Heart Fox Bite

or

Our Spirits, Ribboned Into Shining Scraps, Float Away From Us

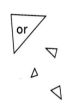

The Dinosaur Boy Blues

After the events at Camp Emet it feels to Taban like time moves unbearably quickly. And yet every morning he wakes feeling like an age has passed since the day before. The Caleb-like Husk has been moved to a hospital where it is now being examined by baffled doctors. Everyone who witnessed the event had the common sense to concoct stories more believable than what had actually happened. But, of course, all those stories contradicted one another. So the adults came up with their own theories that they have told to Ann and which Taban has overheard. Here are some of them →

Hilde's parents, Casper and Birgitta Andreassen – 'Ann. We hate to say it, but it was probably drugs. Caleb's not a bad kid per se, but he's always been rough around the edges and you know he's been through a lot lately with his father passing away. This was most likely some kind of "experiment" gone wrong. Probably Hendrick's idea. Kid's a thug.'

Hendrick's dad, Pieter Boeker – 'Sut, Ann, you know our children. They weren't up to anything too raucous. What I think happened? I think something frightened the life out of them. You know kids. Have very active imaginations. So it was probably half in their heads as well. They say fear can *literally* kill you. Read it in an article in *True Science SA*. So I think what happened is something scared Caleb so much his mind decided to just *vooooom* – vacate the premises. But you know I think he'll come back in time. God's got a plan, Ann. I know it.'

Daisy's parents, Buck and Maxine Johnson – 'It was a punishment from God. I'm sorry to be blunt, Ann, but your nephew, Caleb ... well we saw how his parents let him dress. Some of the bands they let him listen to. It wasn't a good

Christian household. God will only tolerate blasphemy for so long before bringing his wrath to bear. We're not saying this to be cruel. We just worry for you and your son. You're both good people. It would be terrible if your ... *proximity* ... to all these sinful energies were to cause you further hardship. We couldn't live with ourselves if – by being too afraid to be up front – we didn't let you know that there *is* another way. It's never too late. We can arrange a baptism for yourself and Taban at the Church of Emet by the end of the week. Please consider it.'

Gertrude – 'It's your fucking son, Ann. He's always been off. Bleeding. Fainting. Fucking weird schizo episodes. Whatever the hell he's got going on he's given it to Cal. It's the only thing that makes *any* sense. I'm sorry, but I don't want either of you to come near us ever again.'

And so on.

The only parents Taban's not heard offer up an opinion are his own. As far as he knows the one time the incident was discussed by them was a brief exchange over whether they should have allowed him to go to the camp in the first place – given his condition. It was a discussion that could've happened at any time about any occasion. A push and pull debate that has gone on ever since his symptoms started. 'We don't know what he has or what's causing it. It's dangerous. He might get hurt.' Versus: 'We can't let him stay indoors his entire life.' His parents have seesawed between these two positions for as long as he can remember.

In a way it is comforting. The country is falling apart. The farm invasions – which began early last year – have set off a chain reaction that has crashed the economy and unleashed waves of political violence. Ann and Cormack's marriage is now in question – destabilised by Justice's shocking accusation. The death of Athel and Caleb's 'coma' has estranged them from their extended family. And those are just the calamities that his parents are aware of.

And yet they continue on – putting on a performance of normality.

In a way it is terrifying. Terrifying that there is no one else to turn to. While Taban and Hilde call each other on the phone daily to discuss their theories about the House of Foxes, the adults are away. Off in their own little world. A world they are failing to manage.

Such is the way.

One day, about six weeks after that awful night at Camp Emet, this unnerving stasis ends. It stops when Cormack walks into the living room and says, 'Hey son – would you like to go to the museum today?'

'Huh?' Taban looks up from a book on historical architecture – *From Stonehenge to Great Zimbabwe: The Religious Significance of Ancient Structures.* Another text from Hilde he's poring over looking for clues to the House of Foxes' location.

'The Museum. I thought you might want to go.'

'Why?'

'Well you always said when you were a kid you wanted to go see the dinosaurs at the museum. I always said I would take you one day and … well I guess today's got to be the day.'

'Can we spare the fuel?'

'Ja. It's not a problem.'

'Okay. Thanks Dad. Let me just grab my coat.'

'Cool beans. I'll meet you by the car.'

Taban goes to his room and gets his blue tracksuit top and white takkies out of the closet. He also decides to change out of his shorts and into some jeans. It's been an oddly cold November with surprisingly strong winds. Satisfied, he walks out back to the car where his dad is leaning on the bonnet – nursing a cigarette.

'All ready to go?'

'Ja. Sure.'

Cormack stubs out his smoke and puts it in the front pocket of his denim jacket.

They climb into the car.

'You bringing that?' asks Cormack. He points to the big book tucked under Taban's arm.

'Oh.' Taban hadn't even realised he was still holding it. 'Ja. Is that okay?'

'Sure. No worries. You studying for something?'

'Yes. Yes I am.'

'Okay.'

For a moment Taban thinks his dad is about to say something more.

Instead he starts up the engine.

The drive to the museum takes an agonising thirty minutes during which only one clipped exchange passes between the two of them. It happens after they are forced to swerve around a particularly large pothole.

'You know Mark? The guy who used to work in the office next to my studio? He emailed me a photo the other day. Dead funny. It was of this huge pothole. Must've been a metre wide. And this poor madala's car had almost completely fallen in. Like you can only see the back half of it. And his expression. Aw, it was priceless. You feel bad for him, but you got to laugh.'

'Yes. It's awful how bad the roads are. Like the earth beneath our feet is falling away.'

Taban's tone is extra flat – even for him.

They are silent for the rest of the car ride.

Taban reads his book. Cormack keeps his eyes on the road.

They arrive. From the outside the museum looks unassumingly plain. Perhaps a community hall in another life? A smiling woman in a red uniform waves them through the entrance. Inside, glass cases filled with green-grey bones sit on podiums illuminated in oven-yellow. The specimens they've come to see are suspended by wires in dramatic poses in the centre of the room. Megapnosaurus. Three metres in length. Pack hunter from the late Triassic. Indigenous.

'Impressive beasty, isn't it?' says Cormack.

'Ja,' replies Taban.

'So … I'm not sure if Mom has let you know yet, but tomorrow I'm going to be catching a plane.' He turns to the guard by the door. 'Are we allowed to smoke in here?'

'Yes. No problem, shamwari.'

'Peace.' He lights up his half-finished cigarette from before.

Taban and Cormack observe the dinosaur.

'So …' Cormack continues. 'Things have been rough. We're broke basically. The government want one hundred thousand U.S. from me – which they know I don't have – or they're not going to let me buy airtime on the radio any more. Licensing fee they say. Though I suspect even if I did somehow get the money together the fee would magically go up. And the DJ and technician side jobs just aren't steady enough to keep us afloat on their own unfortunately. Inflation has buggered our savings. And Mom's teacher's salary isn't going up in line with the situation. We'll be lucky if it's enough for a week's groceries come new year …'

Cormack fizzles. He looks to Taban expectantly. Taban

doesn't know what his father wants from him – so instead he focuses on the display in front of them. The placard below has an artist's rendition of what a living Megapnosaurus would've looked like. The gulf between this illustration and the actual fossil is impossible to ignore. The feathered dinosaur in the picture is spry, lively. The artist has done a good job of making the wiry scavenger appear vital and immediate with its vibrant plumage and dramatic mid-leap pose. By contrast, the fossil appears all the more dead – a grey forgery so delicate it might break apart at any moment.

'So …' Cormack starts up again. 'Um. The plan is we're going to move to the UK. I have a job lined up in Scotland that seems steady and I've sorted out the visas. Some old friends of your mom's have arranged us accommodation. I'm sure once we've got a foot in the door we can make it work. No. Um. We *will* make it work. *I'll* make it work. I promise.'

A long plume of ash at the end of Cormack's cigarette drops to the floor.

'Anyway, that's the plan. I just wanted to make sure you were up to speed. You and Mom are going to be joining me a little later. You'll be spending Christmas with her friend. You know Dr Green? He's booked a lodge up in Nyanga. Should be scenic. Anyway. Er. Seeing as we won't be having Christmas together I thought I'd give you your present from me in advance.'

Cormack produces a branded shoe box from a shopping bag Taban hadn't noticed him carrying. Taban forces a neutral-smile – looks inside.

'Reeboks?' he says, inspecting a pair of black track shoes with red and white highlights.

'Ja. I thought your shoes seemed pretty knackered and

we've never really got you any fancy clothes. Thought you'd find it nice to have something premium for a change.'

'Thank you, Dad.'

'No worries, Son. Also check the little guy on the back. I think you'll like him.'

Taban rotates one of the shoes. On the heel there is a small image of a dinosaur skull.

'It was a tie-in they did to promote that new Jurassic Park movie from a few years back. *Lost World*? Was that it? Anyway, the guy at the shop said they're quite rare. Reebok Raptors.'

'The skull looks like it's from an allosaurus rather than a velociraptor.'

'Maybe the shoe guy got the name wrong. Do you want to try them on? Might need to return them if they don't fit.'

'Sure. I'll need a place to sit though.'

'I think there's a spot over by that exhibit in the other room.'

Taban and his father walk into a different section labelled 'Ancient Zimbabwean Civilisation'. It is mostly photographs along with a few examples of stonework, pottery, and iron tools. They sit on a bench and Taban puts on his new shoes. He paces back and forth – jumps up and down a little. 'They fit,' he declares, putting his old shoes in the empty box.

'I'm glad,' says Cormack. 'Shall we take a breather here? Then maybe head back?'

'Sure.'

Cormack nods – fishes out a fresh cigarette. The filter disappears behind his thick moustache – which has grown bushy and unkempt.

An uneasy quiet falls between them once more. Cormack blows smoke rings for a minute or two. Then he speaks. 'Can I tell you something, Taban? It's something I've never told anyone before. It's a bit of a long story so it might be a drag to sit through. It's about something I encountered during the Bush War that has weighed on my mind for a very long time.'

Taban stares at his father. The man's expression is unreadable. 'If … if you feel like that's something you can do, Dad. Something you *want* to do … Ja. Go ahead.'

'Okay.' Cormack takes a deep breath. 'Where do I begin? Towards the end of the war I was stationed out in the wilderness by this old crank's farm. He was a friend of some minister I think. I don't want to make it seem like more than it was. Most of the time me and the other guys patrolled around the area and nothing really happened. It wasn't exactly a prime target for the forces of ZANLA or ZIPRA. But one night on patrol we got ambushed. In the confusion I got separated from the others and ended up getting lost in the bush. I don't know how long I walked. According to the officer I was missing for three days, but it felt much longer. With no tent and all the beasts hooting and howling around me I was too scared to sleep. I've never understood your mother's side of the family. Their fascination with camping and game watching and all that crap. The way I see it Nature doesn't want us all up in her business. We should leave her be.

'Anyway, after a while things became … fuzzy. One moment bled into another. I think I was going mad with how tired I was. How *pissed off* I was. Shit, me and the guys weren't there by choice. Mostly. We weren't proper soldiers. Just dumb kids only a bit older than you are now. Got conscripted into a mess engineered by *supposedly* greater minds. And so much of what we were doing felt pointless. Save some folks in a church. Get called away to handhold a politician. Come back a month later to a congregation full of bullet holes. Funny turn of phrase that?

Full of holes. Full of absence – though I guess we humans can be full of emptiness, so it sort of tracks. It was all so ridiculous. Like trying to hold too much water in your hands – it just slips through the cracks between your palms. Though I suppose the guys we were fighting remember it different. They remember their own "churches". Innocent folks dragged out for "interrogation" in the dead of night. I'm sure they must have felt just as desperate and frail and mortal and we must have seemed horrible to them. It was all so fucking stupid. Maybe we all should've just shot our commanders and called the whole thing off? Would the final outcome have been any worse?'

Cormack sucks in air – as if to smother something inside. His cigarette has burned halfway – barely touched like the last.

'Alone, tired, losing my mind, I came upon a clearing and … what I saw was strange … mad. A black guy in full armour head to toe. Weird armour. Silver. Futuristic but somehow ancient at the same time. He looked battered. Defeated. Falling to bits. His big sword dragged behind him like a cross. He spoke in a language I couldn't understand. He seemed lost. I think he was searching for something. Or *somewhere*. Poor guy. Probably just trying to find his way home. Assuming he wasn't just my tired mind playing tricks on me. Probably was. It was probably me who wanted to go home. Though I don't know why my mind would summon up a noble phantom like him. He was dignified and solemn while I was sweating, stinking, mad with fear. All that was going through my mind was that I was exhausted. That I was going to die. That when I shut my eyes they would never open again.'

Cormack pauses again, breathes deep through his nostrils like he's running a marathon, then continues. 'And yet they did open again. And when I awoke, my knight was gone. And I was alive. *Aching,* but alive. It sounds silly, but I think he watched over me while I lay there like a useless sack of shit. I sometimes wonder whether he found his way home. If there was some plan God had in store for us that night. And whether ... whether I did what was expected of me? I don't know. Is he still out there? Was I meant to help him? Guide him home?' The last of Cormack's cigarette falls to the floor. 'Anyway, that probably all sounds crazy.' He forces a smile. 'That's why I've never talked about it before today. I thought ... Taban ... I've not been really ... really there for you. So I ... I wanted you to know. To share my ... Christ, I don't know what I'm saying.' The man buries his face in his hands.

'It's okay, Dad,' Taban says. 'I think I understand.'

Cormack's eyes well up. For a moment Taban thinks he might bawl, but instead he simply coughs. 'Haaaah. It feels good to get that out. Though I think maybe a therapist should've heard it first. That or a priest.'

He stands.

'We should go. I need a leak first though.'

'Okay Dad. I'm good. I'll just wait here.'

Cormack nods and walks off. Taban exhales. He lightly slaps his cheeks to rouse himself and stands up. Absently, he browses the displays – eyes tracing the silhouettes of spearheads and clay pots. Then, he spots something. A photograph that makes his heart thump. Fear and excitement and nausea and relief pump through his veins. The plaque below reads: 'The House of Foxes. A stone structure of unknown origin. Situated roughly midway between Nyanga National Park and the Ziwa ruins, it has baffled archaeologists for generations. The "fox" statues within do not resemble any native species. Historians only know to identify them as such

273

due to inscriptions around the base of the statues. These were translated by P. A. Andrews in 1962. Andrews' translation remains controversial.' The black and white picture hazily depicts a small dome-like structure inside which lupine figures are arranged in a circle.

'I'm back. What you looking at Taban?' Cormack peers over his shoulder at the photo. 'Cool. If this is by Nyanga maybe you and Mom could go visit while you stay there? Might make for a fun day trip.'

'Yes,' Taban says. 'I think it might. Dad, do you think you could ask the woman at the door if she's got a pen? I'd just like to write some of this info down for Hilde. This is her sort of thing.'

'Oh. Ja. Sure.' Cormack goes to negotiate with the guard.

Taban leans close – strains to make out what he suspects is hiding in the grainy image.

Yes.

The foxes are smiling.

<<<

Our Outlines Traced By Ash-Dipped Fingers

Midnight. Just north of Nyanga National Park, just east of Mount Nyangani. After an hour's walk along the river, Taban arrives at the location he saw in those photos five days prior – the House of Foxes Conservation Site. It is down a slight slope – in a clearing cushioned on every side by lush parasol-like tree-ferns with rough pineapple textured trunks. A flimsy metre-and-a-half-high wire fence encircles it. There is a little wooden gate by the entrance with a large illuminated sign boldly warning, 'The House of Foxes. Do Not Enter Without Permission! This site is under the protection of the Zimbabwe Historical Sites Preservation Agency. If you would like to arrange a visit please ask the Security Guard for a form and contact our Head Office in Bulawayo.' Beyond the gate an illuminated dorm with a truck parked outside evidences the existence of said guard.

Taban is thankful he decided against asking his mom to take him here yesterday. He thought perhaps he could scope out the place under the pretext of a day out, but ended up ditching the idea. He couldn't risk involving her in something dangerous. He hadn't even considered that there might be administrative hurdles as well. Would've been a waste of time.

'You're late,' says Hilde, stepping out from behind what looks like the delicate silhouette of a lonely dwarf msasa tree. Taban can just about make her out. Sturdy leather boots. Camo trousers. A green jacket with lots of pockets. On her back is a large satchel and strapped to her hip is a homemade scabard for the dagger they found in the quarry temple. Taban immediately feels underprepared.

'What are you wearing?' she asks.

He shrugs. 'The same thing I always wear. Jeans and a tracksuit top.'

'We're going to another dimension not a shopping mall.'

'It's not like dressing like Rambo is going to do anything. Solomon can crush our brains with a thought.'

Hilde frowns. 'We should do an inventory.' She opens up her satchel. 'I've brought a map, compass, binoculars, watch, provisions, bandages, antiseptic cream, water bottle, tissues, torch, pen and paper, and scissors. And you?'

'Snacks. Torch. Water bottle. Oh and a watch too.' He holds up his arm – revealing a cheap purple wristwatch.

'God. How did you even find your way here?'

'I'm not an idiot. I read the map before I left. You just keep following the river from the lodge and you get here eventually. Don't exactly need to be a park ranger to manage.'

'And what if … *literally anything* … went wrong?'

'Well it's not like planning everything out step by step has been working out for me either!' Taban realises he raised his voice. 'Sorry. I didn't mean to snap. I'm just a bit rattled.'

'I know. It's crazy. You almost emoted there.' Hilde smiles. 'Don't worry. That was a joke. You've never been good at telling when I'm just teasing.'

'You're hard to read sometimes.'

'That's rich coming from you. You've got like three expressions.'

'Three? Normally people say I've got two.'

'Nope. Three. One where you're totally blank. Another where you've got a slight smile – sincere, but a bit strained. And one where you've got a slight smile, but it's a total facade. Very sarcastic. That last one is rare though and hard to pick up on so I can understand why everyone says you've only got two expressions.'

'I'm surprised you're able to read me so well.'

Hilde looks wounded. 'I have known you since we were kids.' She takes out her binoculars and hangs them around her neck.

Taban suspects he's said something insensitive, but isn't sure what. He changes the subject. 'So how did you get here yourself? Are you also staying at a lodge nearby?'

'No. I stole my dad's car and ran away from home. Drove here all the way from Harare.'

Taban is not sure what to say.

Hilde grins. 'That was also a joke. My parents are archaeology nerds. We come to Nyanga practically every other holiday so they can visit Ziwa. They know a guy who owns a place around here.' She peers through the binoculars at the Security Guard's dorm. 'Anyway, we should check how diligent this guy is at his job. Looks like he's—'

'Reading a book?'

Hilde frowns.

'You don't need binoculars. He's only like twenty or thirty metres away in a brightly lit room. You can see him pretty clearly.'

Hilde lowers her binoculars. 'You're no fun.' She sighs. 'Anyway, we can probably sneak by if we're quiet.'

Hilde hunches down and moves swiftly and quietly towards the gate – a ripple through the chalky-coloured feathertop grass. Taban follows after. They climb over with little trouble – though Hilde does mime an expression of frustration when Taban lands on the other side with an inelegant thud. They sneak across the grounds towards the ancient dome. Up close the House of Foxes is much larger than the grainy photos suggested. At first glance the exterior is fairly innocuous, but it becomes eerier the closer you look. Smooth clay walls. An immaculately curved archway. Very different from the other ruins in the region. The few books Hilde managed to find about the place mostly focused on debates as to whether or not the construction was an elaborate hoax. Other than these, there seemed to be little interest. That felt ominous at the time and even more so now with the 'House' looming up ahead. Surely you'd expect lots of books to be written about an unusual structure like this? Instead there was an unsettling ambivalence. As if something was warding people off.

Taban and Hilde peer inside.

Darkness obscures the interior.

They take out their torches.

Hilde looks surprised. Then realises. 'Oh yeah. You did say you packed a torch.'

'Ja. I can't see in the dark like before.'

'I guess after following you in that tunnel for so long I just got used to you having night vision.'

'Ja. I think I would've preferred to keep the vision and lost these damn bites.'

He rolls up his sleeve. To his eyes his arm appears like a garish kaleidoscope – marks of all different shapes and sizes with no coherence or harmony. If he focuses on any one bite then sensations trickle in – tastes, sounds, smells, specific to that mark.

'You know you've talked a lot about these "fox bites", but I can't see anything, Taban.'

'I know,' Taban says, his neutral mask hiding disappointment.

He's about to roll his sleeve back down when Hilde speaks again.

'Why don't you describe one of them?' she asks.

'Huh?'

She slides her hand up to the end of his forearm. Her fingers are dry – laced with flecks of soil. She taps a spot by his elbow. 'Is there one here?'

He looks where she's indicating.

'Yes. Nearby. It's got a sort of wooden colour. When I touch it it's like I'm gently scratching my nails over my old desk back in Grade 3. Its shape … It's hard to describe. Let me show you.'

He crouches, flicks on his torch. With a stray twig he quickly draws something in the dirt.

It looks like this →

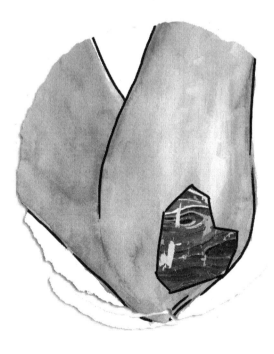

Hilde considers the sketch. 'It looks like a heart. But jagged. Like someone's sliced off all the rounded edges.'

'That's a good way of putting it.'

Taban stares at the shadowed archway of the House of Foxes and thinks about how wonderful it would be to simply walk away. He closes his eyes, does the breathing technique Chenjerai taught him – short inhale, long exhale. Then he stands up – points his torch into the darkness. 'Okay. I think we ought to go in now. Are you still sure you want to come with?'

Hilde's expression is sad, but determined. 'Yeah.' She turns on her torch as well. 'Let's go get Cal back.'

The two step inside together.

Somehow the interior is even more intimidating when lit. Foxes – carved from soapstone, ivory, bronze, and wood – beam their centuries-eroded grins down on them. Above Taban can just about make out a sequence of images engraved on strips of wood hanging from the ceiling. A six-winged angel gifting a seed. A man swallowing a seed. A fox devouring a man who in turn devours the fox. A seed sprouting from a man's belly. Tendrils reaching down from the moon. Tendrils that look like branches. Tendrils that look like roots.

The further Taban goes inside the more he feels surrounded.

'Yuck.' Hilde shivers. 'This place give me the creeps.' She walks towards one of the statues – a large one carved from blueish rock. There is a faded cuneiform-like engraving around its base. She traces her finger along it. 'The *Gate* of Foxes,' she reads aloud. 'Looks like that Andrews guy mistranslated it.'

'How are you able to read that?' Taban asks.

Hilde looks baffled. Her eyes twitch for an instant then stop. 'I'm not sure. I feel like since we made the offering in the quarry

– since I picked up this dagger.' She gestures to the sheath on her hip. 'Like … these fragments of information pop into my thoughts. But when I try and grasp them they fade. You know how dreams slip away in the morning no matter how hard you try to hold them? Like that.'

She turns back to the statue.

'Anyway, I know this language. Somehow. It's a weird mishmash. I'm not an expert like my parents, but it feels to me like it's got both a Hebrew vibe *and* an Old Norse vibe somehow. But with an abundance of "Zah" and "Zee" sounds and a hint of Swahili. It's all over the place.' Her brow furrows. 'I'm going to try something.'

Hilde steps back – gestures for Taban to follow her lead. She mumbles some lah-lah-lah sounds as if loosening her tongue, then utters a phrase Taban does not comprehend. Above there is a slicing sound like a blade cutting flesh. A gust of cold air. Then hot air. Then cold. Hot. Cold. Hot. What looks like a wound opens in the ceiling. It undulates.

'What did you say?'

'I told it to open.'

'Looks like the cut that appeared in the moon when they took Caleb. I guess this is the way in? How do we get up there?'

'I think if you boost me I can reach it.'

'Uh, maybe you should boost me instead? You are kind of bigger than me.'

She raises an eyebrow. 'Exactly. You're scrawny. No upper body strength. How would you pull me up once you got in?'

'Point taken.'

Taban kneels beneath the portal – hands in a webbed cradle. It's a stance he's only ever seen in films and he's not sure he's got it right. Hilde steps into his meshed palms. Then her other foot comes down onto his shoulder with a thump and she kicks upward.

Taban looks up just in time to see Hilde's legs vanish. 'I said I would give you a boost. Not be a step lad— Shit!'

Taban yelps as Hilde abruptly reaches out of the portal and pulls him up. Once he's through, she hooks her other hand under his arm. For a moment she holds him an inch or so off the ground like a little baby. Then she places him down – expression searingly smug.

'Sometimes I think you engineer situations like this to make yourself look cool,' he says neutrally.

She laughs. 'I don't need to *look* cool, Taban.'

Taban is about to reply with something sarky when he notices the sky.

'Hilde, look up.'

She gasps. 'What? Oh God. No, no, no, no, no.'

The sky is full of moons. Teeming. Overlapping. All at different phases, sizes, hues. Some of them are drooping like the moon did that one fateful morning at Camp Emet.

Taban takes in the rest of their surroundings. The 'ground' they are standing on is actually the roof of a ruined building. Looks like a hospital. In every direction he can see the toppled tower blocks and empty streets of what was once South Sun.

'Hey Taban.' Hilde gestures for him to come over to the edge of the roof. 'Come take a look at this.' She passes him the binoculars. 'What do you think this is all about?'

Peering through, Taban sees nestled in the devastated cityscape, a twisted multi-coloured structure. It's like someone has somehow coiled together many different materials into a lopsided prismatic cone. Angular growths sprout from it – grasping at the sky.

'I've spotted these all over place. What do you suppose they're for?'

'I'm not sure. In the last dream where I was Solomon I caught glimpses of something similar rising from the earth.'

'Yeah? And what about that big one over there?' Taban aims the binoculars where she is pointing – feels his heart pump faster when he spots the structure. Gold and bronze. Obsidian and ruby. All at once. Shifting like a mirage. At the base a ramp leads to a massive doorway and several elaborate pipes feed out on to the street. Exhausts? Chutes? Perhaps for waste? The structure curls upward like a mangled tree. Spires shoot out like twisted branches. Or twisted roots? It shimmers. It looks as if it's slowly, imperceptibly, moving. A triangular drill-head juts out at an impossible angle from the top-most spire.

Abruptly, the drill-head jolts up and punctures one of the drooping moons. There is a popping so loud Taban *feels* it more than hears it, followed by a screaming hiss, at once mechanical and unnervingly organic. The stale air churns into wind. It crackles with electricity. The temperature begins to drop then rise – drop then rise. The drill-head bulges then subsides – bulges then subsides. A steady rhythm. Breathing? Drinking? No. *Extracting*.

Silence.

Then – shaking. A sound somewhere between human wailing and crashing waves.

Then – dust. Clouds dense and ashen billow out of the exhaust-chutes below the spire and out onto the desolate streets below. The clouds climb higher and higher until they form a towering wall advancing through the city.

Taban and Hilde duck and shield their heads as the wave of dust passes over – covering them and everything around them in a thick layer of grey. The substance is fine, powdery, warm to the touch – like fireplace ash. For a minute or two they stay fearfully hunched – little round coals in a burnt-out pit. Then they stand – sooty noses and wide eyes emerging from a leaden sea. Taban tries to shake off the dust – only causing more of it to billow up in his face. Hilde lets out a wheezy cough.

'So,' Taban says, gesturing to the strange drill-headed structure in the distance, trying and failing to look composed. 'I reckon that "big one" might be where we need to go.'

< < <

The Girl In The Shadow

It takes Taban and Hilde a long time to navigate the crumbling stairwell down onto the street. Once there, traversing the ruinous environment does not become any easier. The closer they get to 'The Big One' – the more piles of mysterious ash block their path. Eventually they find themselves forced to scale a huge mound of the stuff – a feat made difficult by its flowing, ebbing, sand-like quality. As they crest the top, Taban gets his foot stuck in something.

'Hilde,' he says. 'Could you help?'

'Sure.' She grabs his hand and tugs.

His foot emerges entangled in a ribcage.

'Ah!' Taban yanks his foot away and falls onto his backside. The whole top layer of the mound starts sliding. Hilde snatches Taban's arm to stop him sliding with it. As it peels away, sloughing to the street below, more bones reveal themselves. Hundreds if not thousands. Femurs and clavicles and tibias and sternums and even whole spinal columns. All knotted together like the tails of a rat king. They are different sizes and vary in colour and condition, but they all have one thing in common – they're from humans.

'Christ.' Hilde unconsciously makes a little crossing motion over her chest.

'Ja,' Taban half-speaks, half-sighs. 'Thank you for catching me.'

Hilde nods, eyes still locked on the tangle of human remains. 'God. God. God. Let's take a breather on the other side. I need to sit for a moment.'

They carefully inch their way down the hill of bones.

At the bottom Taban sits on a street sign that's been bent

horizontal. Hilde flops cross-legged on the ground. Rummages in her backpack. Takes out her lunchbox.

'Well at least my sandwiches didn't get dust in them.' The scent of fish paste and olives wafts into the air. Taban usually wouldn't care for the smell, but right now he finds it strangely comforting. Soon though his attention is drawn back to the bone hill behind them. Something beyond the pure horror of the sight unnerves him. Then he realises.

'Hilde, do you see any skulls?'

'What?'

'I don't see any skulls. Like, you'd think there would be at least some skulls in there. In my dreams Solomon absorbed skulls to get people's knowledge and memories. So I wonder if that's what's happened to all of them. And maybe that drill thing at the top of that spiral structure goes into other worlds and gets fresh—'

'How much water do you have left?' Hilde interrupts.

'Um.' Taban checks his water bottle. 'Maybe a little under half a bottle?'

'Okay. Make sure to keep some in reserve for the journey back.' Hilde packs away her now empty lunchbox. 'These look nice.' She points at Taban's shoes. 'Well. At least they would if they weren't covered in dirt and god knows what.'

'Thank you.'

'Are they new?'

'Ja. Dad got them for me. Early Christmas present.'

'And you took them to *this* place?'

'Might as well wear them while I still have the chance.'

'Why do you say that?' Hilde voices this question like an accusation.

Taban forces a neutral-smile.

'Cut that out. I can see right through it. Why do you keep talking like you're not coming back?'

The boy's mask slips to neutral. 'Hilde, I'm going to give myself up in exchange for Caleb.'

'Why?'

'What do you mean "Why"? Isn't it obvious?'

'Not to me.'

Taban stands – paces back and forth.

Hilde also stands – follows him, arms folded.

'What else am I meant to do?' he asks.

'Not give that … *thing* … what it wants.'

'So let Caleb die then? Worse in fact – let Solomon use whatever … *part* … of Caleb he stole to make some kind of gateway to our world?'

'No. I didn't say that.'

'Then what?'

'We stop him.'

'How?'

'We'll figure it out. I have a feeling.'

'I thought you were the rational one.'

'It's more rational than doing something that will allow *this.*' She points to the bone hill. 'To happen our world *quicker.*'

'I caused all of this, Hilde!' Taban's voice rises, yet somehow still fails to crack through its characteristic flatness. He feels light-headed. He tries Chenjerai's breathing exercise, but can't focus. He sits on a centuries-old trashcan – stares into the ground. 'Look, Hilde, I didn't tell you and Cal everything. The terrible things I did. That Solomon did … *through* me. I didn't tell you—'

'And you don't need to.'

Taban looks up. Hilde is standing over him, eyes fixed on his

287

eyes, hand pressed down firmly on his shoulder – as if to stop him from floating away. 'I know already. I know you, Taban. I've known you for so long. I know you're not the innocent victim you pretend to be. Hendrick was right about that at least. But there's a difference between taking responsibility for your actions and throwing yourself to your death because you can't live with the guilt. I'm sure if Caleb were here he'd tell you the same. Now can you please trust me when I say there is a way this can all work out?'

'Okay.' Taban gently brushes away her hand. 'But I just don't understand your optimism.'

Hilde smiles, sits next to him. 'I don't really understand it either. I've never exactly been the optimistic type. But … there's something weird going on with me. Like what I mentioned earlier – when I figured out the trick with those statues. There are all these fragments in my head now. I don't know if that person from the vision in the quarry gave them to me, or if they were always in there, waiting to activate. The closer we get to that spiral, the more these fragments meld together into something that makes sense. I get this *feeling*. Like I'm on the cusp of realising something *big*. That there's something I – or another "*I*", *a me* within me – can do to bring an end to this. I don't know how to explain. It's like when you're looking at a jumbled puzzle. You can't tell exactly where every piece goes, but you have an idea of the overall picture.'

Hilde has a wild cheerful look that feels totally alien to their desolate surroundings.

'Could you recite one of these "fragments" for me?' Taban asks.

'I'm not sure if any of them would mean anything to you.'

'Don't worry about that. After all I described one of my fox bites to you – and those aren't exactly easy to understand either.'

'Okay. Let me think.' She pauses for a moment – clearly searching through her memory for something ideal. 'Alright,' she continues. 'Here's one that's almost coherent start to finish.'

Hilde's voice becomes formal. Like she's reading in front of class.

'Heed our warning. Shun the winged apostles who come bearing gifts of power. They are merely pollinators for the Tree. Shun the whisperers who come cloaked in canid forms. They are the tillers for the Tree's soil. The Tree whose roots reach down from alien skies to drink the blood of worlds. We have learned through folly. We have learned through suffering. Done our best to cull, to burn, to clip. But the Tree's roots are long and deep. Wherever darkness touches it waits. Listening. Patient. Only a single seed needs come to fruition for it to have a way in. It enters through the mouth – the gut. It exits through the mind – the heart. It comes back roaring to life again and again filling up the horizon with waxing and waning moons of sadness and consumption, consumption, consumption. When it takes hold there is only one—'

Hilde falls silent. Smiles awkwardly. 'After that it gets sort of jumbled. Something about a tool called a "Focus" and "Divine Implements of Culling". It's all fuzzy. Like trying to tune into a distant radio station.'

Taban realises he has leaned in close to Hilde. Their hands are almost touching.

'Taban,' she says, suddenly sounding a little out of breath. 'You know that favour you owe me for lending you the book?

That very important book of which there are only three copies and which you returned to me scuffed with creased pages?'

'Um. Yes. I do.'

'Well.'

She nudges her hand closer.

Then abruptly pulls away and stands bolt upright.

'Actually never mind. It's not important right now.' She slings her satchel over her shoulder. 'We should get moving. I think we're getting close.'

'Okay then.' Taban does not really know what to make of her behaviour.

For the next hour they travel across the ruined city in relative silence. With the one exception. A moment when Taban asks Hilde the following question →

'Hilde, back in Grade 3, after Cal moved schools, why did you stop hanging out with me?'

She frowns. 'You don't remember?'

'No. I mean I always assumed it was because you only wanted to be Caleb's friend and with him gone you didn't see any reason to keep putting up with me.'

'Well firstly – it's not that I didn't want to *ever* hang out with you *ever* again. I was just mad at you for a while. I thought that after some time you'd come back to hang out and maybe you'd apologise for the stupid thing you said. But you *never* did! And that made me more mad and so I ended up staying mad for years.' She laughs. 'Though really I guess it was silly of me to expect any emotional intuition from you. You have a really black and white way of reading people. They either hate you or they don't. There's nothing in between.'

'What was the stupid thing I said that upset you so much?'

She stares. 'You really don't remember, do you?'

'No.'

She sighs. 'One time, when you came round my house to play after school, my mom asked you how I got on with the other kids at Highveldt and you told her I was in love with Caleb.'

'Oh. Ja, that must've been really embarrassing. But it was *very* obvious though. Even to me. You were always hanging around us at break time. Everyone could see it. Still I shouldn't have outed you to your folks like that.'

'I didn't like Caleb, Taban.'

'Really? Not even a little? I mean he's really cool though.'

'No. I mean ... I didn't *like*-like him. I wasn't upset because ... Forget it. This is torture.'

Taban's neutral-smile slips into neutral. 'I'm sorry, Hilde.'

Hilde looks him up and down as if assessing a broken keepsake – internally debating if it can be repaired. 'It's just ... It's *always* about *Caleb* with you. Caleb, Caleb, Caleb. You edit me out of things. Make me feel like a background character in your story about how cool you think Caleb is. So much so that I've just come to expect it. I hate it. And sometimes you even seem to think of yourself as a background character too. It's messed up. You're so obsessed with Caleb, and Caleb's approval, and Caleb's way of being cool, that you've made your life miserable and have never been able to see that some people have always liked ... *Whatever.* I'm just rambling now. Let's keep moving.' She averts her eyes and hurries ahead – trudging over a waist-high pile of rubble with a stumbling stop-start urgency, as if repressing a desire to sprint away.

Taban searches for something to say. He knows he needs to say something.

'Hilde,' he calls after. 'I've always thought you were really cool as well.'

Hilde stops abruptly – every limb rigid like she's been electrocuted. Without turning to face him she replies with a clipped, 'Thank you,' and resumes walking at a brisk pace.

Taban can't see her expression, but hopes she is smiling. He tries to catch up but ends up lagging behind slightly for the rest of the journey.

<<<

Let Go

Eventually Taban and Hilde arrive at the base of The Big One. Up close its immensity feels overwhelming – as does its wavering, hazy, unsettled quality. As they approach the ramp that leads to the entrance, figures emerge from within the twisting walls.

Foxes. Foxes of all of sizes and colours. Foxes that are at once foxes and yet not foxes. Foxes with smiles that do not fit in their mouths, skin that does not fit in their fur, eyes that do not fit in their lids. Foxes that are like congealed amalgams of every lupin nightmare humanity has had since its first fretful conscious thoughts. Foxes that are the dark dream of foxes.

One steps forward from the teeming mass. Taban immediately recognises it. White fur. Familiar human-like eyes. Near black. Like his.

We've been expecting you.

The ramp transforms into stairs in a shimmering flick. Taban and Hilde ascend – each footfall hesitant, as if the steps might disappear at any moment. Once they reach the top the lupin mass parts and the lead fox motions with its head for them to follow.

Come.

Taban looks to Hilde – seeking approval.

She nods.

They follow.

Nausea. Every metre closer to the archway entrance sends a wave of it through Taban's synapses. His heart kicks to an alien rhythm. Duduk. Duduk. He hears a high-pitch drone. Feels a headache coming on. He represses. Ignores. They are so *close*.

They pass through the archway and into a long corridor with a high, vaulted ceiling. It looks like the central aisle of a church. A nave, Taban thinks they're called. At least he remembers being lectured about it by one of the Camp Emet supervisors who was strangely heated about the subject.

Yes. It is like a church. But also like a tree – turned inside out and upside down.

Meshed into the walls, pulsing with sickly green light, are thin branch-like structures. Near the apex of the ceiling, some of these stems sprout outward. Little fleshy orbs dangle like ripe fruit from the tips. Taban spots one of them crack. A familiar winged being hatches from within. Clutching a seed, it uncurls like a waking bat, flutters into a dark corner of the roof, and vanishes.

The focal point from which all these branches emerge is at the far end of the chamber – growing out of the floor. A bronze throne with thick tubes and wires jutting out the back. No. Not tubes. *Veins*. Veins that curl upward into a massive capsule. It undulates like living skin but is clear like a plastic saline bag. It hangs suspended from the ceiling by a thick artery.

It is full of skulls.

The scene is so alien and overwhelming that it takes a moment for Taban to even notice the pale figure slouched not *on* the throne, but *in* the throne. Merged at the thighs. Left elbow melted into the arm rest. His neck bent crooked to rest on his shoulder.

Taban realises this person is Solomon. Or what is left of him. Most of his flesh has rotted away and what little remains is so withered and pale it's indistinguishable from bone. The only thing still vaguely recognisable is the face – barely visible in the mess of decay and mysterious organic machinery.

Suddenly one of the skulls in the saline-flesh-bag disintegrates. The ceiling-artery pumps in a replacement. The room fills with the sound of a relieved, breathy, 'Aaaaah'. Solomon's silver eyes creak open. 'I thought you'd never come,' he says, voice deep and resonate. 'White August 96 – please bring in the substitute candidate.'

The fox disappears through an adjacent doorway, then returns dragging a small water-tank-like device by a chain in its maw. The device is filled with red and yellow liquid and attached to a long copper and green cable – the end of which is connected to a collar around Caleb's neck. Or, rather, Caleb's *spirit's* neck. At least that is the only way Taban can comprehend the perfect double – as his spirit. It floats upside down – like gravity affects it in reverse. It looks exactly like Caleb, but if all his edges were bright and hazy – as if glimpsed underwater on a cloudless sunny day. The only detail that is sharp and clear is its expression – pain. Closed eyelids tremble. Jaws clench in a rigid grimace. Thin wisps of red smoke leak from the tips of its fingers and other extremities. The fluids inside the tank gurgle in response – as if drinking in his suffering.

'What are you doing to Caleb?' asks Taban.

Solomon raises a rotted brow, like he has heard an incredibly stupid question. 'Making him into a Conduit, of course. He's not a willing host sadly so it's an agonising, centuries-long process. Of course he won't need to experience it any longer – *provided* you're willing to re-commit your vows and fulfil your half of the contract. If you agree to that I can sever his link to this place and his consciousness will float up to whichever of the many moons above is the double of your world's. I forget which it is. There are so many planes of existence I am infiltrating at present. Under my stewardship, the World Tree's roots now stretch out into all corners of the cosmos. It might take a long time for your friend's essence to return to him. Maybe a month. Maybe fifty years. As with many things in life there is a high variance of possibilities.'

'Why are you even doing any of this?'

Solomon looks even more baffled. 'Because it's the right thing to do.'

'What? How?'

'People die, boy.' Solomon snaps his fingers. The click reverberates around the chamber then fades into nothing. 'They die and then they are gone and everything they've experienced is gone too. Even if their life is religiously documented the best that will ever give you is a vague approximation of their experiences filtered through the artifice of language and storytelling. And that is *even* if you if assume that people are always honest. That they don't have experiences they'd rather be forgotten. Secrets they want to hide. But with this power,' he taps his forehead – unkempt nails clinking against a patch of exposed bone, 'they can live forever in me and in the World Tree.' Another skull in the container above fizzles away and is replaced. Solomon lets out a gasp that expresses something between weary relief and uncomfortable delight.

Taban shakes his head. 'You're not the Solomon from my dreams.'

'Solomon? Oh. It's been a while since I heard that name. I've grown so far beyond it. Thousands of years have passed since my contract was fulfilled and I became the Nexus of the World Tree. And also only a few moments. For time flows differently in all the worlds and I am in all the worlds *simultaneously*. Taban? Was that your name? You are *merely* a prospective

Conduit. And a child no less. How could you understand? How could I explain?'

Solomon rolls his silver eyes upward. Gently nibbles what remains his lower lip. Makes a long *hmmmmmm* – like an absent-minded professor searching for the right words.

'How do I put this? In your dreams of me you felt my pain. You wept for my losses. You were moved. As I *intended.* But know that at the same time I also peered into your life. And I did not weep. I was not moved. I have watched your story unfold and found it of little consequence. Don't misunderstand me. I will store and preserve your experiences – but you must understand – while there has been only one Solomon in your life there have been many Tabans in mine. Let me give you a glimpse.'

Millions of images storm through Taban's brain. Many planets. Many people. Wounded people. Vulnerable people. Desperate people. Eating the seeds. Using powers they do not understand. Glowing marks accumulating across the galaxy. Bodies slowly transforming until – in a final pained spasm – erupting into pillars that reach up. Up to meet roots coming down from the sky. Worlds upon worlds upon worlds. Churned into shit. Then soil. Then ash.

The boy throws up.

Solomon sighs. 'I know. It's painful. As a mortal I, too, was manipulated by forces greater than myself. But such deception is necessary. Just as adults lie to children – Gods must lie to mortals. Mortals are too egotistical. They treasure their limited agency far too much. They will not give it up freely. If you want them to become part of something greater you have to lure them in. You have to tempt them with power. Only then will the seed gro—'

He coughs. Blood and viscous ichor trickles from his nose in a perfect red-green swirl. For a moment the spell of his deep commanding voice is broken. In the walls above and around, Taban sees the gleaming eyes and grinning teeth of foxes peering in. Watching. Judging. Laughing at all of them. The king looks frail – dwarfed by his throne.

Solomon sighs – wipes pink mucus from his pallid chin. 'I grow tired of this conversation.' He makes a cutting motion with his hand. Behind them a small wound-like portal opens.

As if on cue a seraph flutters down from the ceiling. It hovers in front of Taban. Spindly hands – coral red with gold nails – offer up a fresh seed.

Solomon clears his throat. 'Here are your options, boy. Renew your contract, restate your desire for your world's end, and become a Conduit for the World Tree – freeing your friend from his suffering. Or don't. Just leave. It doesn't really matter in the long run. The difference of a few hundred years means little to me. But hurry up. I can't keep the portal open forever.'

For once Taban feels like his neutral mask conveys the feeling he wishes to get across with a 100 percent accuracy. 'You're just a vessel – aren't you?'

Solomon frowns. Ancient teeth show through a little gap in the corner of his mouth. The way his jaw curves up gives the effect of a sort of half-frown, half-smile. 'Quit stalling,' he groans. 'There's nothing you can say that's going to change things. I've heard so many trite truisms over the millennia. I doubt you have anything novel to say.'

'Well perhaps *I* do! Does the name "Shamira" ring any bells?'

Taban's gaze snaps toward Hilde. His mind races – processing what she's just said.

A baby found in a quarry. Doors between dimensions. Tinashi embracing the earth.

A me within me.

Solomon's semi-sepulchral jaw goes slack. 'Shamira?' he echoes, sounding for a brief spell like the Solomon from Taban's dreams. 'I haven't heard that name in so long. My daughter?'

'Yes, Father. I have returned.'

'But you are lost?'

'No. Tinashi took me to another world where time flows slow – like a dammed river in a drought. But I have come back.'

Solomon beckons with a skeletal finger. 'Come.'

Hilde approaches – eyes fixed on Solomon, posture open and unguarded, smile obsequious, fawning, convincing. Taban, however, sees her hand subtly gesture towards Caleb's agonised spirit. He takes the hint and slowly edges towards the thrumming device and the long cables ensnaring it.

'Come, Shamira,' pleads Solomon, his silver eyes welling up. 'At last you can be one with your mother and me.'

Hilde tenderly strokes the old man's corpse-cold cheek – kneels.

Solomon reaches out his palm – thumb and forefinger extended like fangs. 'At last!'

Hilde's sickly obedient smile flattens into a placid line.

Like this → '–'

A tiny incision. A little minus – signalling removal. A little dash – signalling connection. Or separation. Or held in silence for twice the length to signal an abrupt conclusion, like—

Neutral. So many interpretations.

She pulls the stone dagger from its sheath and slashes.

A new line – this one less ambiguous.

There is a sound somewhere between a scream and tearing paper. The dagger goes not just through Solomon, but through the very physical space he occupies – leaving a rip in mid-air. Hilde quickly chucks the dagger to Taban. It clatters on the floor next to Caleb's chained spirit.

'Now!'

Taban snatches the dagger – cuts across the cable.

Slice.

The end still connected to the device thrashes like a bisected worm. It spits silver-blue sparks then dies. The tank bubbles desperately for a moment then goes dim and still. Yellow cools to orange. Red cools to black. The collar around the spirit's neck drops off like a dead tick. Then Caleb's essence flies up and phases through the ceiling – an untethered balloon of radiance and warmth.

Angry howls. Hundreds of foxes begin squeezing into the chamber – their gnashing jaws poking out from the walls.

What have you done?

The giant fox designated White August 96 jumps on Taban and pins him.

Jaws unhinge. Hot drool drips on Taban's forehead.

Teeth descend.

Taban stabs upward. Instead of hitting flesh it feels like the dagger punches through thin fabric. The fox freezes – a puncture in space where one of its near-black near-human eyes should be. The dagger spins in the socket. The air fills with the smell of salt and burning metal.

Hands grab his shoulders.

'Taban!' Hilde drags him out from beneath the fox. Rather than slumping to the floor the beast hangs mid-air – as if pinned in place by the blade. 'We've got to move. I think this whole world is about to collapse!'

'What!?' Taban scrambles to his feet.

A deafening sound blasts through the chamber – white noise and thunder. The cut Hilde made through Solomon and his throne widens into a metre-high gash beyond which there is only an ominously still white void. Its edges peel further and further back – like dissected skin being pried apart by a surgeon's hands. One metre becomes three metres becomes ten. The massive throne with all its tubes and machinery folds inside – disappearing.

Taban feels a strong pull – like a current is dragging him towards the tear. He runs toward the portal Solomon opened at the far end of the chamber – the portal that is slowly sealing up. But, every step he takes, the tear in the world behind them pulls him back by half. He dares not look back, but he can feel it expanding – catching up. Taban sees Hilde – running beside him, then slowly overtaking. Good. One of them will get out. And it deserves to be her. If anyone deserves to live it is Hilde. Though really can anyone ever truly *deserve* life or death? What could anyone ever do to *deserve* such a gift? What could anyone ever do to deserve being *robbed* of such a gift? Taban feels like laughing. We're really foolish. We're really foolish and *arrogant. I've* been really foolish and arrogant. I am *still – most likely,* no *most definitely –* foolish and arrogant.

The exhaustion he's been repressing blows through him like a squall. His legs ache, wobble. They're about to give out. Hopefully, Caleb's spirit has found its way back to their world by now. Or at least blundered into a parallel world that's not crumpling in on itself. That would be just like him. Poor Hilde will no doubt be left waiting for him a long time while his soul dream-walks its way home through countless fantastic dimensions.

Neutral-smile. A little dash barely curling at the corners – desperately hoping you welcome it as a bonafide grin.

Taban's eyes begin to shut.

Then – a grip around his wrist.

A yank. A shove.

The next thing there is dirt on his face as he lands with a thud on the floor of the House of Foxes. He jumps to his feet.

Hilde.

Hilde isn't with him.

He looks up to see a hand reaching out from a tiny gap in the air above. He grabs it and pulls with all his strength. Her head emerges. Then shoulders, arms, torso, and—

A dash can also be a cut.

The portal shuts.

There is no blood. No viscera. Only brilliant particles of light pouring out from where her legs should be. Hilde floats in mid-air. Her expression slowly changes from shock, to sadness, to amused acceptance. 'Damn,' she says, chuckling. 'Well I'm not sure I could've stayed here anyway. I mean I'm not really from *here* after all.'

A bit of her shoulder glows, breaks off, and floats up. It folds into itself like origami – smaller and smaller until it is gone.

'But still,' she continues. 'I would've liked to have tried. It would've been nice. I've always been unhappy – feeling like I was from two places at once. But it turns out I actually *was*. It's good to understand yourself.'

Hilde is now nothing more than a pair of arms and a smiling face drifting upward. Radiant shards peel off – melting into morning air.

'Taban, you know Hendrick was full of shit, but he was right about one thing. You are cruel sometimes. So this is my request

– the favour you owe me for the book and everything else – try not to be cruel from now on. And *please* …'

She is now just a hand and a stern but loving voice.

'Let go.'

The last shimmering particle folds and disappears.

Taban is alone. His hand holds on to nothing.

Hilde is gone.

There are footsteps outside the door – though Taban doesn't really register them. He simply stands. Hand aloft. Looking at the space where Hilde once was. Trying to locate some tiny speck of her.

'Ann! I've found him!' shouts a familiar voice. Chenjerai? He didn't think they would track down where he'd gone so soon. Perhaps they found the note he left? The one he hid in a spot where it would eventually be found in the likely event he didn't come back. The one that said, 'I love you Mom. I'm sorry. I've gone to get Caleb from the House of Foxes.'

Suddenly, there are arms around him. Taban hears his mother crying. 'I was so worried.'

Bright things. Is it Hilde coming back? No. They're marks. Multi-coloured marks all along his mother's shoulders. Fox bites? Has she always had them? Had he just not noticed? He wants to ask about their origins. But instead he blurts out, 'It hurts. I don't understand. It doesn't make sense. I'm sorry, Hilde. I'm so sorry, I'm …'

'Who do you mean, my boy?'

Taban feels a cold energy pooling inside. Rising. Erupting. Everything. It's all coming out. His body can't contain it any more. His face clenches like a fist. His neutral mask mangles into something new. His mouth makes sounds he hasn't heard from it before. His body trembles. His face is wet. Are these tears?

Yes.

They are.

How unfair to only get them now.

'My boy, these marks … Oh God. You too.' Ann squeezes him tight.

Taban tries to speak. Tries to explain. But he can't stop what is pouring out of him long enough to get a word out. So he stops trying to explain – hugs his mom.

In the cold morning light, Taban and Ann Grayson's fox bites glow – a display of colour and radiance that only they can see.

<<<

About a week later
In late afternoon traffic
On the way to
Harare International Airport

Out Of Orbit, Our Cracked Hearts Bleed Out

Red light. Chenjerai brings the car to a halt. A girl rushes from the sidewalk – wet rag bunched in a small hand. Before he has the opportunity to decline she is zigzagging the cloth across the windscreen. Whether this makes the glass more or less clean is uncertain. Ann pulls some change from their wallet.

'Here you go,' they say, gently placing coins into the girl's palm.

She nods and darts back to the sidewalk.

Green light. They drive off.

Taban wonders where the windscreen-washer will sleep tonight. It is uncommon to see a girl doing that sort of thing. Taban recalls hearing his dad grumble once that whenever you have dealings with so-called 'street kids' what enters your mind – along with pity – is an ugly poisonous fear that if you say, 'No,' you will come back to find your car broken into, but, if you say, 'Yes,' they will brand you an easy mark. Taban wonders where that phrase 'street kids' comes from. How it got into his brain. After all, many of these so-called 'kids' were actually men. Young men, but definitely *men*. Like a lot of idioms Taban has inherited, 'street kids' comes from a perspective alien to him. It's as if some august father figure is speaking through him. Hands outstretched to give, to rob. Eyes peering down – peering *in* – to judge. Increasingly, Taban has begun to ponder where these people – condemned by this unseen father to be eternal children – go at the end of the day. They have a weight which must be laid down. Where do they go? Where can they go? The city around them is all concrete and hard angles. And their bodies are soft – built of bone which breaks, flesh that rips, muscles that wither. Taban wonders if they too have bites no one can see. They must do. Even if the moon is not visible it is still there.

It seems to him as if until recently he has been living in a network of bubbles. His house. His suburb. His school. His parents' car. All designed to put space around him – place air and silence between him and this city of noise and cast-out children. Now those bubbles are all pierced. Cracked like eggs. The outside air is pouring in and it is revolting and beautiful and revoltingly beautiful. Outside is a world full of life and pain. Tiny crystalline moments of joy and misery. A world he is at once disgusted by and yet is so pathetically, pitifully, shamefully grateful is still here. Thank you, Hilde. I'm so sorry, Hilde. It hurts. It doesn't make sense. Oh God. Thank you. I'm sorry. Thank you.

They arrive at Harare International Airport. Chenjerai helps them carry the few bags they have to the front entrance. An old movie poster hangs on the wall by the sliding doors – edges frayed, plastic encasement cracked. It's for a film that finished its theatrical run years ago. *From An Angelic Height.* A romantic drama starring Jodie Foster and Sean Bean. In it Foster plays a surgeon who lost her husband in a terrorist bombing and has developed a morphine addiction. She is hired by a cutting-edge medical institute to perform experimental reconstructive facial surgery on a patient played by Bean. At first they don't get along, but gradually they fall in love and he helps her kick her drug habit. The third act twist – because there is always a third act twist in this kind of story – is that Sean Bean is a former undercover cop who helped carry out the bombing that killed her husband. He'd infiltrated the revolutionary group responsible intending to uncover their plans. But when he found no evidence of any terrorist plot, his superiors got him to create one by pushing the organisation in a more extreme direction from within. It had all been planned as a big setup with the police swooping in at the last minute to foil the conspiracy. But it went horridly wrong.

Taban can't remember exactly how the film ended. If Bean survived the surgery. If Foster ever forgave Bean. He'd only half-watched it many years ago over a TV dinner with Mom and Aunt Gertrude. Ann's review was that it was middling and a bit convoluted. Gertrude's review was that Sean Bean is a dish even under an inch of unconvincing prosthetics. He can blow up my husband any day, etc. Such is the way.

In the poster, Bean lies in a hospital bed looking up at Foster. Bandages artfully frame his glittering green eyes. Foster's pristine doctor's coat billows slightly – like a cape. She wears a stethoscope. So you know she's a doctor. They gaze at each other romantically. There is a golden sunrise superimposed behind them. The tagline below reads, 'Scars are beautiful. They are signs of healing.'

Taban thinks perhaps there is a germ of wisdom in this cornball insensitive statement. Or perhaps he is clinging to the hope that he has something more to look forward to than just survival. Though really survival is beautiful too. Or, maybe not *beautiful* exactly. *Precious.*

Who could ever deserve such a gift?

Chenjerai passes the last bag over to Ann.

'If there are problems get in touch with my friend Chipo in London,' he says. 'She will be sure to help. Please let me know when you've arrived safely. I'll be keeping an eye on my emails.'

'Thank you, Green. You've always been so good to me.'

Chenjerai gives Ann a big hug. 'I'm so happy you think that, old friend. It's a great look by the way.'

'Hmmm?' Ann seems to take in their own appearance for the first time. A blue denim jacket over black denim dungarees. Hair shaved short. Earrings replaced with simple studs. 'I guess I just felt like a change. I'm fed up of fussing with my hair all the time.'

Chenjerai nods then turns to Taban. 'Make sure to look after your mom okay. And also yourself. If you have any weird flare-ups while you're on the plane be sure to take the medicine I gave you.'

'Thank you Green.'

For a moment Chenjerai's lip quivers like he might cry again, but then he recomposes himself. 'Well. You better get going. It will be check-in time shortly. Safe journey you two.'

He walks back to his car and drives away – waving goodbye out the window as he does.

Ann and Taban enter the airport, check in, and go through to the departure lounge.

There they sit in a cafe and wait in a slightly dazed, slightly meditative silence.

Outside – a plane. A 152,000-kilogram shell, comprised of composite metals and plastics, containing more than 10,000 kilograms of human meat, excrement, and consumer goods. It sets down on the runway and runs a little way before coming to a halt. It hatches and its chattering mortal cargo spills out into the sticky afternoon. After the passengers have been led away, uniformed people move in to scrub the aeroplane's guts – prepping it for its next multi-national pregnancy. Soon its metal stomach will be filled with new life. With foreign journalists, clutching their passports tight, holding their breath as they slip through customs. With tourists adorned in bright shirts and local trinkets – gawking over holiday snaps of dangerous beasts. With exhausted middle-income families – fed up and leaving for good, heavy black bags dangling beneath their eyes. With rich children – the sons and daughters of the elite, off to Western lands to shop, feed, fornicate.

Taban wonders if any of those people coming off or getting on to the plane have fox bites.

He sips his hot chocolate and tries not to think about it.

On the table in front of him, scribbled in pencil in an old school notebook, is an unfinished attempt to turn everything that led up to that horrid night in Solomon's world into a story. To make sense of what happened. He started writing it last night. He couldn't sleep. The first page has a short description of the old family laptop – a DOS-powered brick. When he was six he played *Ultima VII* on it. Now, eight years later, he writes about playing *Ultima VII* on it. In another eight years will he write about writing about playing *Ultima VII* on it? In another eight years will he write about writing about playing *Ultima VII* on it? Taban feels like a chunk of debris falling out of orbit. Drifting from its star. Further and further from fire and motion and the memory of heat. Ever slower. Ever closer to stillness. It doesn't make sense. I'm sorry, Hilde.

Tok. The sound of an empty cardboard coffee cup being placed on the circular glass table. Ann looks at him. Smiles. 'Trying to work out your thoughts?' they ask.

Taban nods.

'Well if you need any help figuring things out.' They lean back in their chair, stretch their arms. 'I'm willing to answer any questions you might have.'

'Okay. Whatever happened to Ms Cowley?'

'Cowley? June Cowley? Didn't we tell you?'

'No.'

'She had a breakdown. Quit. Last I heard she'd eloped to Greece with a woman from Yugoslavia. Her family was outraged. Called me up out of the blue a few years ago asking if I had her contact details, but June and I didn't really get on so I didn't know any more than they did.'

'Oh.'

'Did you think something else had happened?'

'It's just ... I had a dream shortly after ... it all started.'

'Aw, my boy. I'm sorry. You'll learn. The world is big. Not everything is about you. Thank God.'

Taban feels an odd swell of emotions. Relief that Cowley most likely still lives, but also joy. Joy that perhaps she no longer desires to straighten kids out with rulers. That perhaps she has grown as he has grown. That her heart is now big enough to contain regret.

Learning can never come 'Too Late.'

Neutral-smile.

'I love you, Mom.'

The words come out easy.

Ann discreetly plucks a tiny crystal teardrop from the corner of their eye.

'Love you too, my boy.'

A beep. Ann's phone. They check it. After a few chunky Nokia clicks they smile.

'It's from Gertrude. She says Caleb's stabilised. She wants to wish us well on our journey to the UK. She also says sorry for what she said the other night. She wants to keep in touch.'

There are a few more clicks as Ann punches in a reply. Then they put the phone away.

Taban checks his satchel once again – a supermarket school bag containing all his treasured possessions. When he looks up he sees the fox. It's standing a few feet away by the window. Planes take off and land behind it. Its white patchy fur catches the sun – refracting light around the room.

'Do you see it as well?' Ann asks.

'Yes.' Taban reaches over and squeezes his mom's hand. 'Do you suppose it will follow us all the way to the UK?'

'I don't know,' Ann replies, squeezing back. 'We should go. They'll be calling for us to board any minute now.'

The two gather up their things and begin walking to the terminal. Taban glances back at the fox. Its eyes are deep near-black hazel. Human. His eyes. They have a sad pleading quality.

You can't be free of me. I am born from you and you from me.

Taban looks away and does not look back again. He follows after his mother – linking hands with them. They guide him to a door where a smiling woman checks their tickets and passports. As the woman inspects his green booklet, Taban sees his name and for the first time is struck by how odd it looks in print. Like a typing error. There is a story behind it of course. Due to a blood type incompatibility Taban was born prematurely and nearly died. His parents wanted to name him after the doctor who saved his life. That man's name was Thabang, which meant, 'To bring joy,' in his language. But Cormack misheard him. Thabang became Taban. By the time the mistake was realised Taban was already a year old.

The inspector looks at the name – mutters, 'Fake?' under her breath – but nonetheless waves them through.

'It was a mistake,' Taban mumbles.

The woman smiles, shakes her head. 'No, no,' she says. 'Lovely country. Never a mistake.'

Taban responds with a nod. Then he heads with his mother down the passage, outside, and over hot asphalt towards the aircraft. Emblazoned on the plane's tail and flank is the symbol of Zimbabwe. A golden bird. The image of an ancient sculpture. Itself fashioned in imitation of a living thing that once hopped, fluttered, flew. Bateleur Eagle or African Fish Eagle? No one is certain of the long-dead artist's intentions. It is an ambiguous reconstruction.

As he ascends the ladder and enters the craft's belly, Taban looks back one last time over the land he's called home his entire life. Part of him yearns to see some spectacle to mark the occasion. Instead the land is quiet. Indifferent. Such is the way.

Thank you \ I'm sorry, Eve.

Thank you \ I'm sorry, Athel.

Thank you \ I'm sorry, Hilde.

It doesn't make sense.

It hurts.

I'm sorry.

Thank you for everything.

Thank you.

I love you.

Taban's heart longs for their forgiveness. But the dead cannot forgive.

He turns away, goes to his seat, hugs his school bag. He sits and stares into space while next to him his mother talks about the changes to come – half to him, half to themselves. The plane starts to ascend. He gazes out the window at the great metal wings lifting them into the sky. The plane soars – an eagle adorned with gold and red. Late afternoon crosses the threshold into early evening. Taban's fox bites in all their myriad colours begin to glow under the auspices of the rising moon. If you had been there – and had the right eyes to see them – then they would've looked like this →